TALES BEYOND BEL
OW!
MW01622707
TOMB
No. 1
JUNE
TOMB
OF
TERROR
PDC
OF TERROR
10¢
WILL YOU
BE ABLE TO
LOOK AT...
THE THING
FROM THE
CENTER OF
THE EARTH!
MAIN ST.

TOMB OF TERROR, June, 1952, Vol. 1, No. 1, is published monthly by HARVEY PUBLICATIONS, INC., at 420 DeSoto Avenue, St. Louis 7, Mo. Editorial, Advertising and Executive offices, 1860 Broadway, New York 23, N. Y. President, Alfred Harvey; Vice-President and Editor, Leon Harvey; Vice-President and Business Manager, Robert B. Harvey. Application for second-class entry pending at the Post Office at St. Louis, Mo. Single copies, 10c. Subscription rates, 10 issues for $1.00 in the U. S. and possessions, elsewhere, $1.50. All names in this periodical are entirely fictitious and no identification with actual persons is intended.

You have come! You have pushed your way through the fiendish fog that envelops the ghastly grave-yard. You have fought the wailing wind that groans its song of misery. You have passed grave-stones that tell a tale of yesterday, and warn of today!

Now you shudder! Now you gasp! Now you feel your blood boil and curdle as if in a pot of evil! Ha, you have arrived at this place long sought! You look around, and you know . . . that this is the **TOMB OF TERROR!!!**

Formless figures weave in and out this compartment of cruelty. Madness reigns as the undead tear at each other and twisted tentacles reach out from the world beyond to encompass it all in one slimy swoop!

***TOMB OF TERROR** will bring to you thrills and chills comparable to Frankenstein's monster, the Mummy, the Wolf-man, the Zombie, Dracula, and The Thing.*

The vault will be opened and the ghouls of the unknown will spring forth in a dreadful clamor! Tales never told before will clutch at your sanity!

But, as the stories unfold, you will know, you will realize that no human imagination— no matter how great — could have thought of these tales. You will know that they are TRUE! And you will be right!

The clock strikes the twelfth hour. Midnight swarms in with its weird and treacherous meaning. Mortals rush for shelter. Shutters are clamped tight to keep out night's horrible hour.

And you find your retreat . . . a retreat with no exit. You are caught in the web of horror . . . You are trapped in the . . . ***TOMB OF TERROR!***

No. 1
JUNE

TOMB OF TERROR

IN THIS ISSUE

NEWS REPORTER, NOAH BRANDT, WAS GIVEN AN EERIE ASSIGNMENT WHICH LED HIM TO FACE A HORROR THAT MOVED AND LIVED FOR THE LUST OF KILLING... FOR IT WAS...

THE THING FROM THE CENTER OF THE EARTH!

MOURNFUL VOICES ECHOING IN THE SINISTER DARKNESS OF THE NIGHT... A COLD WIND THAT STRIKES WILD TERROR AT THE HUMAN HEART... THE GHASTLY SIGHT OF A FACE RISING FROM THE DEPTHS OF EVIL... ALL THIS IS EVIDENT AT THE FATEFUL TIME WHEN...

THE DEAD AWAKEN

WELCOME TO MY WATERY GRAVE, ALAN!!!

WE HAVE BROUGHT HIM AS YOU COMMANDED!! WE MUST RETURN TO THE LAND OF THE DEAD!!

SHEILA!! NO!! IT COULDN'T BE!!!

DO YOU THINK IT ODD FOR PUPPETEERS TO USE LIVE PUPPETS? BUT THEN YOU HAVEN'T HEARD THE HALF OF IT!!! COME WITH US AND WITNESS THE SAGA OF...

THE LITTLE PEOPLE

HA-HA, LITTLE FRIEND! STRUGGLING WILL DO YOU NO GOOD!

THE KARNOS ARE A FAMILY OF RENOWNED PUPPETEERS... BUT THEY HAVE KNOWN BETTER DAYS...

PEOPLE CAME, LAUGHED AND POINTED, BUT THEIR BACKBONES WOULD HAVE SHIVERED WITH FEAR, AND THEIR EYES BULGED WITH TERROR, IF THEY ONLY KNEW THE SECRET OF THE ...

WAX MUSEUM

NO! NO- DON'T DO IT!! DON'T

DAAAAAAAH!

WE DARE YOU TO READ
YOU'LL THRILL! YOU'LL CHILL!
EVERY STORY COLORFULLY FILLED WITH SPINE-TINGLING BLOOD-CURDLING ADVENTURE!!
FOLLOW THE NEW SUSPENSE-CHARGED MAGAZINE EVERY ISSUE!
THRILL TO...
BLACK CAT MYSTERY
STRANGEST TALES OF FEAR AND TERROR!
BLACK CAT MYSTERY
JACK OF HORROR!
APR. ISSUE NOW ON SALE!
STRANGEST TALES OF FEAR AND TERROR!
BLACK CAT MYSTERY
WEIRD! DIFFERENT! AMAZING!
GET YOUR COPIES!!!
JUNE ISSUE ON SALE SOON!

MOURNFUL VOICES ECHOING IN THE SINISTER DARKNESS OF THE NIGHT... A COLD WIND THAT STRIKES WILD TERROR AT THE HUMAN HEART... THE GHASTLY SIGHT OF A FACE RISING FROM THE DEPTHS OF EVIL... ALL THIS IS EVIDENT AT THE FATEFUL TIME WHEN...
THE DEAD AWAKEN
WELCOME TO MY WATERY GRAVE, ALAN!!!
WE HAVE BROUGHT HIM AS YOU COMMANDED!! WE MUST RETURN TO THE LAND OF THE DEAD!!
SHEILA!! NO!! IT COULDN'T BE!!!
A BRIGHT SUMMER'S DAY--AND TWO YOUNG LOVERS ROW CALMLY AND HAPPILY DOWN A PLACID LAKE--UNAWARE OF THE FATE THAT LURKS FOR THEM IN THE SILENCE!...
YOU'D BETTER WATCH WHERE YOU'RE PADDLING, DEAR! THIS BOAT FEELS SORT OF SHAKY TO ME!!
DON'T BE FOOLISH, SHEILA!! IT COULDN'T POSSIBLY...
SUDDENLY, A SHARP WIND CUTS AT THE FRAGILE BOAT, AND...
ALAN!!
THE BOAT'S TURNING OVER!!

HELP!! SHEILA!! I CAN'T SWIM!!
HOLD ON, ALAN!! I'LL GET YOU--!!
ARE YOU ALL RIGHT, DEAR??
I--THINK SO. I--FEEL--SO STRANGE--AND WEAK...
I WAS SO FRIGHTENED!! I THOUGHT YOU WERE GOING TO--TO...
FOR A MINUTE--I THOUGHT I DID!!! I'M GLAD YOU--
SUDDENLY, THE COUPLE IS CONFRONTED WITH A SHOCKING SIGHT, AS THE MERCILESS WATER GIVES UP A WRETCHED AND BLOATED VICTIM!...
L--LOOK!! IT'S THE BODY OF A MAN!!
WHERE COULD IT HAVE COME FROM???
ALAN!! HE LOOKS LIKE--LIKE YOU!!
HE DOES!! UGH-H-H!!!
WHY, HE'S GOT MY NAME IN HIS WALLET!! HOW COULD HE---
I DON'T KNOW, ALAN! IT MUST BE SOME HORRIBLE MISTAKE!!
IDENTIFICATION CARD
Alan Granger
126 Carolina Ave.
East Overshoe, Vt.
2

GAZING AT THE HIDEOUS, TWISTED FEATURES OF THE CORPSE, THE GIRL QUICKLY REALIZES THE TERRIBLE TRUTH--AND A NUMBING TERROR SEIZES HER!!...
GOOD LORD!! ALAN MUST HAVE ACTUALLY DROWNED IN THE WATER--AND THESE ARE HIS REMAINS!!! SOMEHOW HE MUST HAVE CONTINUED TO EXIST IN HIS HUMAN FORM!! BUT HE'S DEAD!! DEAD!!
DARLING!! WHAT'S THE MATTER??
DON'T TOUCH ME!! DON'T COME NEAR ME!! I NEVER WANT TO SEE YOU AGAIN!!
THE VIOLENT, ANGRY WORDS--COMING WITHOUT WARNING--TURN ALAN'S GENTLENESS TO ANIMAL FURY!
WHY, YOU---I OUGHT TO KILL YOU!!--
OH-H-H-H!!!
SHEILA!! HER HEAD HIT A ROCK!! I DIDN'T MEAN--BUT I'VE KILLED HER!! I--I'VE GOT TO GET RID OF THE BODY!!
THIS LAKE IS VERY DEEP!! THEY'LL NEVER FIND HER!! AND I'LL NEVER COME HERE AGAIN!!
BUT AS HE LEAVES, HE HEARS THE MURMUR OF STRANGE VOICES--VOICES FROM OUT OF A WATERY SHROUD--THAT CALL TO HIM AS BROTHER TO BROTHER!...
THE DEAD CANNOT LEAVE THE DEAD!! NEVER FORGET!!
I COULD HAVE SWORN--BUT I'D BETTER BE GOING!!
3

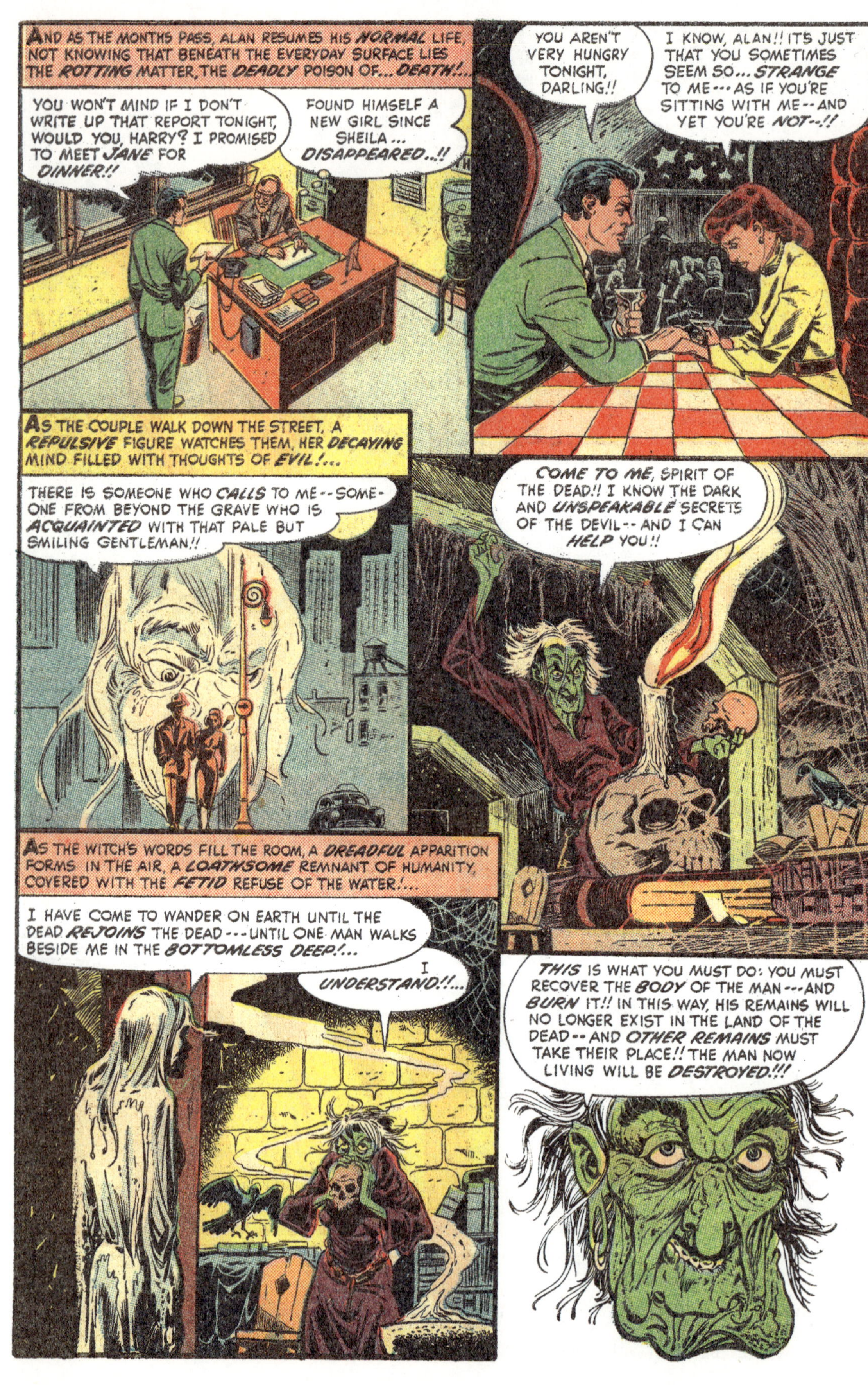
AND AS THE MONTHS PASS, ALAN RESUMES HIS NORMAL LIFE, NOT KNOWING THAT BENEATH THE EVERYDAY SURFACE LIES THE ROTTING MATTER, THE DEADLY POISON OF... DEATH!...
YOU WON'T MIND IF I DON'T WRITE UP THAT REPORT TONIGHT, WOULD YOU, HARRY? I PROMISED TO MEET JANE FOR DINNER!!
FOUND HIMSELF A NEW GIRL SINCE SHEILA ... DISAPPEARED..!!
YOU AREN'T VERY HUNGRY TONIGHT, DARLING!!
I KNOW, ALAN!! IT'S JUST THAT YOU SOMETIMES SEEM SO... STRANGE TO ME--- AS IF YOU'RE SITTING WITH ME-- AND YET YOU'RE NOT--!!
AS THE COUPLE WALK DOWN THE STREET, A REPULSIVE FIGURE WATCHES THEM, HER DECAYING MIND FILLED WITH THOUGHTS OF EVIL!...
THERE IS SOMEONE WHO CALLS TO ME-- SOME-ONE FROM BEYOND THE GRAVE WHO IS ACQUAINTED WITH THAT PALE BUT SMILING GENTLEMAN!!
COME TO ME, SPIRIT OF THE DEAD!! I KNOW THE DARK AND UNSPEAKABLE SECRETS OF THE DEVIL-- AND I CAN HELP YOU!!
AS THE WITCH'S WORDS FILL THE ROOM, A DREADFUL APPARITION FORMS IN THE AIR, A LOATHSOME REMNANT OF HUMANITY, COVERED WITH THE FETID REFUSE OF THE WATER!...
I HAVE COME TO WANDER ON EARTH UNTIL THE DEAD REJOINS THE DEAD--- UNTIL ONE MAN WALKS BESIDE ME IN THE BOTTOMLESS DEEP!...
I UNDERSTAND!!...
THIS IS WHAT YOU MUST DO: YOU MUST RECOVER THE BODY OF THE MAN---AND BURN IT!! IN THIS WAY, HIS REMAINS WILL NO LONGER EXIST IN THE LAND OF THE DEAD-- AND OTHER REMAINS MUST TAKE THEIR PLACE!! THE MAN NOW LIVING WILL BE DESTROYED!!!

THE NIGHT HAS JUST BEGUN!! I WISH HER SUCCESS IN HER--UNDERTAKING!!
THAT NIGHT, A FIGURE IN WHITE MOVES BESIDE THE LAKE-- CASTING NO REFLECTION ON THE QUIET WATER--ITS FEARFUL CRY LOST IN THE DEEPENING GLOOM!...
I MUST FIND THE BODY!! THE B-O-D-Y!!!
AT LAST!!! I MUST DESTROY IT NOW!!
DEVOUR HIM QUICKLY!! DESTROY THE POOR HUMAN SHELL THAT REMAINS AFTER DEATH!!
AS THE FIRE EATS AWAY AT THE FLESH, THE DEAD SPIRITS THAT LIVED IN THE BODY RUSH DESPERATELY FROM THEIR HOME--THEIR SIGHTLESS EYES STARING WILDLY, THEIR MOUTHS AGAPE WITH HORROR!...
WHY HAVE WE BEEN SUMMONED FROM OUR SLEEP OF DEATH?? WE CANNOT THRIVE WITH NO BODY TO FEED UPON!!
THEN YOU MUST LISTEN TO ME!!
AND AT THAT VERY MOMENT...
I WANT TO MARRY YOU, JANE!! THERE'S NEVER BEEN ANOTHER!!
I KNOW, ALAN!!

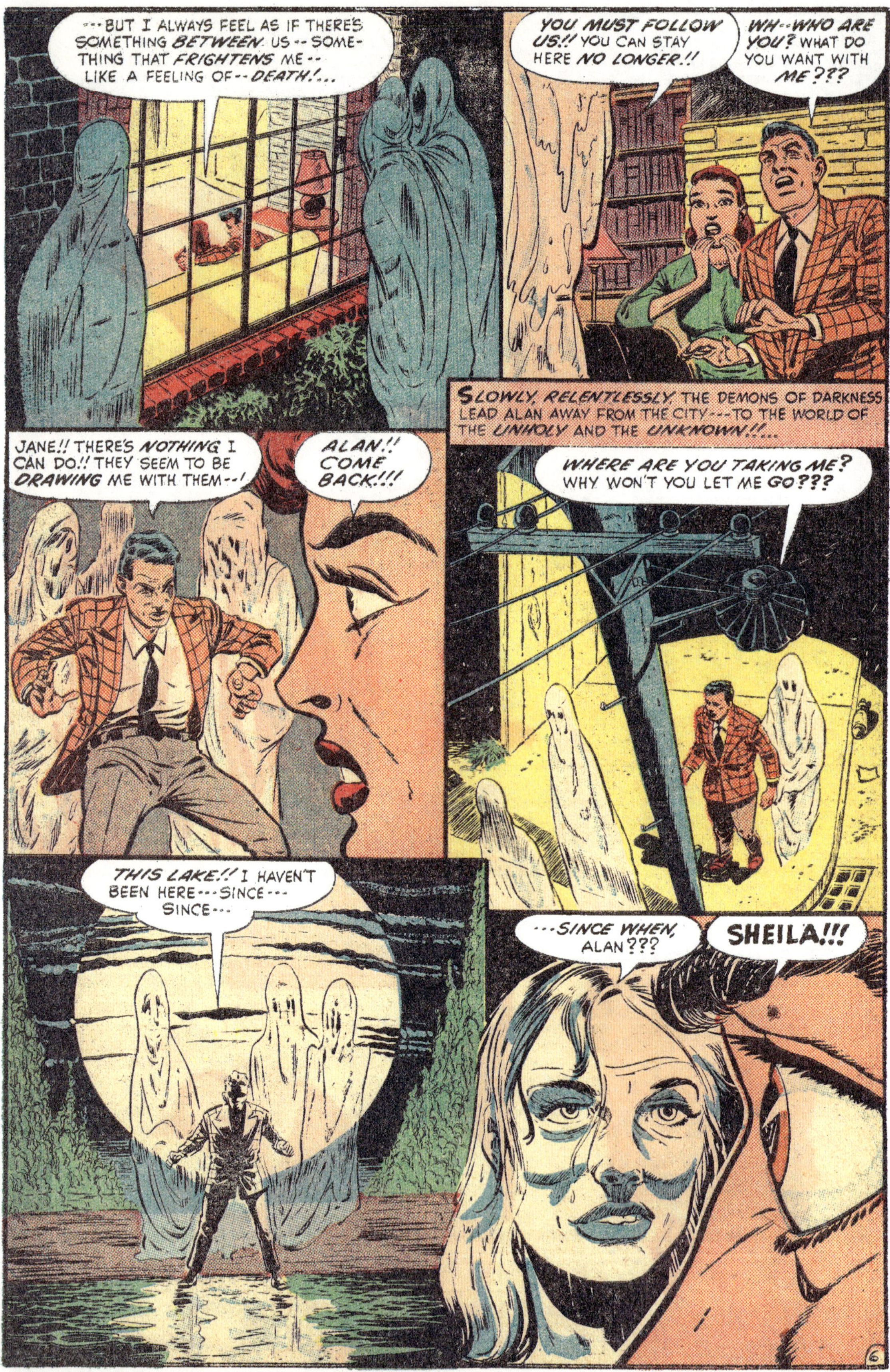

---BUT I ALWAYS FEEL AS IF THERE'S SOMETHING BETWEEN US -- SOMETHING THAT FRIGHTENS ME -- LIKE A FEELING OF -- DEATH!...
YOU MUST FOLLOW US!! YOU CAN STAY HERE NO LONGER!!
WH--WHO ARE YOU? WHAT DO YOU WANT WITH ME???
JANE!! THERE'S NOTHING I CAN DO!! THEY SEEM TO BE DRAWING ME WITH THEM--!
ALAN!! COME BACK!!!
SLOWLY, RELENTLESSLY, THE DEMONS OF DARKNESS LEAD ALAN AWAY FROM THE CITY---TO THE WORLD OF THE UNHOLY AND THE UNKNOWN!!...
WHERE ARE YOU TAKING ME? WHY WON'T YOU LET ME GO???
THIS LAKE!! I HAVEN'T BEEN HERE---SINCE--- SINCE---
---SINCE WHEN, ALAN???
SHEILA!!!

THE TIME HAS COME FOR YOU TO JOIN ME IN ETERNAL DARKNESS.!! YOU HAVE LIVED IN SHADOW TOO LONG.!!
WH--WHAT DO YOU MEAN??
YOU NEVER EMERGED FROM THE LAKE ALIVE!! ONLY THE FORM OF YOU SURVIVED!! AND NOW THAT YOUR BODY IS ASHES, THE FORM MUST REPLACE IT IN THE LAND OF THE DEAD!!!
NO!! NO!!
COME WITH ME, ALAN!! YOU CANNOT FEAR DEATH-- SINCE YOU ARE ALREADY DEAD!!
I WON'T!! I---WON'T---!!
COME!!! FOLLOW ME!!!
SHEILA!! NO--O-O-O!! N---
---THE APPALLING SILENCE TELLS US THAT DEATH HAS CONQUERED, AS ARM IN ARM WITH THE MONSTROUS CREATURE WHO BROUGHT HIM DOOM, HE MOVES INTO THE DEPTHS WHERE ENDLESS AGONY AWAITS THE EVIL!...
MERCILESSLY, THE WATER RUSHES IN UPON ALAN, CRUSHING THE "LIFE" HE NEVER REALLY HAD, UNTIL ONE FINAL GASP ESCAPES FROM HIS TORMENTED BODY AND...
The End
7

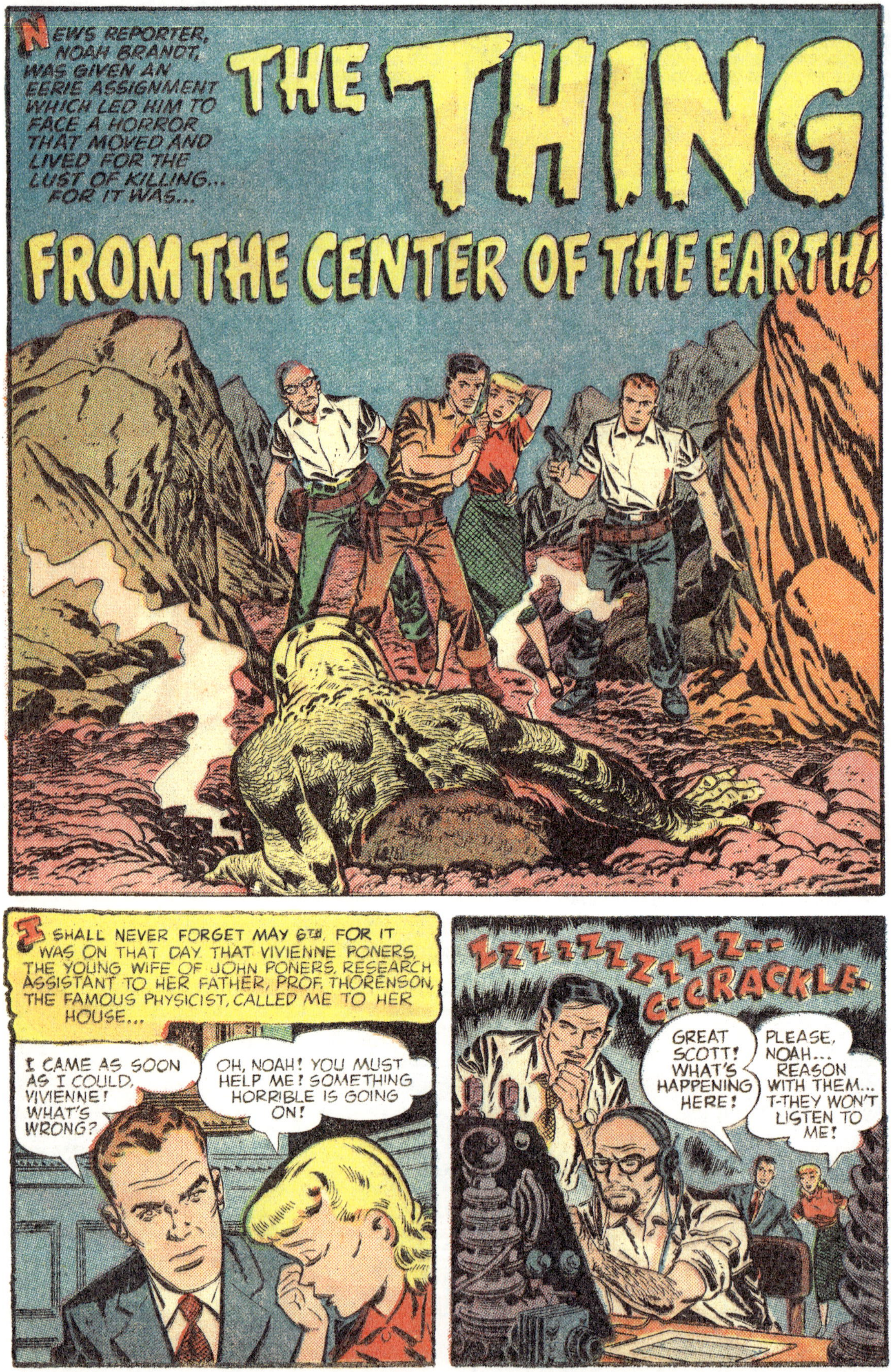

NEWS REPORTER, NOAH BRANDT, WAS GIVEN AN EERIE ASSIGNMENT WHICH LED HIM TO FACE A HORROR THAT MOVED AND LIVED FOR THE LUST OF KILLING... FOR IT WAS...

THE THING FROM THE CENTER OF THE EARTH!

MR. BRANDT! THIS IS INDEED A PLEASURE!
NOAH! WHERE HAVE YOU BEEN HIDING YOURSELF? COME IN! COME IN! YOU'RE GOING TO SEE SOMETHING YOU NEVER DREAMED ABOUT!
SO I UNDERSTAND FROM VIVIENNE!

JOHN PULLED ME EXCITEDLY TOWARDS A CLUSTER OF WEIRD-LOOKING INSTRUMENTS THAT FLICKERED ON AND OFF AT REGULAR INTERVALS INTER-LOCKED WITH A SERIES OF SOUND SIGNALS THAT ROSE AND DECREASED IN INTENSITY!
NOAH...WHAT IF I TOLD YOU THAT THERE'S SOME SORT OF LIFE DEEP WITHIN THE EARTH... A LIFE WE'RE NOT EVEN AWARE OF?
I'D SAY YOU'RE EITHER JOKING OR WORKING TOO HARD!
BBEEEPP EEEP

NO, I ASSURE YOU...I NEVER WAS MORE SERIOUS IN ALL MY LIFE! PROF. THORENSON AND I HAVE MANAGED TO CONTACT THIS "BEING" OR WHATEVER IT IS WHEN WE FIRST NOTICED IRREG-ULARITIES IN OUR RADAR SIGNALS WITHIN THIS AREA!

AS YOU KNOW, WE WERE FIRST TRYING TO FIND HOW DEEP, MODIFIED ELECTRICAL IMPULSES CAN PENETRATE THE EARTH'S CORE FROM THE RETURN IMPULSES OF THESE WAVES. THEN WE STARTED GETTING INTELLI-GENT RESPONSES. WE EREC-TED A DEVICE THAT ENABLES WHATEVER IT IS TO REACH THE SURFACE VIA OUR BEAM!

THAT'S WHY I CALLED YOU HERE, NOAH! YOU MUST STOP THEM! I JUST KNOW SOMETHING IS TERRIBLY WRONG HERE! I HAVE SUCH A-A STRONG FEELING OF DANGER!
YOU'RE RIGHT, VIVIENNE! SHOULDN'T YOU CONTACT THE PROPER AUTHORITIES ON THIS DISCOVERY, PROF?

YES, EXCEPT FOR ONE THING! WE HAVE NO VISIBLE MEANS OF PROOF...AND BEFORE WE COULD SET UP THE NECESSARY BATTERY OF TESTS TO ES-TABLISH OUR FINDINGS, WE'LL LOSE THE SIGNAL, PERHAPS FOREVER!

I COULD SENSE THE THRILL OF PENETRATING THE UNKNOWN MYSELF... BUT UNDER THIS EXCITEMENT WAS A FAR MORE SERIOUS MOTIVE! WHAT WOULD THEY FIND? I DECIDED TO STICK WITH THEM, AND A FEW DAYS LATER, WE SET OUT FOR THE REGION WHERE THESE IMPULSES WERE STRONGEST...

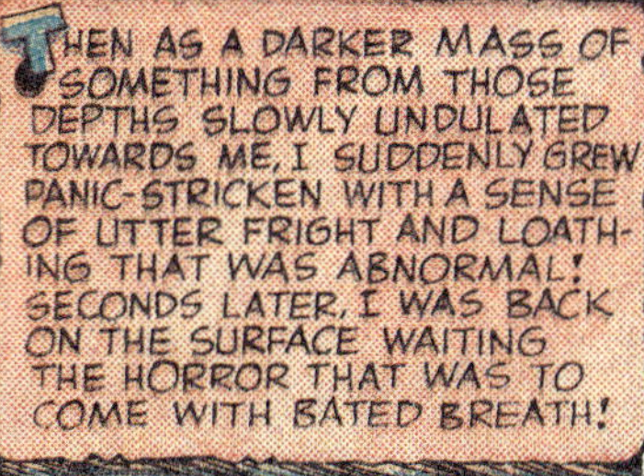
THEN AS A DARKER MASS OF SOMETHING FROM THOSE DEPTHS SLOWLY UNDULATED TOWARDS ME, I SUDDENLY GREW PANIC-STRICKEN WITH A SENSE OF UTTER FRIGHT AND LOATHING THAT WAS ABNORMAL! SECONDS LATER, I WAS BACK ON THE SURFACE WAITING THE HORROR THAT WAS TO COME WITH BATED BREATH!

NOAH! WHAT IS IT? DID YOU SEE ANYTHING DOWN THERE!
WAIT...DO YOU HEAR IT? IT... IT'S COMING UP!

E-E-EEEE! IT'S A PAIR OF HANDS. T-T-THEY'RE AS BIG AS OUR OWN ARMS!
DON'T LOSE YOUR NERVES! KEEP CALM! WATCH!

AAAARRRRGGGHH!!

GOOD LORD! IT...IT HAS A HUMAN SHAPE...BUT... BUT THAT FACE...UGGH! IT'S THAT OF A SENTIENT INTELLIGENCE, NOT HUMAN!
BACK... GET BACK TO THE SHACK! HURRY!
AAAARRRRGGHH

ONE LOOK WAS ENOUGH FOR ME! THIS WAS NO ORDINARY CREATURE... IT SEEMED RATHER TO BE A THING THAT HAD BEEN INCREDIBLY ALIVE FOR HUNDREDS OF CENTURIES...FILLING ALL WHO LOOKED AT IT WITH NAMELESS DREAD!
JOHN...I TOLD YOU NOT TO VIOLATE THE SECRETS OF NATURE! I TOLD YOU... OHH!
DON'T LOSE YOUR COURAGE HONEY! WE'LL THINK OF SOMETHING TO CONTROL THAT...THAT BEAST! WE MUST!

CRASH!
WELL... RIGHT NOW...I'D GRAB THESE RIFLES IF I WERE YOU! THAT BABY OUT THERE MEANS BUSINESS!
OHHH... HE'S SMASHING THOUSANDS OF DOLLARS WORTH OF EQUIPMENT! WE CAN'T JUST STAND HERE! WE MUST STOP IT!

BUT THERE WAS NO STOPPING THIS MONSTER THAT BROUGHT TERROR AND FEAR TO THE HEARTS OF EVEN THE BRAVEST OF US! WE WAITED PARALYZED, FOR THE MOMENT IT WOULD TEAR DOWN THE DOOR, AND STALK IN TOWARD US...!

YES, WE WERE THROUGH WITH THE HORROR, BUT WE HADN'T FORGOTTEN IT. WHEN PEOPLE STOP AND KID ME ABOUT MY GRAY HAIR, I ALWAYS KID RIGHT BACK...FOR THIS IS ONE STORY, I, NOAH BRANDT, CAN NEVER WRITE FOR POSTERITY!

THE END

THE MARRIAGE OF THE MONSTERS

"Groth, when I push this lever down one million volts of electricity will flood into the body of this woman. The electricity will be as a life blood to her. I will have created my second being. I . . ."

"But, doctor, what about your first . . . ah . . . being? It has escaped and is prowling about free in the forest around our castle."

"Fool! What do you think I created her for? If I tried to capture him now he would probably kill himself trying to get away. He is far from perfected. But, he has all the emotions of a human being and as we, seeks a mate. Well, here is his mate. And when she lives, he will know and come for her. Then, we will get him. However, enough of this idle mumbling. Check the voltage. I am ready to begin."

As Groth shuffled over to a huge panel on which jutted out numerous levers and dials, the movement of his body creased the deep shadows that choked the laboratory.

"All is ready, master!"

"Good! Good!"

The veins stringing Doctor Drakov's right arm tightened and rose as the doctor began to pull the lever down.

A second later, the two gigantic electrodes seemed to explode in an orgy of flashing light. A million volts of electricity coursed down thin wires and into small electrodes driven into the neck of a corpse.

Then, as the slashing electricity flared to an even higher brilliance, gashing deep ravines of fear in the faces of the two men looking on, the "dead" woman lying on the crude wooden table began to tremble!

First, her eyelids moved. Then, her ghostly white skin took on a pinkish color as the searing electricity pulsing red hot through her body burned life into her. Finally, a low moan slithered through teeth originally jammed shut by DEATH!

"Enough, Groth. Stop the current. She lives!"

The two men ran to the operating table and began to loosen the electrical apparatus which had cheated death.

"Ha, look, Groth. Another example of my genius. Do you remember when they threw me out of the convention? Mad they said. Impossible to bring the dead back. Well, look, Groth. Am I mad? Is not that life you see before you?"

Then, quickly realizing that certain things had to be done to maintain life in this "being," Doctor Drakov bent over his creation ready to administer a stimulant.

But . . .

"AAARRRGGGHHH!!!"

Smashing through the heavy oaken door of the laboratory with one hand came the male monster. He had come for his mate.

"M-master! Torg has c-come to claim her!"

"No, no! I did not think he would come now. Quick, Groth, when he steps on the trap door pull the lever. Pull . . ."

Drakov could not finish for the monster knew of the trap door. With human intelligence he circled it and advanced on the cringing men!

"Back! Back! I have created you. I am your master!"

"Aiieehhh!"

Groth crumpled to the ground, his neck smashed by one blow from the monster. And as he backed away, Drakov came into contact with a live wire. When the flash had dimmed, a blackened corpse lay sprawled on the floor.

Then, Torg staggered over to the table where his mate lay. Sweeping her up in his arms he stumbled out of the laboratory.

But, already, he felt a strange feeling of weakness in his body. His life-giving electricity was sputtering out.

Soon, Death will have conquered again!

Strange Superstitions

MAGICAL INFLUENCE–
WHEN THE *OJIBWA INDIAN* WANTS TO BRING *SICKNESS* TO THE BODY OF AN *ENEMY*, HE MAKES A SMALL WOODEN *IMAGE* OF THE PERSON AND *PIERCES* ITS *HEAD* AND *HEART* WITH *NEEDLES*, BELIEVING THAT HIS ENEMY WILL EXPERIENCE THE SAME FATE. IF THE PURPOSE IS *TO KILL*, THE *IMAGE* IS *BURNED*.

OMEN OF DEATH–
THE *HOWLING OF DOGS*, THE *LOWING OF CATTLE*, AND THE *CROWING OF ROOSTERS* AT NIGHT, ARE SUPPOSED TO *FORETELL* THE *DEATH* OF A PERSON AS THESE ANIMALS ARE SAID TO BE ABLE TO SEE *DEATH* ENTER THE HOME OF THE *DOOMED* ONE.

WITCHES
MANY PEOPLE THINK OF A *WITCH* AS A PERSON OF *EVIL*. BUT, FOR MANY CENTURIES, THEY WERE CALLED UPON TO RELIEVE THE *MISFORTUNES OF ILLNESSES, CHILDBIRTH*, AND, IN MANY WAYS, ASSUMED THE ROLE OF A *DOCTOR*.

TABOOS
ALL OVER THE WORLD, *KNOTS* ARE CONSIDERED OBJECTIONABLE. THE *PARLIAMENT OF BORDEAUX*, IN 1718, HAD A PERSON *BURNED* ALIVE FOR CAUSING THE *RUIN* OF A FAMILY BY MEANS OF TYING *KNOTS*.

THE WEREWOLF
"SKIN CHANGER" AND *"TURN COAT"* WERE TERMS USE BY THE *ROMANS* TO DESCRIBE THE *WEREWOLF*. DURING THE *MEDIEVAL AGES* PEOPLE BELIEVED THAT WHILE THE *WEREWOLF* WAS IN HIS *HUMAN FORM* HIS *HAIR* GREW *INWARDS*, AND WHEN HE CHANGED INTO A *WOLF* HE JUST *TURNED* HIMSELF *INSIDE OUT*.

Have Fun! Thrills! Romances!
Anyone Can Learn to Dance
Square Dances
Fox Trot
Jitterbug
Samba
Waltz
Rhumba
Why put off learning to Dance—NOW Here's a much EASIER WAY than YOU ever SAW!
No longer do YOU have to sit and watch while others enjoy dancing NOW you can join the fun! Think of the great pleasure. You'll get. SURPRISE and AMAZE your friends when they see you do the latest dance steps with ease. Learn from simple lessons by Betty Lee, one of America's foremost dance authorities.
LEARN THE FOX TROT, COUNTRY DANCES, RHUMBA, SAMBA, CALL SQUARE DANCES!
16 COMPLETE DANCE COURSES—each worth as much as you pay for the entire book. Join thousands who have learned to dance with the help of this amazing book. Written in simple language full of easy-to-follow illustrations—You Learn to Dance in the Privacy of Your Own Home.
LEARN TO DANCE IN 5 DAYS OR PAY NOTHING Here's a wonderful offer. Test this exciting book 5 days — See how it can help you become a smooth dancer and be admired. Yes, You Dance in 5 Days or return book for prompt refund of purchase price.
If You Can Do This Step — You Can Dance in 5 Days!
Simple as ABC
Here's how this exciting book can help you become a smooth dancer. It's full of easy-to-follow diagrams and instructions.
Dancing
ONLY $1.98 POSTPAID
MAIL THIS COUPON TODAY
FUN PARADE INC. DEPT. W-6
1860 Broadway New York 23, N.Y.
Please rush my copy of "Dancing" in plain wrapper. If I am not satisfied, I may return book in 5 days for full refund of purchase price.
Send C.O.D. I'll pay postman $1.98 plus postage.*
I enclose $1.98, you pay postage. Same guarantee applies.*
NAME
ADDRESS
CITY
STATE
LEARN THE FOX TROT, COUNTRY DANCES, RHUMBA, SAMBA, CALL SQUARE DANCES!
Canada and Foreign $2.25 in advance

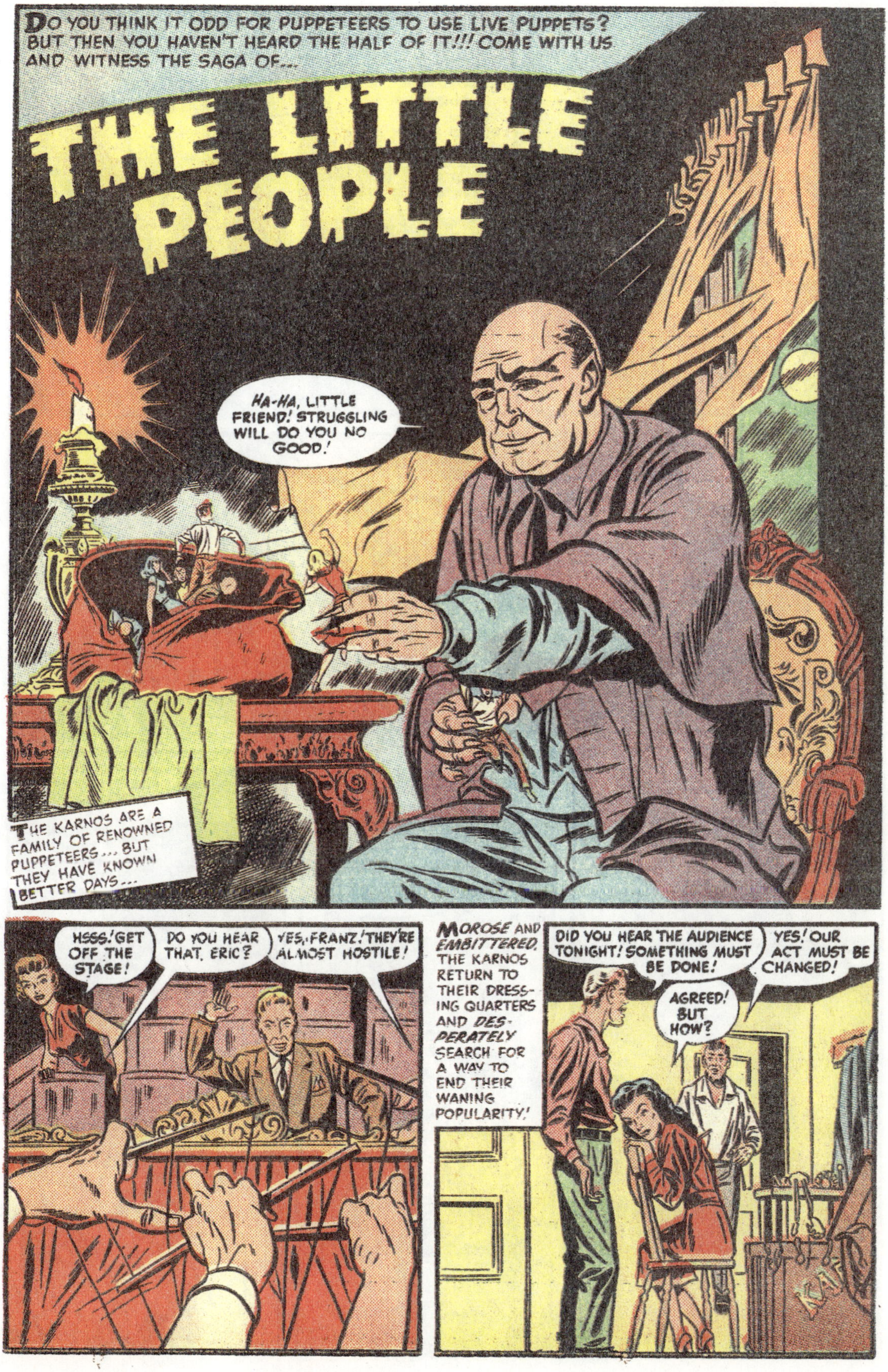

DO YOU THINK IT ODD FOR PUPPETEERS TO USE LIVE PUPPETS? BUT THEN YOU HAVEN'T HEARD THE HALF OF IT!!! COME WITH US AND WITNESS THE SAGA OF...

THE LITTLE PEOPLE

HA-HA, LITTLE FRIEND! STRUGGLING WILL DO YOU NO GOOD!

THE KARNOS ARE A FAMILY OF RENOWNED PUPPETEERS... BUT THEY HAVE KNOWN BETTER DAYS...

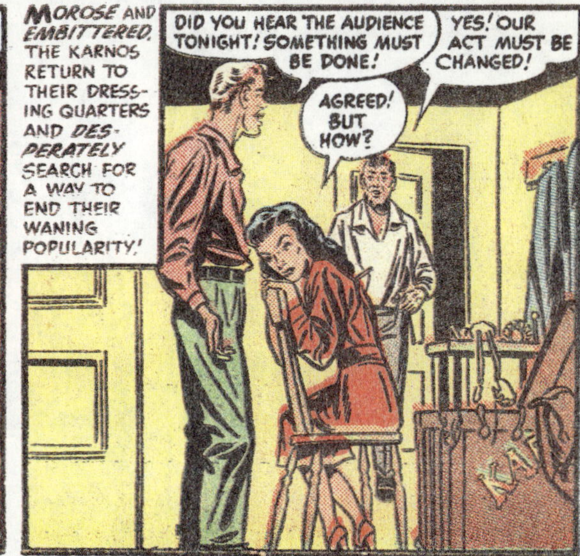

THERE MUST BE A WAY! THERE MUST OR WE'LL BE RUINED!
WE'RE NOT FAR FROM THAT NOW!
BE REASONABLE. HOW CAN A MARIONETTE ACT BE CHANGED? PUPPETS ARE PUPPETS!
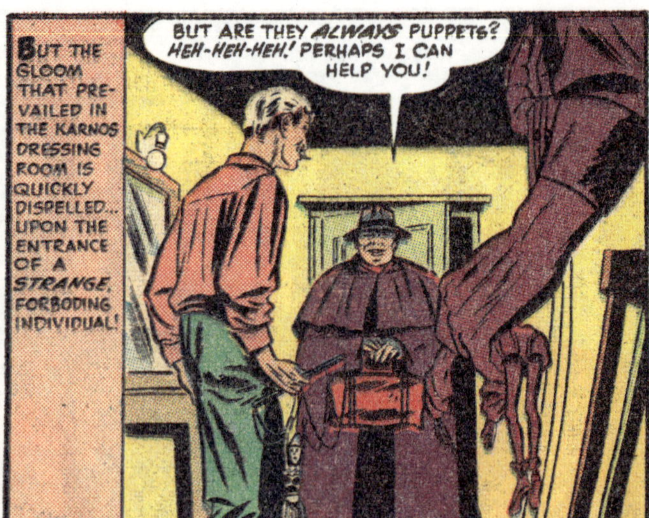
BUT THE GLOOM THAT PREVAILED IN THE KARNOS DRESSING ROOM IS QUICKLY DISPELLED... UPON THE ENTRANCE OF A STRANGE, FORBODING INDIVIDUAL!
BUT ARE THEY ALWAYS PUPPETS? HEH-HEH-HEH! PERHAPS I CAN HELP YOU!

AND AS THE OLD MAN REACHES INTO HIS SATCHEL, THE KARNOS WATCH IN SPEECHLESS AMAZEMENT!!
HEH-HEH-HEH!!
HELP!! PUT US DOWN!!

THEY'RE ...ALIVE!
WONDERFUL! LIVING MARIONETTES!
HELP!

INSTANTLY, FIENDISHLY... THE KARNOS' PERVERTED BRAINS FUNCTION IN UNISON AS THE SAME DIABOLICAL THOUGHT REGISTERS WITH EACH! TO THE OBVIOUS SATISFACTION OF THE STRANGER!
IN OUR ACT THEY'D BE A SENSATION!
REAL PUPPETS! HA HA! WE'LL TIE STRINGS TO THEM!

FOR THE RIGHT PRICE, THEY'RE YOURS!
ANYTHING! WE'LL PAY ANYTHING FOR THESE LITTLE PEOPLE! HA-HA!

SPLENDID! AND REMEMBER--I'LL HAVE MORE FOR YOU AS YOU NEED THEM! HEH-HEH-HEH!

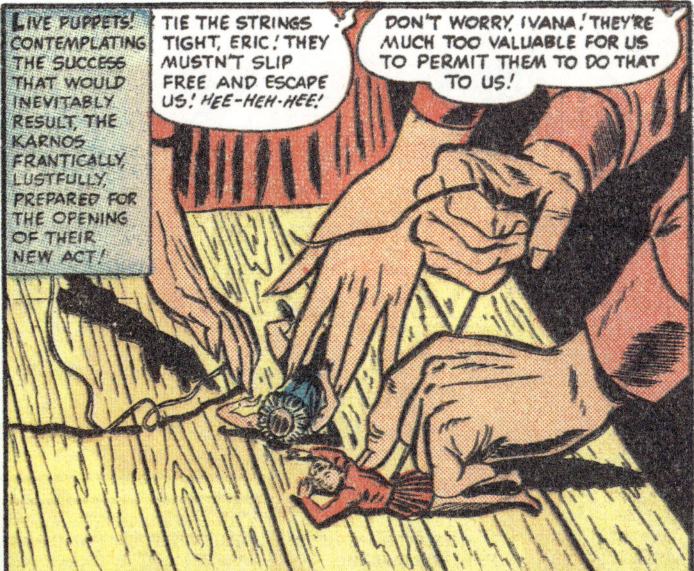
LIVE PUPPETS! CONTEMPLATING THE SUCCESS THAT WOULD INEVITABLY RESULT, THE KARNOS FRANTICALLY, LUSTFULLY, PREPARED FOR THE OPENING OF THEIR NEW ACT!
TIE THE STRINGS TIGHT, ERIC! THEY MUSTN'T SLIP FREE AND ESCAPE US! HEE-HEH-HEE!
DON'T WORRY, IVANA! THEY'RE MUCH TOO VALUABLE FOR US TO PERMIT THEM TO DO THAT TO US!

AND WHEN THE STRINGS WERE FASTENED THE LITTLE PEOPLE WERE HERDED OUT FROM THE WINGS ONTO THE STAGE TO REHEARSE THEIR ACT! AN ACT OF VIOLENCE AND DEATH TO BE PERFORMED WITH BREATHTAKING REALITY BY THE KARNOS' LIFE-LIKE MARIONETTES!!
ALL RIGHT! NOW AS I'VE INSTRUCTED YOU! LEAP AT ONE ANOTHER BRANDISHING YOUR WOODEN DAGGERS AS IF THEY WERE REAL!
DON'T CRY! IT'LL BE ALL RIGHT. IT'S ONLY AN ACT
OOHHH! (SOB)

AND LATE THAT NIGHT...
DON'T BE FRIGHTENED! YOU SAW THEY HAD US USE WOODEN DAGGERS! THEY DON'T MEAN US ANY HARM!
I-I'M SCARED, JOHNNY!

BUT BACKSTAGE BEFORE THE PERFORMANCE ITSELF, THE FORLORN SOULS LEARN THE GHOULISH TRUTH!!
PLACE THE REAL DAGGERS IN THEIR HANDS, ERIC! HA-HA-HA!
THE DEATH SCENE PERFORMED BY OUR PUPPETS WILL BE HIGHLY REALISTIC!
HELP! NO OOO!

SILENCE! ALL OF YOU! OR I'LL DO AWAY WITH YOU MYSELF!
HEE-HEE-HEE!
HELP... STOP!

AND THE CURTAIN RISES UPON THE FIENDISH PERFORMANCE!
AIEEE!
AGGGHHRRR!!! DON'T KILL...ME...AGGHHRR...!
I'M NOT DOING...NOT DOING...IT... AIEEEE!
NOOOO! DON'T PLEASE--- DON'T! AIEEE!!
I CAN'T HELP IT! MY HAND! THEY'RE MAKING ME DO IT!
THE INITIAL REACTION OF THE AUDIENCE WAS THAT OF STARTLED SHOCK...AS THE MINUTE FIGURES ON THE STAGE REAPED BLOODY CARNAGE UPON ONE ANOTHER!!!
EEEK!
NO!
STOP IT!
BUT IT WASN'T LONG BEFORE THEY "REALIZED" THAT IT WAS ALL MERELY A CLEVERLY DEVISED ACT...COMPELLING IN ITS REALISM!! AND THEY APPLAUDED IT AS SUCH!
BRAVO! KARNO
AND THAT EVENING AFTER RECEIVING A TREMENDOUS OVATION THE KARNOS RETIRE IN DIABOLICAL GLEE TO DISPOSE OF THE BROKEN LITTLE CORPSES OF THE PUPPETS WHO HAD PERFORMED SO WELL!
HA-HA-HA! IT WAS SUPERB! DID YOU EVER HEAR SUCH A REACTION, IVANA?
NEVER, FRANZ! AND WE STILL HAVE ENOUGH LEFT FOR TOMORROW'S SHOW!
YES! THINGS ARE WORKING OUT WELL!

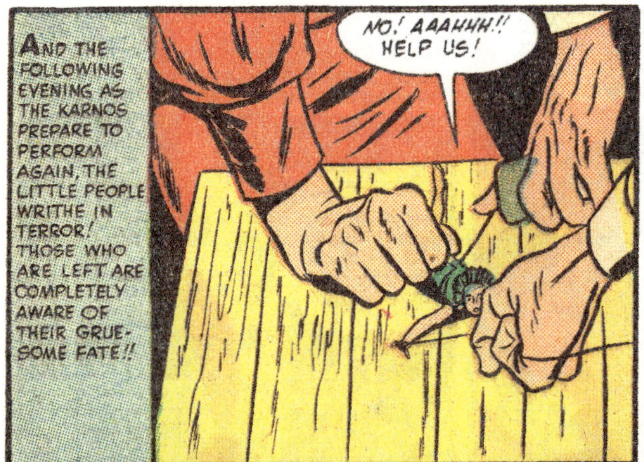
AND THE FOLLOWING EVENING AS THE KARNOS PREPARE TO PERFORM AGAIN, THE LITTLE PEOPLE WRITHE IN TERROR! THOSE WHO ARE LEFT ARE COMPLETELY AWARE OF THEIR GRUESOME FATE!!
NO! AAAHHH!! HELP US!

SEE HOW THEY WRIGGLE, ERIC! THEY SEEM RELUCTANT TO PERFORM!
THEIR ARTISTIC TEMPERAMENTS, PERHAPS! HEE-HEE!

AND THE SECOND PERFORMANCE IS NO LESS SPECTACULAR THAN THE FIRST!
DON'T... DON'T... AGGGHHRRAA!

DON'T-DON'T-- AIEEE!!

AIEEEE!!
BRAVO! HOW REALISTIC!

THE KARNOS RETURNED TO THEIR DRESSING ROOM JUBILANTLY AFTER THEIR SECOND STUNNING PERFORMANCE, AND THEY TOAST TO THEIR HIDEOUS SUCCESS!!
TO THE KARNOS! WHOSE MARIONETTE RERFORMANCES ARE UNEQUALLED FOR REALISM! HA-HA-HA!
OR FOR FINANCIAL SUCCESS!

AND THE OMINOUS INDIVIDUAL RETURNS TO A CITY OF THE "LITTLE PEOPLE" TO COLLECT MORE HUMAN MARIONETTES TO BE SACRIFICED SO BRUTALLY FOR THE PROFIT OF HIMSELF AND THE KARNOS... AND THE EDIFICATION OF THEIR AUDIENCE.

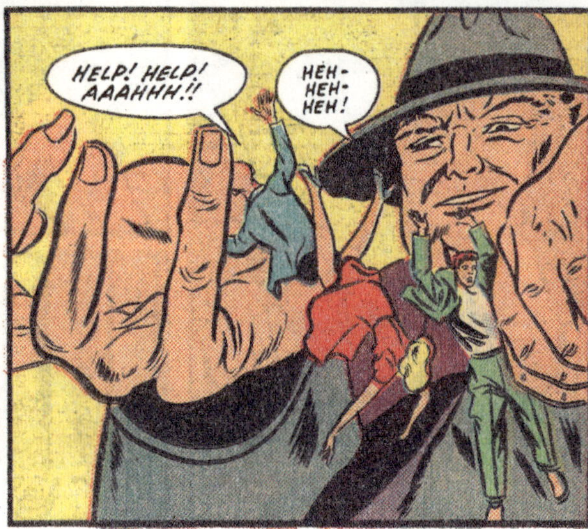

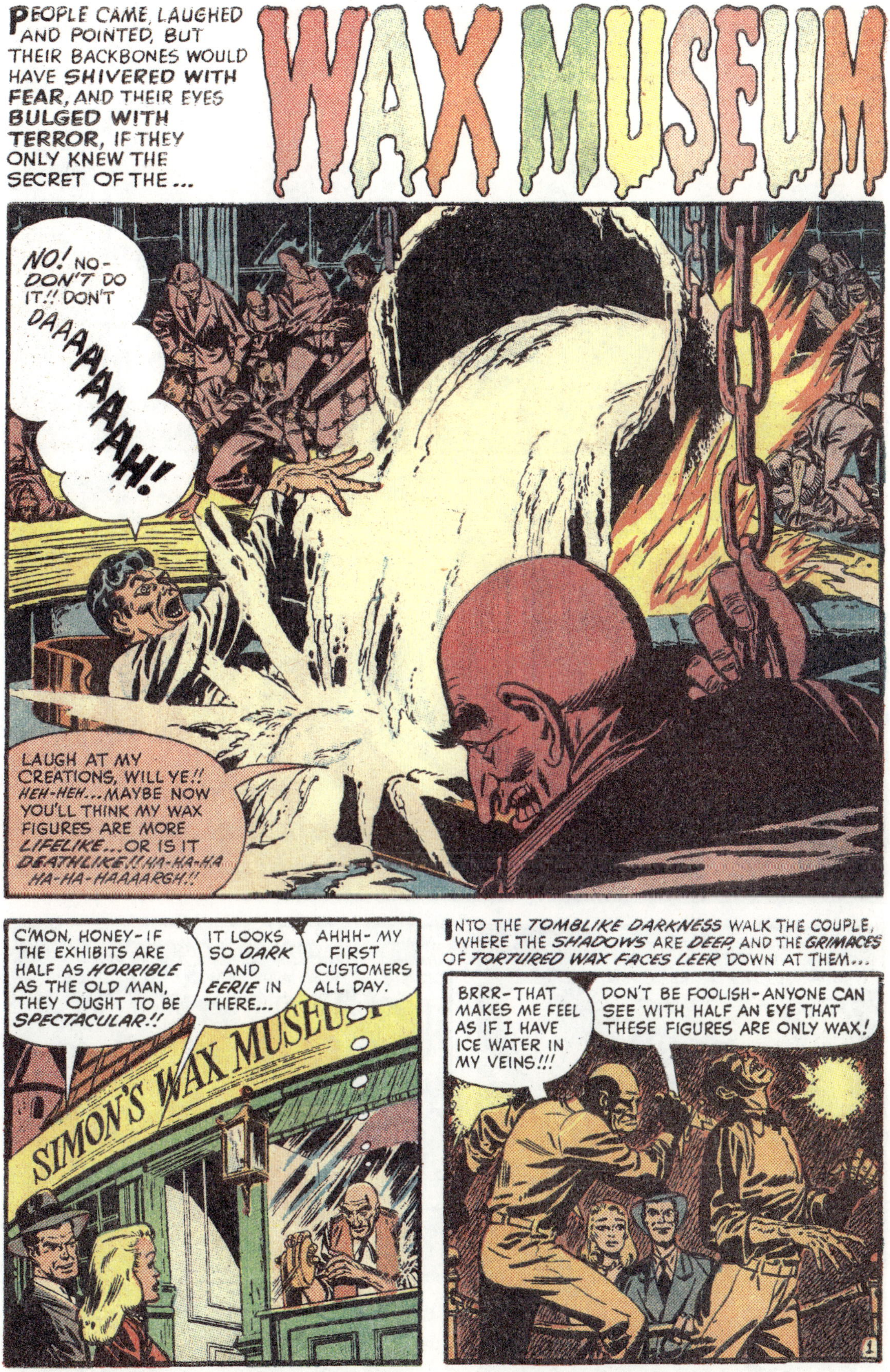

PEOPLE CAME, LAUGHED AND POINTED, BUT THEIR BACKBONES WOULD HAVE **SHIVERED WITH FEAR**, AND THEIR EYES **BULGED WITH TERROR**, IF THEY ONLY KNEW THE SECRET OF THE ...

NO! NO-*DON'T* DO IT!! DON'T DAAAAAAAAH!

LAUGH AT MY CREATIONS, WILL YE!! *HEH-HEH*... MAYBE NOW YOU'LL THINK MY WAX FIGURES ARE MORE *LIFELIKE*... OR IS IT *DEATHLIKE!! HA-HA-HA HA-HA-HAAAARGH!!*

INTO THE *TOMBLIKE DARKNESS* WALK THE COUPLE, WHERE THE *SHADOWS* ARE *DEEP*, AND THE *GRIMACES* OF *TORTURED WAX FACES LEER* DOWN AT THEM...

WELL, WELL, WELL- DO YOU LIKE MY EXHIBIT? I AM AN ARTIST IN WAX, AS YOU CAN SEE. IT TOOK YEARS OF LONG, LONELY WORK TO LEARN THE TRADE!
YOUR FIGURES HAVE GROWN OLD AND MUSTY, SIMON! NO WONDER YOU HAVE SO FEW CUSTOMERS! THEY HAVE NO LIFE!

SOMETHING SNAPS IN THE OLD MAN'S MIND, A MIND TOO LONG TURNED IN UPON ITSELF DURING THE LONG HOURS OF WORK! FIENDISH THOUGHTS ENTER THE CRACKED BRAIN...
MY WORK WILL NEVER GROW OLD - IT IS DEATHLESS, D'YA HEAR ... DEATHLESS!!

LET'S GET OUT OF HERE... I THINK YOU GOT THE OLD MAN MAD!
AHHH, THE HARMLESS OLD FOOL!

NAAAAAH!! KEEP AWAY... KEEP AWAY!

NOT LIFELIKE, EH?? HEH-HEH... NOBODY WILL BE ABLE TO SAY THAT ABOUT MY WORK AGAIN!!

UMMFF... UMMM... OOMFF!
IT MUST BE SCALDING HOT- HOT ENOUGH TO SEAR THE FLESH FROM YOUR BONES!!
2

SLOWLY THE SISLING LIQUID SLITHERS TOWARD THE THROAT AND BLANKS OUT THE EYES, HARDENS THE MOUTH INTO A *GAPING EXPRESSION* OF *HORROR*...

SOON THE FAME OF SIMON'S LIFELIKE EXHIBIT SPREAD THRU THE CITY, AND HIS MONEYBOX SWELLED ALONG WITH HIS *INSANE PRIDE*. BUT ONE DAY...

SEE, MABEL- IT WAS EASILY EXPLAINED! BUT IT SURE DID FEEL LIKE WARM, STICKY BLOOD!
LET'S GET OUT OF HERE! THIS PLACE IS TOO MUCH LIKE A LIVING GRAVE-YARD!
SO THE BLOOD IS STILL HOT IN THEIR VEINS!! THEY ARE STILL ALIVE AND THEY SUFFER!

SO YOU TWO CAN STILL HEAR ME!! HA-HA-HA! I THINK I'LL GIVE THE TORTURE RACK A FEW MORE TURNS-

BUT IN THE DEAD SILENCE OF THE NIGHT, THE MAN CALLS ON HIS REMAINING STRENGTH AND...
CRRRRRACK...
CRRRRR RUNCH

SWIFTLY, THE HALF-HUMAN, HALF-WAX FIGURE, WITH THE SMELL OF DEATH HANGING ABOUT IT, SLIPS INTO SIMON'S BEDROOM, AND..
YOUR TIME HAS COME, OLD MAN!!

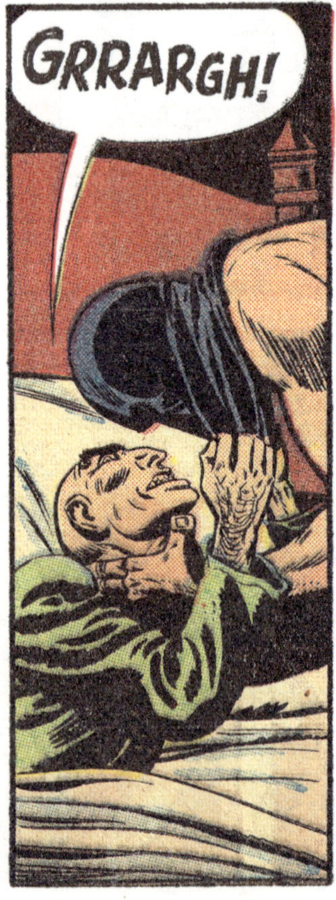
GRRARGH!

SIMON'S CLUTCHING HANDS, CLUTCHING FOR LIFE, SUDDENLY RIPS AWAY THE HANGMAN'S HOOD, AND...
AIEEEEE!! A DEMON FROM HELL HAS COME TO CLAIM ME!
4

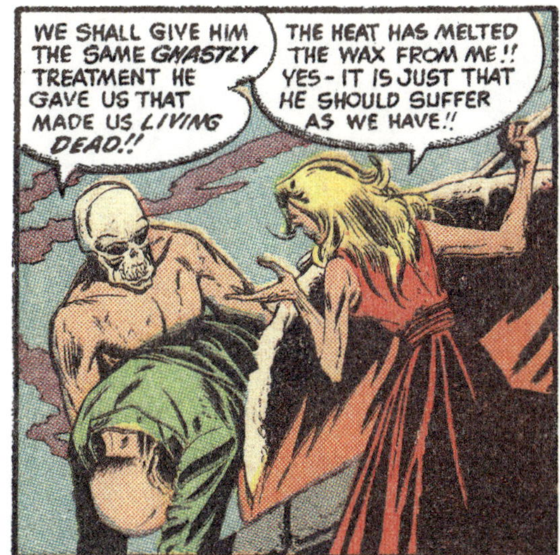
WE SHALL GIVE HIM THE SAME GHASTLY TREATMENT HE GAVE US THAT MADE US LIVING DEAD!!
THE HEAT HAS MELTED THE WAX FROM ME!! YES - IT IS JUST THAT HE SHOULD SUFFER AS WE HAVE!!

NO! DON'T!! PLEASE - HAVE MERCY!! HAVE M... AHHHHGLUG!!
THE SAME MERCY YOU HAD FOR US. FIEND!!

OHOOOOOO!!
THE PLACE IS ON FIRE!! MY SKIN GROWS HOT!!
THE WAX IS PART OF US! WE HAVE TO GET OUT OF HERE - OR WE'LL MELT!!

HELP!! HELLLLPPP...
MELTING!! WE'RE MELT... ...I... NNGGGGG!!

AND AMID THE RAGING FIRE, THE TWO GROTESQUE FIGURES MELT DOWN LIKE BURNING CANDLES, EXTINGUISHING THEIR STRANGE EXISTENCE, AND THE WAX MAKER'S SECRET FOREVER...

HEY, JOE - LOOK AT THIS EXHIBIT! THE FIRE DIDN'T GET THIS ONE. SAY, THAT GUY WHO RUNS THIS PLACE MUST HAVE SOME IMAGINATION TO MAKE SOMETHING LIKE THIS!! ARRRGH - IT'S GRUESOME... ALMOST LOOKS REAL!!
YEAH! THERE'S NOTHING ALIVE HERE! LET'S GO-
THE END
5

the LIVING DEAD

George felt a hand touch his shoulder.

"Who's there?"

No one was there. There was nothing but the eerie expanse of the graveyard.

"That's what happens when you decide to walk by a graveyard... for a pleasure stroll."

"Do you think so?",

"Who's that?? Who are you??? Where are you???"

"Right next to you, my friend! Don't be frightened!"

"I'm going crazy! There's nothing here! Blast this horrible place!" George started to walk fast—and then run!

"Don't run... I'll follow you! Stop!"

George was brought to a stop by an invisible hand that broke out of the blackness!

"Please listen to me! Don't be frightened!"

"Who are you??? I can't see you!!"

"Of course, you can't. I am invisible! And I need you to help me. Just listen to me, my friend. Give me a chance!"

"Talk. Talk, whoever you are!"

"Many years ago, an evil witch—yes, there are witches, my friend—cast a terrible spell on me and gave me this invisible shape! I must roam the world in this way until I can find someone who has enough faith in me to lend me his body for a minute. Then I will be free!"

"You want *me* to lend you my shape? Why has no one done it before?"

"If men have no trust in mortal men, how can you expect them to trust one from the unknown? Help me, my friend!"

George was frightened. He trembled in the thought of being invisible. But, he believed this strange creature of the night—and was sorry for him.

"All right, I'll help you. Take my body!"

"Thank you, my friend. You shall be repaid!"

A great blast shook the night as phantoms danced in the darkness!

"What happened?? Where am I? My body—*I'm invisible!!* How much longer must I stay like this???"

"Hah, hah, hah!!! Possibly forever, my friend ...or until you find someone as trustworthy as yourself! You have loaned me your body for a minute—and now I am free! But, I never said I would give it back to you! Thank you, my invisible friend!"

George looked at himself—and saw nothing. He watched his body run away into the distance, and he realized his fate!

"Why do you have to be so cruel? Haven't we enough money?"

"Enough money? My dear, do you think I can ever have enough money? No, no! I want more and more and more!!!"

"But Stephen—you can't take it with you!"

"So I can't take it with me? Hah! Go away, my foolish wife! So you think I can't take it with me?? Hah! Well I won't leave my money for you or any of those children! Get out of my sight!"

Gilda Watson moved out of the sight of her husband's ravenous eyes. She walked out of his study and left him alone with his greed.

Watson picked up the telephone.

"Get me my factory... Hello, Somkin! I want production doubled by the end of the month! I don't care how hard it will be! No, of course, no new help. Let them twist and writhe in the dust of the factory—and if they don't like it, let them seek work elsewhere! I want more money!... You, too! So I can't take it with me? Hah! Good-bye, you fool!"

There was silence for a moment. Then the door opened.

"I heard all that, Stephen. I've heard enough of your madness!"

"Gilda, put down that gun! What are you trying to do??"

"Isn't it obvious, Stephen? I don't care what happens to me. Perhaps your money will be used for good—when we're both gone..."

"Stop, stop! I'll change, I'll change!"

"You could never change!"

BANG! BANG!

Gilda Watson placed the gun against her forehead.

BANG!

Then silence, and two dead bodies...

A week later, Stephen Watson's will was read.

"This is strange, very strange," said the lawyer. "I've asked him many times to change it—but he refused. All of Stephen Watson's millions are to go toward the purchase of a bejeweled and gold glittered coffin!"

A voice semed to echo through the room: "So I can't take it with me!"

NOW PUBLISHED MONTHLY!
CHAMBER OF CHILLS
MAGAZINE
THE PIT OF THE DAMNED
DEAL OF SATAN
2 MASTERS IN MYSTERY TO THRILL, CHILL YOU!
WITCHES TALES
WE DARE YOU
WEIRD TALES OF UNSEEN TERRORS
FATAL STEPS
BOTH ON SALE AROUND THE 15TH OF EVERY MONTH!
NO MORE WAITING TWO MONTHS FOR THESE SUSPENSE-CHARGED MAGAZINES!
BE SURE TO GET YOUR COPIES!

WEIRD FACTS

IN NEW YORK, JUST TWO YEARS AGO, A PAIR OF DETECTIVES CORNERED A SUSPECT ON THE EIGHTH FLOOR OF A BUILDING. THE SUSPECT LEAPED FOR THE WINDOW AND DIVED OUT INTO SPACE! HIS BODY WAS NEVER FOUND!

IN MUSCATINE, IOWA, A ROCKING CHAIR TOOK IT UPON ITSELF TO ROCK FOR 37 DAYS! MORE THAN 200 PEOPLE SWORE THAT THEY SAW THIS IMPOSSIBLE ACTION... BUT NO ONE COULD DARE ANSWER WHY IT HAPPENED!

ONCE MORE, IN THE NEW YORK METROPOLIS, JUST MONTHS AGO, A MAN LEAPED INTO THE PATH OF AN ONRUSHING TRAIN! SEARCH AS THEY MIGHT, THE POLICE NEVER FOUND THE BODY!

EXPRESS

IN THE 1920'S THE TOMB OF TUTANKH-AMEN, THE GREAT EGYPTIAN PHAROAH, WAS OPENED BY THE CARNARVON EXPLORERS. SOON AFTERWARD, MANY OF THOSE CONNECTED WITH THE EXPLORATION BECAME SICK... AND DIED! WAS THE PHAROAH'S CURSE AT WORK?

THEN, ONLY A YEAR AGO, A YOUNG ENGLISH ARCHEOLOGIST WAS SUDDENLY TAKEN SICK. HE BEGAN BABBLING OF AN EGYPTIAN COURT OF ANCIENT DEAD THAT FOUND HIM GUILTY OF ABUSING THE PAST! HE SOON DIED FROM THE SICKNESS... A SICKNESS THE DOCTORS COULDN'T NAME!

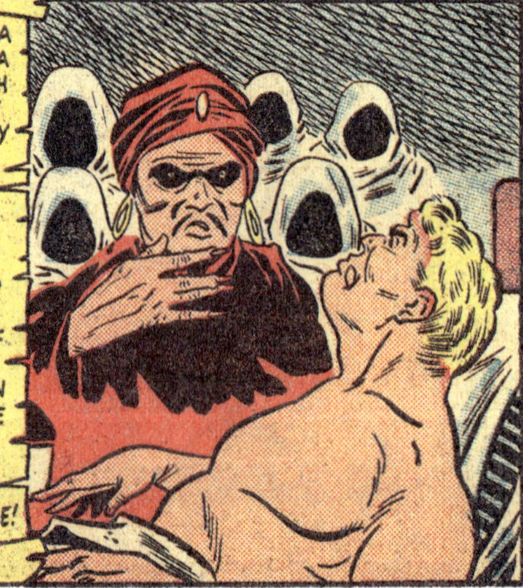

"Scram! You SKINNY Scarecrow!
the boys shouted at me
ONLY A FEW WEEKS AGO!
"I was a SKINNY, scared, girl-shy skeleton. Now I feel and look great. Pal, do as I did, right NOW! Mail the Coupon below.
I gained 53 lbs.
of MIGHTY MUSCLE
6½ inches on my CHEST; 3 inches on each ARM. You can do it in 10 minutes a day!"
—NewYork
Roger D. Hirsch
YOU CAN WIN THIS 15" TALL SILVER TROPHY AS THEY DID! 10 MINUTES OF FUN A DAY IS ALL YOU NEED!
ROGER HIRSCH was an 112 lb. 6 ft. weakling LOOK AT HIM NOW!
"They used to call me,
'SKINNY, SKINNY'
But look at me now —an All-American Jowett Champion"—says John Sill, Utah, who like millions, mailed me 10c and a coupon like the one below YOU MAIL NOW!
"This is The GREAT CHANGE You made in me in 90 DAYS! From a SKINNY WEAKLING to a MIGHTY MAN. With ONE hand I can now lift overhead a boy weighing 145 pounds. I can bend a 1½ inch IRON BAR around my neck. Jowett gives you muscle quality as well as quantity."
Yours,
Jobie Jackson Jr.
ARKANSAS
Jobie Jackson NOW!!!
Jobie Jackson Only 90 DAYS ago!
"NOW, I am a NEW STRONG MAN. It's wonderful! I never dreamed I could live to have a big 49 inch CHEST!! powerful 17 inch ARMS!! a small 32 inch WAIST the big 17 inch difference between my chest and waist attracts everybody's admiration at the beach."
Felipe Mendoza
—CALIFORNIA
MAN! aren't YOU as SICK and TIRED as I and thousands of MIGHTY JOWETT HE-MEN WERE OF BEING SKINNY?
Then, Come on, Pal, do as they did! Give me 10 Pleasant Minutes a Day and I'll give YOU a NEW HE-MAN BODY for your OLD SKELETON FRAME.
NO! I don't e how skinny or flabby you are; if you're a teen-ager, in your 20's or 30's or over; if you're short or tall, or what work you do. All I want is to MAKE YOU OVER by the SAME METHOD I turned myself from a wreck to a Champion of Champions.
YES! You'll see INCH upon INCH of MIGHTY MUSCLE added to YOUR ARMS. Your CHEST deepened. Your BACK AND SHOULDERS broadened. From head to heels, you'll gain SOLIDITY, SIZE, POWER, SPEED! You'll become an ALL-Around, ALL-American HE-MAN, a WINNER in everything you tackle—or my Training won't cost you one single cent!
Develop YOUR 520 MUSCLES
Gain Pounds, INCHES, FAST!
Friend, I've traveled the world. Made a LIFETIME STUDY of every way known to develop your body. Then I devised the BEST by TEST, my "5-WAY PROGRESSIVE POWER" the only method that builds you 5-ways fast. You save YEARS, DOLLARS like movie star Tom Tyler did. Like Champ Roger Hirsch . . . Like MANY THOUSANDS like you did. SO . . .
HURRY TO MAIL COUPON!
George F Jowett Whom experts call "Champion of Champions"
How to Build MIGHTY ARMS
How to Build A MIGHTY CHEST
How to Build A MIGHTY BACK
FREE Photo Book How to Achieve Nerves of Steel, Muscles of Iron
How to Build MIGHTY LEGS
How to Build A MIGHTY GRIP
How to BECOME A MIGHTY HE-MAN
This may be Your LAST chance to GET AMAZING NATIONAL EMERGENCY OFFER! All these for only 5 Picture Packed COURSES on He-Man Building while supply lasts! MILLIONS have been sold for $1 & more
10¢
BOTH FREE FOR QUICK ACTION
1. Photo Book of STRONG MEN
2. MUSCLE METER
DEPT. HA-25
"Jowett Courses greatest in World for Building All-Around HE-MEN". —R.F. Kelley Physical Director
JOWETT INSTITUTE OF PHYSICAL TRAINING
230 FIFTH AVENUE, NEW YORK 1, N.Y. HA-25
George Send me FREE Photo Book of Strong Men, a Muscle Meter, plus all 5 HE-MAN Building Courses 1. How to Build a Mighty Chest; 2 Mighty Arm, 3 Mighty Grip; 4 Mighty Back; 5 Mighty Legs—all in One Volume How to Become a Mighty He-Man." I enclose 10c (No C O D's)
NAME ____ AGE ____
ADDRESS ____
CITY ____ ZONE ____ STATE ____

For Boys - Girls - Hunters - Campers - Everybody!
THE MOST AMAZING SUN WATCH IN THE WORLD!
JUST LOOK AT WHAT IT DOES!
TELZALL 9 IN 1
THE TIMEPIECE OF ADVENTURE!
1. TELLS TIME the truly scientific sun dial way
2. WEATHER FORECASTER secretly concealed, changes colors to predict weather
3. GLOW-IN-THE-DARK COMPASS tells directions day or night
4. STRAP is durable plastic 8" measure
5. 6-POWER MAGNIFYING and burning glass, secretly concealed
6. WORLD'S SMALLEST BALL POINT PEN writes thousands of words
7. SIGNALLING DEVICE on the back
8. CONSTELLATIONS Chart shows how to find the North Star
9. MORSE CODE engraved on the back
Amazing Value $1.98
You'll be the envy of all your friends when you wear this sensational 9-way wonder — the amazing, patented new TELZALL SUN WATCH. It's the only watch of its kind in the world. This tickless time piece tells the sun time . . . nothing to go out of order.
The gracefully designed case of gleaming jeweler's bronze with durable red plastic 8" measuring strap looks like an expensive watch on your wrist. The weather forecaster and the magnifying and fire-starting glass are secretly concealed inside the case.
You'll marvel at the other fascinating features of this wonderful new invention. It may even save your life—with the Morse Code permanently engraved on the back, a glow-in-the-dark compass, signalling mirror, all right on your wrist in case of emergency! What fun, too, being able to predict the weather at a glance, measure objects, write with the world's smallest ball point pen, and locate the North Star and other constellations. Don't delay — rush your order today to be sure of prompt delivery.
SEND NO MONEY! Wear the 9-in-1 Telzall Sun Watch on your wrist. See how perfectly it operates. If you don't agree it's worth many dollars more than the small cost, simply return within 10 days for full refund of purchase price.
MONEY-BACK GUARANTEE — ORDER TODAY
Fun Parade, Inc., 1860 Broadway, New York 23, N. Y.
© 1950 Arkay Enterprises
Patent Pending
10-DAY TRIAL COUPON
FUN PARADE, Inc., Dept. T-1
1860 Broadway, New York 23, N. Y.
RUSH
Gentlemen: Rush ☐ 9-in-1 Telzall Sun Watches described above — on your no-risk 10-day money-back guarantee offer. On delivery I will pay postman only $1.98 each plus C.O.D. postage, with the understanding that if I am not completely satisfied I may return within 10 days for full refund of purchase price.
Name
(please print)
Address
City Zone State
☐ I enclose $1.98 for each — send the Telzall 9-in-1 Sun Watch all postage charges prepaid — on money-back guarantee.

TALES BEYOND BELIEF AND IMAGINATION!
TOMB OF TERROR
No. 2
JULY
TOMB OF TERROR
PDC
10¢
I KNOW IT'S COMING BUT I-CANT-GET-OUT! WHAT! F-FOOT STEPS BEHIND ME! AHHHH...IT IT'S THE QUAGMIRE BEAST!
LEE ELIAS

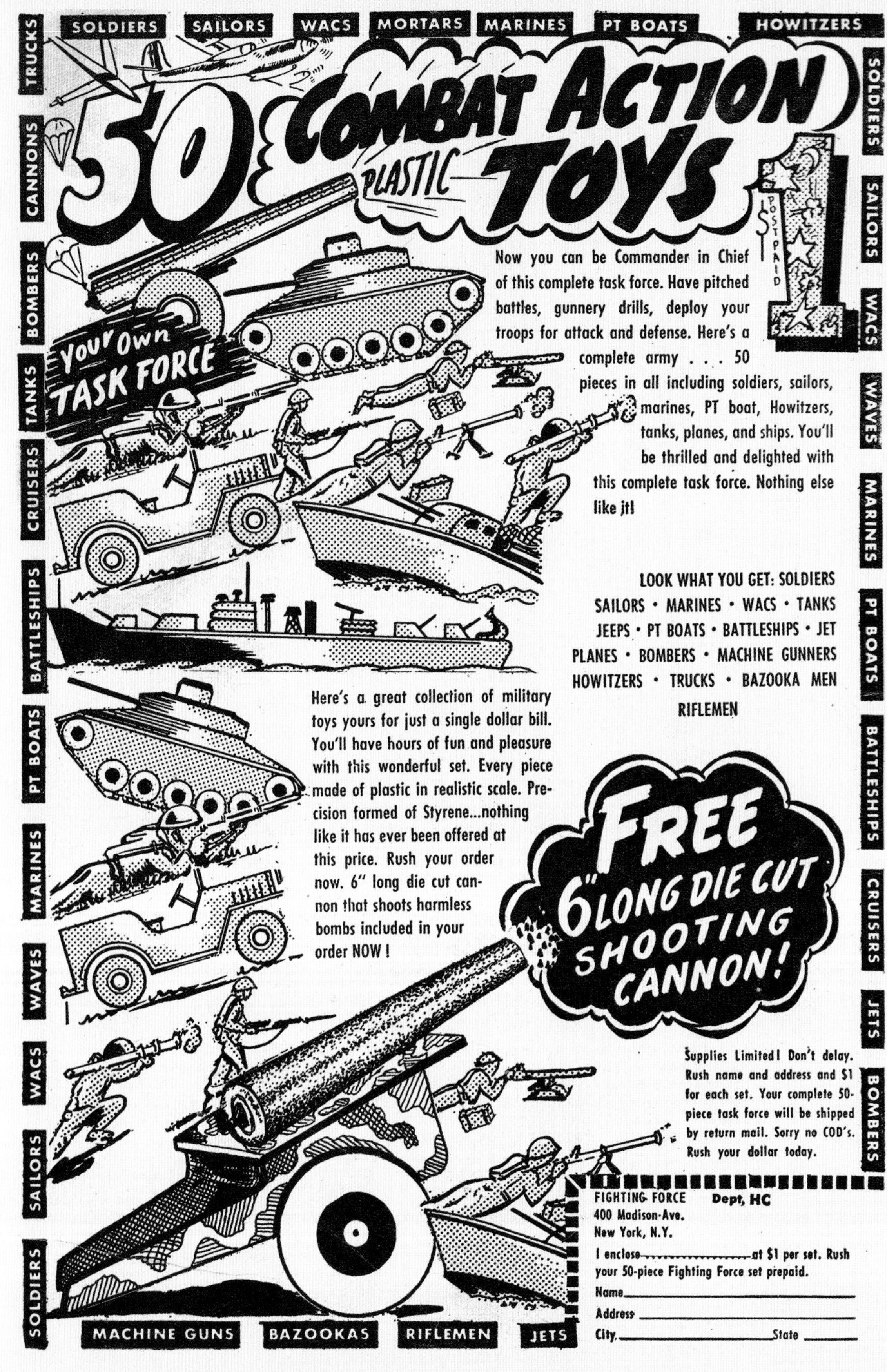
SOLDIERS
SAILORS
WACS
MORTARS
MARINES
PT BOATS
HOWITZERS
50 COMBAT ACTION PLASTIC TOYS
$1 POSTPAID
Your Own TASK FORCE
Now you can be Commander in Chief of this complete task force. Have pitched battles, gunnery drills, deploy your troops for attack and defense. Here's a complete army . . . 50 pieces in all including soldiers, sailors, marines, PT boat, Howitzers, tanks, planes, and ships. You'll be thrilled and delighted with this complete task force. Nothing else like it!
LOOK WHAT YOU GET: SOLDIERS SAILORS • MARINES • WACS • TANKS JEEPS • PT BOATS • BATTLESHIPS • JET PLANES • BOMBERS • MACHINE GUNNERS HOWITZERS • TRUCKS • BAZOOKA MEN RIFLEMEN
Here's a great collection of military toys yours for just a single dollar bill. You'll have hours of fun and pleasure with this wonderful set. Every piece made of plastic in realistic scale. Precision formed of Styrene...nothing like it has ever been offered at this price. Rush your order now. 6" long die cut cannon that shoots harmless bombs included in your order NOW!
FREE 6" LONG DIE CUT SHOOTING CANNON!
Supplies Limited! Don't delay. Rush name and address and $1 for each set. Your complete 50-piece task force will be shipped by return mail. Sorry no COD's. Rush your dollar today.
FIGHTING FORCE Dept, HC
400 Madison Ave.
New York, N.Y.
I enclose.................at $1 per set. Rush your 50-piece Fighting Force set prepaid.
Name
Address
City
State
TRUCKS
CANNONS
BOMBERS
TANKS
CRUISERS
BATTLESHIPS
PT BOATS
MARINES
WAVES
WACS
SAILORS
SOLDIERS
SOLDIERS
SAILORS
WACS
WAVES
MARINES
PT BOATS
BATTLESHIPS
CRUISERS
JETS
BOMBERS
MACHINE GUNS
BAZOOKAS
RIFLEMEN
JETS

THE BEYOND BECKONS...

The wind grabs at the gravestones as it whirls its eerie way through the yard. It whirls onward sweeping over the stories of yesterday.

The blackness of night closes in wrapping the world in its breast and squeezing out the twilight! Flesh shrivels as the demons of the night pour out from the bowels of the earth.

And all roads lead to one place. All steps march on to the same spot. The winds swirl all up in a huge bundle of horror and drops it at the . . . TOMB OF TERROR!

Shrieking, gasping, panting, screaming, sobbing elements mix together in a Babel of evil that echoes far into the night. Ghosts battle, monsters reign by terror, phantoms appear, spectres dance mysteriously in the . . . TOMB OF TERROR!

Never before has any magazine been received with such praise! And, as a result, to meet the clamoring demand, TOMB OF TERROR can now be had by you every month!

Yes, with pride and delight, the editors announce that: TOMB OF TERROR goes monthly!

The wind lashes out . . . the gravestones give way . . . the crypts open up . . . the world is berserk as mystery leaps out from the TOMB OF TERROR!

Yes, TOMB OF TERROR goes monthly, and the unknown has found its home!

TOMB OF TERROR, July, 1952, Vol. 1, No. 2, is published monthly by HARVEY PUBLICATIONS, INC., at 420 DeSoto Avenue, St. Louis 7, Mo. Editorial, Advertising and Executive offices, 1860 Broadway, New York 23, N. Y. President, Alfred Harvey; Vice-President and Editor, Leon Harvey; Vice-President and Business Manager, Robert B. Harvey. Application for second-class entry pending at the Post Office at St. Louis, Mo. Single copies, 10c. Subscription rates, 10 issues for $1.00 in the U. S. and possessions, elsewhere, $1.50.

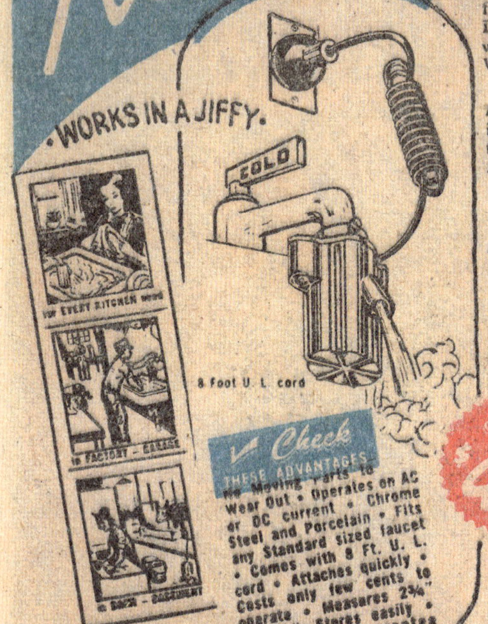

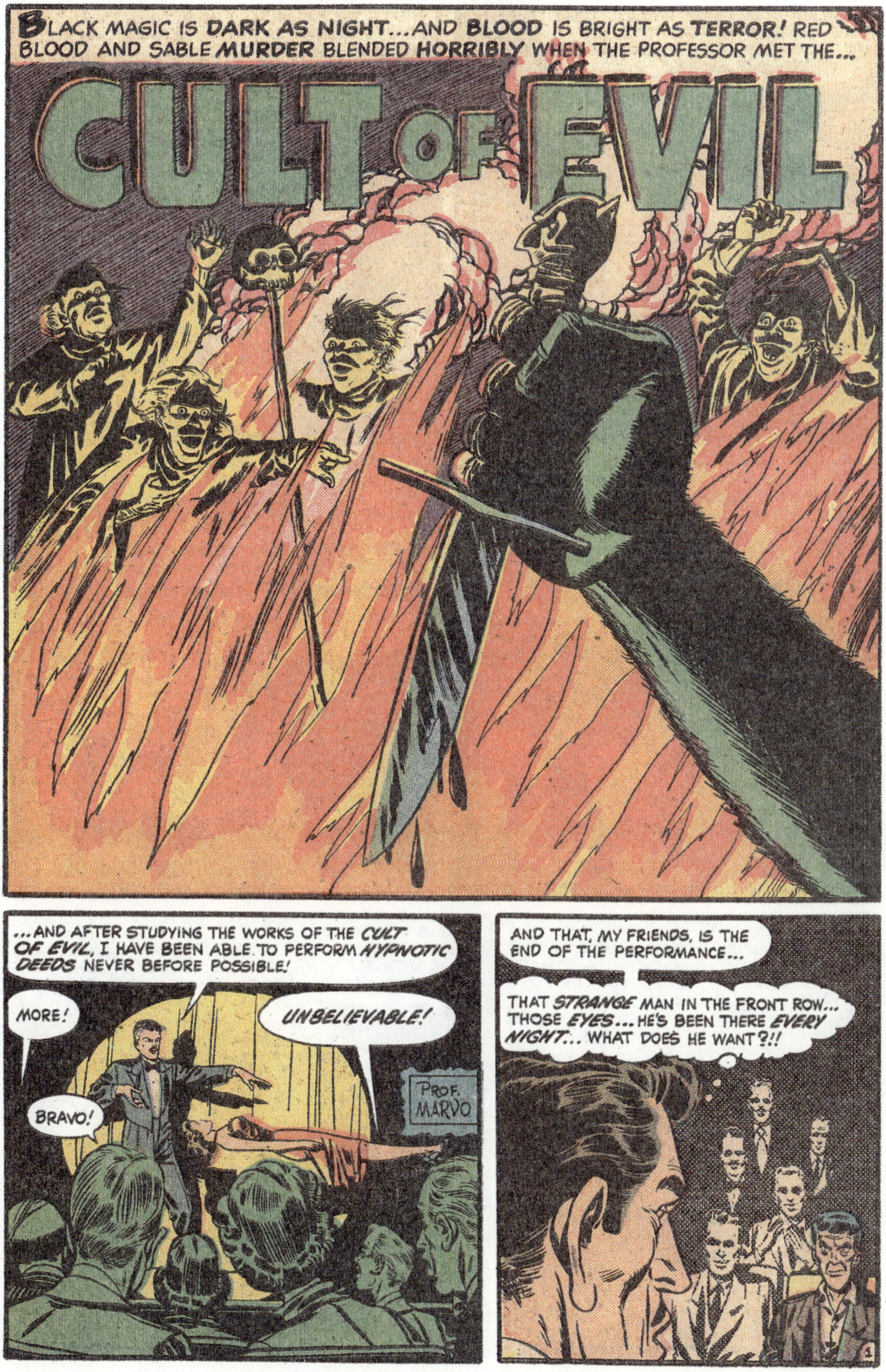

BLACK MAGIC IS DARK AS NIGHT...AND BLOOD IS BRIGHT AS TERROR! RED BLOOD AND SABLE MURDER BLENDED HORRIBLY WHEN THE PROFESSOR MET THE...

CULT OF EVIL

I'M GLAD TO BE HOME FINALLY... THAT WAS A TIRING PERFORMANCE! WHA-! AT THE WINDOW - THOSE EYES AGAIN! NO! NO! GO AWAY!

WHAT'S THE TROUBLE, DEAR! I THOUGHT I HEARD YOU SCREAM!
N-NOTHING, DEAR! JUST MY NERVES... AS YOU CAN SEE, THERE'S... NOTHING HERE...

I WISH YOU'D STOP THIS HORRID BLACK MAGIC... YOU'VE BEEN SO-SO STRANGE LATELY!
NO! LET ME ALONE! I MUST PREPARE FOR TOMORROW'S PERFORMANCE!
THE BOOK... SEEMS TO BE... CALLING ME...
THE CULT OF EVIL

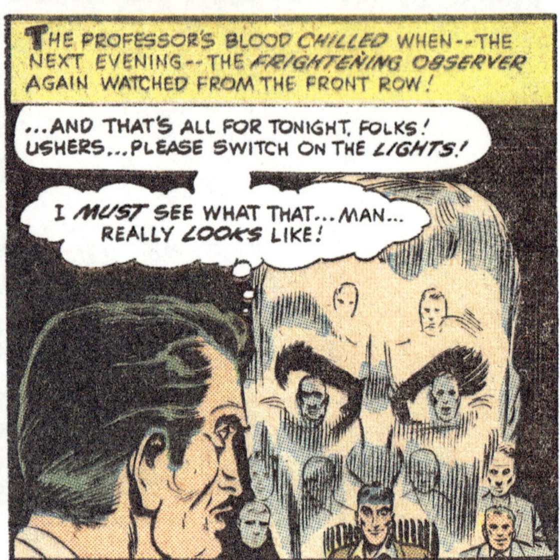
THE PROFESSOR'S BLOOD CHILLED WHEN -- THE NEXT EVENING -- THE FRIGHTENING OBSERVER AGAIN WATCHED FROM THE FRONT ROW!
...AND THAT'S ALL FOR TONIGHT, FOLKS! USHERS... PLEASE SWITCH ON THE LIGHTS!
I MUST SEE WHAT THAT... MAN... REALLY LOOKS LIKE!

MISS CHANDLER! LOOK! THAT SEAT IS EMPTY! THERE WAS NO ONE THERE!
WHY-WHY-- I KNOW THAT, PROFESSOR MARVO... IT'S BEEN EMPTY FOR THE LAST FEW NIGHTS! WH-- WHAT'S WRONG?

LATER
I HAVE WAITED LONG FOR YOU... YOU WILL COME WITH ME NOW, PROFESSOR MARVO!
I-- I COULD HARDLY WALK TO THE DRESSING ROOM... THAT FACE! IF ONLY I... EH! WHA-- WHAT! WH-WHO S-SAID THAT....!

I AM A MESSENGER FROM... ANOTHER PLACE! THE CULT OF EVIL CALLS FOR YOU! YOU WILL COME WITH ME NOW...
YES...YES-SSS... I COME... I CAN'T SEEM TO HELP MYSELF... I AM COMING WITH YOU...

THE CULT MEETS TONIGHT, PROFESSOR! WE ARE ALMOST THERE...AND YOU ARE ALMOST ONE OF US! AH...JUST AHEAD... AND YOU WILL MEET LIVING EVIL!
I COME...I SEE THEM...THEY ARE...MY FRIENDS...

WELCOME, PROFESSOR MARVO...WE HAVE LONG WAITED TO CLAIM YOU AS ONE OF US! YOU WILL DANCE WITH US NOW IN OUR RITES OF DEATH!
I HEAR...O MASTER...I FEEL THAT I MUST BE... ONE OF YOU...

HEE! HEEHEE! WE HAVE TRAPPED HIS SOUL! SOON WE WILL CLAIM HIS BODY! HE IS LOST... AS IS EVERY MORTAL WHO LOOKS TOO DEEPLY INTO THE SECRETS OF DARKNESS!

BEFORE YOU CAN JOIN US, MARVO...YOU MUST COMMIT THE FINAL ACT! YOU MUST SHED HUMAN BLOOD...AND THEN ALL OUR SECRETS WILL BE YOURS! GO NOW...BACK TO YOUR MORTAL HOME!

AS THE CREATURE OF MIDNIGHT SPOKE, MARVO WAS WHIRLED UP...UP...UP THROUGH UNSPEAKABLE VISIONS...INTO THE BLACKNESS...
GO NOW! GO NOW! GO-O-O!
3

THE NEXT NIGHT, MARVO HAD A VAMPIRE'S DESIRE FOR BLOOD! HE FELT STRANGE URGES... DARK POWERS... SURGING THROUGH HIM!
IT'S TIME, PROFESSOR MARVO! WE'RE DUE ON STAGE!
I MUST KILL... BLOOD... CAN'T GET RID OF THAT FEELING... ER--AH... I'M COMING, MISS CHANDLER! I'M READY!

...THE LAST ACT... IS TO SHOW YOU HOW... A GHOUL DRAWS BLOOD FROM HIS VICTIM!
OOOH... I CAN'T LOOK!
THIS LOOKS A LITTLE TOO REAL IF YOU ASK ME!

THAT GUY IS WEIRD... HE REALLY ACTS LIKE A GHOUL!
THEY OUGHT TO BAN THIS SHOW!
PROFESSOR... TH-THAT ACT WASN'T IN THE S-SCRIPT! WHAT'S THE M-MATTER WITH Y-YOU!
NOTHING... COME, MY DEAR... THERE IS SOMETHING I MUST SHOW YOU IN MY DRESSING ROOM!

WHAT DID YOU WANT TO SHOW ME, PROF-- AYEEE!! WHAT ARE Y-YOU DOING W-WITH TH-THAT KNIFE...!
I'M SORRY, MY DEAR... BUT I'M AFRAID I... MUST KILL YOU...

YOU- YOU'RE MAD! NO! DON'T COME NEAR ME! DON'T TOUCH ME!
KILL! BLOOD! BLOOD! HEE! HAAAHAAAHA!

EEEEEEE! I'M GETTING OUT OF HERE! EEEEE!
COME BACK! COME BACK!
4

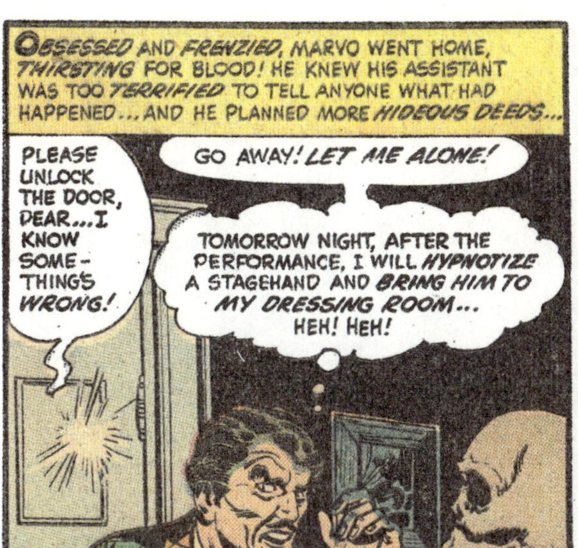
OBSESSED AND FRENZIED, MARVO WENT HOME, THIRSTING FOR BLOOD! HE KNEW HIS ASSISTANT WAS TOO TERRIFIED TO TELL ANYONE WHAT HAD HAPPENED... AND HE PLANNED MORE HIDEOUS DEEDS...
PLEASE UNLOCK THE DOOR, DEAR... I KNOW SOME-THING'S WRONG!
GO AWAY! LET ME ALONE!
TOMORROW NIGHT, AFTER THE PERFORMANCE, I WILL HYPNOTIZE A STAGEHAND AND BRING HIM TO MY DRESSING ROOM... HEH! HEH!

JUST AS I PLANNED LAST NIGHT! THE FOOL WAS EASY TO HYPNOTIZE! AND NOW... LOOK OUT! IDIOT! YOU'RE UPSETTING MY BOOKS!

SOME HEAVY TOMES ON THE BLACK ARTS FELL ON THE VICTIM'S HEAD... SNAPPING HIM OUT OF HIS HYPNOTIC TRANCE OF DEATH!
YOU FOOL! I'LL KILL YOU ANYWAY! ARRRGH!
WHERE AM I... WHA-- YAAAAA! NO! YOU'RE A FIEND!

I-I MUST GET AWAY... GET THE POLICE! HELP! HELP! HE'S A MADMAN!
THE--THE POLICE! NO! STOP, YOU FOOL!

STOP! STOP!... ARRR! I'LL NEVER CATCH HIM NOW! I MUST GET HOME... HIDE!
HE-EE-ELP! POLICE!

PUFF... PUFF... SO I RAN HOME TO HIDE! YOU MUST HIDE ME FROM THE POLICE, MY DEAR... OR I'LL KILL YOU! I'LL KILL YOU!
OH! WHY-WHY... YOU'RE JUST... S-SICK... DEAR...
5

OPEN UP IN THERE! THIS IS THE POLICE! OPEN UP!
SICK AM I? EH? WHAT'S THAT! THE POLICE! I'VE GOT TO GET OUT OF HERE!

THEY'LL NEVER GET ME! HEEEYYAAGH! I MUST GET TO THE WOODS... FIND THE CULT... THEY'LL HELP ME!
CRA-ASH!

COME AND FOLLOW ME, YOU FOOLS... IF YOU DARE! HEE! HEE!
STOP! STOP, MARVO! YOU CAN'T GET AWAY!
BANG!

THEY'LL NEVER GET ME!! I'LL SEEK THE FIENDS OF HELL... TOGETHER, WE'LL BATHE THE WORLD IN BLOOD! BLOOD! BLOOD!

PUFF--PUFF--I FEEL THE PRESENCE OF... UNSEEN THINGS! YES... YES! THEY ARE HERE! ALL AROUND ME... THOSE EYES!

DEATH BE PRAISED! YOU'VE FOUND ME... YOU MUST HELP ME! I AM ONE OF YOU! THE POLICE... THEY'RE AFTER ME!
YOU NEED FEAR ONLY THE BLACKNESS OF YOUR OWN SOUL! WE TAKE YOU TO THE MASTER... BUT YOU ARE NOT YET ONE OF US! YOU HAVE NOT YET SHED HUMAN BLOOD!
6

O, EVIL ONE...MASTER! MAKE ME ONE OF YOU... I NEED YOUR HELP!
YOU CANNOT COME TO US FOR HELP... YOU HAVE SPILLED NO BLOOD!

SO I HAVE SPILLED NO BLOOD, EH? THEN I'LL KILL ONE OF YOU! ARRGH! TAKE THAT! WH-WHAT!... YOU D-DON'T B-BLEED!
HA! HAAHAA! FOOL! DEAD THINGS DON'T BLEED!

BUT YOU, MARVO... YOU CAN BLEED!
NO! NO! DON'T! YEEEAAARGH!

NOW...YOU HAVE FINALLY COMMITTED THE ACT THAT MAKES YOU OUR BROTHER! ARISE, UNHOLY PHANTOM OF MARVO! ARISE... THE MASTER CALLS YOU!

NOW YOU ARE ONE OF US...FOREVER, MARVO! JUST LIKE ALL OTHER KINDRED MEN OF EVIL! COME...BACK TO THE SHADOWLAND OF RESTLESS GRAVES!

YOU NEED RUN FROM THE POLICE NO LONGER, MARVO... THEY WILL NEVER GET YOU NOW...
THE END

BENEATH THE SLIME OF THE QUICKSAND LURKED THE UNSPEAKABLE GOLGOTH... FORGOTTEN FOR TWO THOUSAND YEARS, BUT ALIVE AND GRIMLY WAITING! CARL BORMAN KNEW THAT THE ONLY WAY TO THE ANCIENT TREASURE OF SHABAOL WAS BY SATISFYING THE TERRIBLE HUNGER OF...

THE QUAGMIRE BEAST

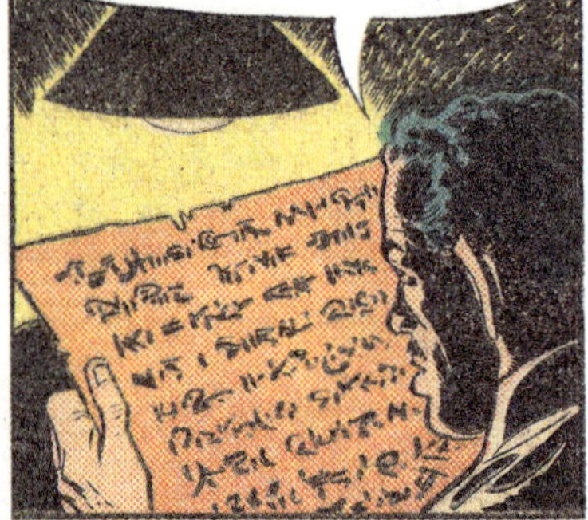

TWO LIVING MEN, EH? HMMM... CLARK AND EVANS... THEY'LL LEAP AT THE CHANCE TO GO WITH ME!

BORMAN TOLD HIS TWO FRIENDS THE ENTIRE STORY BUT SOMEHOW FORGOT TO MENTION GOLGOTH!
THE TREASURE OF SHABAOL! WHY...WE...WE'LL BE THE RICHEST MEN IN THE WORLD!
I'LL PLAN OUT THE DETAILS OF OUR JOURNEY, AND WE'LL LEAVE AS SOON AS WE CAN!

ONLY WEEKS LATER, DEEP IN THE HEART OF THE MUTE AND MENACING JUNGLE...
SHABAOL! WE'VE FOUND IT!
HURRY! TO THE CENTER OF THE CITY...WHERE THE TREASURE CHAMBER IS!

EVERY DETAIL OF THAT ANCIENT MANUSCRIPT WAS TRUE!
AND IS THE LEGEND OF GOLGOTH TRUE, TOO? I WONDER!

THE TREASURE...BUT HOW CAN WE GET TO IT...ACROSS THAT QUAGMIRE?
NONE MAY TAKE THE TREASURE UNLESS HE SACRIFICE TWO LIVING MEN TO THE BEAST OF THE QUAGMIRE! WHO-EVER YOU ARE UNDER THOSE SANDS, I'M DELIVERING THESE TWO TO YOU!

BORMAN! NO! NO!
AARRGHHHH!

RELENTLESSLY THE OOZING QUICKSAND SUCKED THE TWO STRUGGLING FIGURES DOWN TO THE WORLD OF SLIME WHERE GOLGOTH DWELT...
BORMAN, YOU DEVIL! YOU'LL PAY FOR THIS!
I HAVE DONE AS YOU ASKED, GOLGOTH. WHERE IS MY REWARD!

MOMENTS LATER...
IT'S JUST LIKE THE MANUSCRIPT SAID! TWO LIVING SACRIFICES AND THE TREASURE IS MINE! GOLGOTH KEEPS HIS WORD!

SOON, LADEN WITH HIS TREASURE, BORMAN SEEKS HIS WAY UPWARD...
THAT'S STRANGE... THOSE STATUES... THEY WEREN'T HERE BEFORE!
THOSE MONSTROUS BEINGS! THEY... THEY'RE ALIVE!
I...I PAID MY DEBT TO GOLGOTH... TWO LIVING HUMANS... AS THE BOOK SAID...

DON'T YOU RECOGNIZE US? WE ARE YOUR SACRIFICES, BORMAN!
WH-WHAT? YOU... CLARK AND EVANS!
YES, WE SANK DEEP BENEATH THE SANDS, DEEP DOWN TO A WORLD OF SLIME AND HORROR BELOW, AND THEN...

...WE SAW HIM GOLGOTH... THE BEAST OF THE QUAGMIRE!...
WELCOME TO THE LAIR OF GOLGOTH! YOU WILL SERVE ME FOREVER IN THESE DEPTHS BELOW THE WORLD... THE LIVING FLESH OF YOUR BODIES CHANGED BY THE SANDS OF MY QUAGMIRE!

PLEASE! I...I HAD TO SACRIFICE YOU TO GOLGOTH... TO GET THE TREASURE!
OF COURSE! BUT WE MADE A BARGAIN WITH GOLGOTH, TOO. HE GRANTED US A YEAR'S FREE-DOM...TO ENJOY THE LUXURIES WE NEVER HAD... WHICH YOUR TREA-SURE CAN BUY FOR US!

DURING THAT YEAR, YOU WILL SERVE US... USING YOUR TREASURE TO GRANT OUR EVERY WHIM AND WISH
Y-YES! I-I'LL DO WHATEVER YOU SAY!

YOU INTEND TO LIVE IN THAT OLD MANSION ALONE?
YES... ALONE WITH MY STATUES.
ONE YEAR... AND THEN I'LL BE FREE TO SPEND MY MILLIONS...FREE FROM THE HAUNTING HORROR OF THESE MONSTERS!

IN THE MONTHS THAT PASSED, STRANGE RUMOR AROSE ABOUT THE MYSTERIOUS MILLIONAIRE WHO LIVED ALONE WITH HIS STATUES...BUT NONE WAS STRANGER THAN THE TRUTH...
HERE ARE THE RECORDS AND BOOKS YOU WANTED ME TO SEND FOR.
AHH... MY FAVORITE MUSIC. PLAY THEM WHILE WE EAT!
YOU CAN READ TO ME LATER.

SET IT DOWN, BORMAN... AND I HOPE IT'S WELL DONE ...FOR YOUR SAKE!
I...I HOPE SO...I SPENT ALL DAY PREPARING IT!
IT'S INTOLERABLE... WAITING ON THEM HAND AND FOOT ALL DAY... NEVER KNOWING WHEN THEY MAY TURN ON ME AND DESTROY ME!

I HAVEN'T READ THE MANUSCRIPT SINCE I RETURNED WITH THE TREASURE. MAYBE I CAN LEARN SOMETHING THAT WILL FREE ME OF THOSE MONSTERS...BEFORE THE YEAR IS OVER!

ONCE AGAIN, BORMAN EAGERLY POURED OVER THE ANCIENT MANUSCRIPT, AND...
WHY...IT...IT SAYS THAT GOLGOTH GIVES HIS SERVANTS FREEDOM IF THEY PROMISE TO BRING BACK SOMEONE ELSE! THAT MEANS THEY INTEND TO TAKE ME BACK IN EXCHANGE FOR THEIR LIVES!

I...I MUST HIDE...SOMEWHERE SO THEY CAN NEVER REACH ME... UNTIL THE YEAR IS OVER... AND TAKE THE TREASURE WITH ME! THEY'LL KNOW IF I LEAVE THE HOUSE... ONLY ONE THING TO DO!

A LITTLE LATER...DEEP IN A SUBTERRANEAN CELLAR OF THE ANCIENT MANSION...
YEARS AGO THE LORD WHO OWNED THIS MANSION USED THIS ROOM AS A DUNGEON! EVEN IF THEY FIND ME HERE THEY WON'T BE ABLE TO BREAK THROUGH THE THICK WALLS OR THE IRON DOOR!

FOR MONTHS, BORMAN LIVED IN THE DUNGEON, HIS RATIONS GROWING SLIMMER AND SLIMMER...
IN A LITTLE WHILE THEIR YEAR WILL BE OVER...THEY'LL BE FORCED TO RETURN WITHOUT ME...AND THEN I'LL BE FREE...FREE TO SPEND THE TREASURE... AND LIVE!

HA, HA! POUND AWAY! YOU'LL NEVER BREAK THROUGH THESE WALLS! YOU WILL RETURN TO GOLGOTH WITHOUT ME!
BAM
BAM

SUDDENLY...
THE STONE WALLS...THEY... THEY'RE TURNING TO QUICK-SAND...LIKE THE FOUL STUFF OF THE QUAGMIRE... NO! NO! HELP!

YAAAH! THE FLOOR...IT...IT'S QUICKSAND...SPREADING TOWARD ME! IN A MOMENT I..I'LL SINK DOWN!
YES...DOWN TO GOLGOTH!

HE IS COMING, GOLGOTH... TO SERVE YOU, FOREVER!
DO NOT BE IMPATIENT, GOLGOTH. WE BRING HIM!
AAAGH! GOLGOTH! HE...HE IS DRAGGING ME DOWN!
THE END

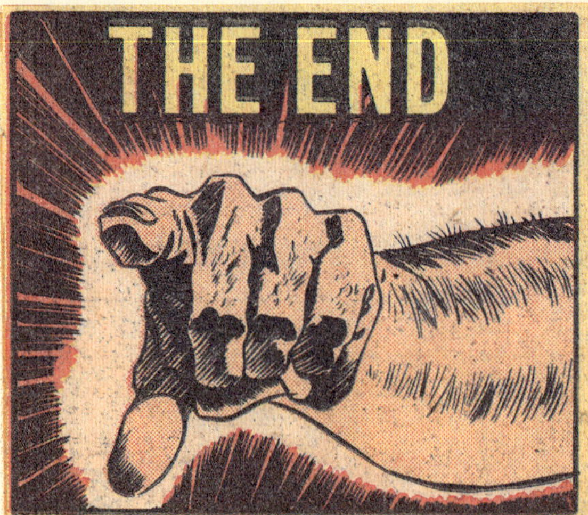

(You are now inside the specially constructed atomic chamber far out on the ice fields of Antartica. Here, scientists can perform atomic tests, explode bombs, if necessary, and observe the results in completely safety behind the thick, lead walls of the chamber.)

"Hello, Washington? What's up? You weren't supposed to check with us until tomorrow."

"Look, you guys, something is happening up here. Do you feel the temperature rising?"

"Are you nuts! This is the South Pole, Buster, not a Turkish Bath."

"Cut the comedy. I'm serious. The temperature here, during the past hour, has risen to 119 degrees. People are beginning to drop like flies."

"Hoky Catfish! Is that right! No, we don't have any change here, but let me check the outside instruments. Hold on!

"Yow!

"Hello, Washington! You're right! Even here the temperature is going up. We can't feel it because we're in this chamber but the instruments do show that something is going on outside. Tell me, what do other spots around the world report?"

"The same. London . . . Paris . . . Moscow . . New Delhi . . all of them report a sudden surge in the temperature. It's as if some giant were holding a flame under the earth. Wait a minute. Here's the latest. Paris reports a temperature of 134 degrees. People are dying as if the plague were upon them!"

"What in heaven's name is going on? What do the observatories show? Maybe it's some kind of an attack from space."

"We thought of that. No s-soap. Hey, cold boys, send some of th-that ice up here. I'm beginning to roast. I . . . ugghhhh . . ."

"Hello, Washington! Hello, Washington! Come in! Come in!

"Hey, guys, either somebody is playing a joke or something, but things don't look so good now. Wait a minute!"

"Hello, Expedition Atomic Ice, operator you were just talking to passed out. Temperature is now up to 128 degrees and climbing. Here, in Washington, all the air conditioning units have been turned on, but they don't seem to help very much. This heat seems to be bringing a peculiar odor with it. A heavy searing odor. Good heavens! I've just been handed a report. Most of the people in Paris are dead and the other capitols are cutting off one by one. What is going on?"

"I don't know, Washington, but another check of our outside instruments show that the temperature has risen sixty degrees. Believe it or not, some of the ice is beginning to melt!

"Hey, Rawlings, have the scientists returned from their field trip yet? They've got to know about this. What? You've lost contact with them! Keep on trying! Hello, Washington!"

"G-go a-ahead . . ."

"What's the matter?"

"Heat . . . h-h-heat . . ."

"Hello, Washington . . . Washington . . . come in, Washington. Come in, London. Come in, Madrid. Come in, Tokyo. Hello, hello. Anybody who is still alive, this is Expedition Atomic-Ice . . . Come in . . . please come in!

"What! The temperature is 100 degrees here! Yeah! Look! The window! That's water splashing against it. The ice has melted. But this is the South Pole. The ice is thousands of feet thick. What kind of heat is it?"

BOOOOMMM!

"Wh-what! How did you get in here? Who are you? Why has it gotten so hot in here? Say something!"

"Keep away from me. Why are you taking off your cape? What ahhhh!"

He turned around to leave. There was still work to do.

ATLANTIS

THIS LAND OF BEAUTY IS STILL SAID TO EXIST AT THE BOTTOM OF THE OCEAN. BEAUTIFUL TEMPLES, GREAT HOUSES -- ALL IN THE GREAT STYLE OF THE GREEK ARCHITECTS -- STAND IN THE WORLD OF WATER.

BUT WHAT HAPPENED TO ATLANTIS TO SEND IT TO ITS WATERY GRAVE? SUPPOSEDLY, A TERRIBLE EARTHQUAKE RIPPED APART THE BUILDINGS, SWEPT DOWN MOUNTAINS, TORE UP LAND AND ALLOWED THE SEA TO POUR IN! DOWN WENT ATLANTIS TO ITS SITE OF NO RETURN!

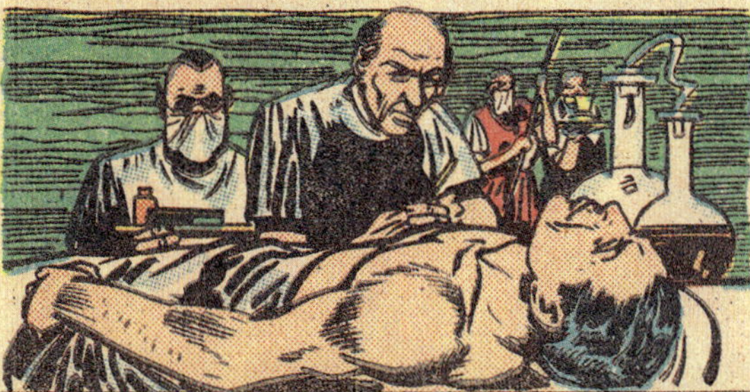

MEDICINE IN ATLANTIS WAS A FAR CRY FROM THE PRIMITIVE SUPERSTITIOUS MEDICINE OF EUROPE. IT IS BELIEVED THAT ATLANTIS DOCTORS USED DRUGS WHICH WE, TODAY, STILL DO NOT KNOW ABOUT!

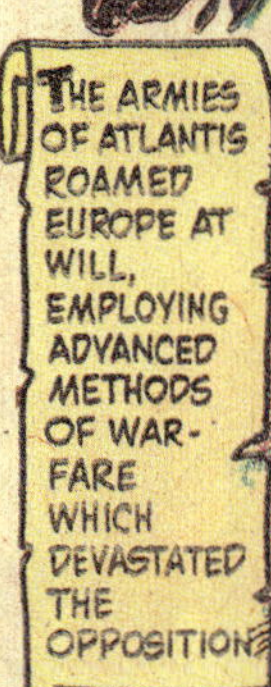

SCIENTIFIC FACT EVEN BEARS OUT THE POSSIBILITY OF OTHER ATLANTISES. OUR OCEANS ARE CONSTANTLY MOVING, LAND SHAPES ARE CONTINUOUSLY CHANGING. MANY THOUSANDS OF YEARS AGO, ALASKA AND SIBERIA WERE JOINED, AS WAS EUROPE AND AFRICA! PERHAPS THERE ARE OTHER LOST LANDS!

IT'S EASY TO HYPNOTIZE...

when you know how!

Want the thrill of imposing your will over someone? Of making someone do exactly what you order? Try hypnotism! This amazing technique gives full personal satisfaction. You'll find it entertaining and gratifying. **HOW TO HYPNOTIZE** shows all you need to know. It is put so simply, anyone can follow it. And there are 24 revealing photographs for your guidance.

SEND NO MONEY

FREE ten days' examination of this system is offered to you if you send the coupon today. We will ship you our copy by return mail, in plain wrapper. If not delighted with results, return it in 10 days and your money will be refunded. Stravon Publishers, Dept. H313, 113 West 57th St., New York 19, N. Y.

Mail Coupon Today

STRAVON PUBLISHERS, Dept. H313
113 West 57th St., N. Y. 19, N. Y.

Send **HOW TO HYPNOTIZE** in plain wrapper.

☐ Send C.O.D. I will pay postman $1.98 plus postage.

☐ I enclose $1.98. Send postpaid.

If not delighted, I may return it in 10 days and get my money back.

Name ....

Address ....

City .... *Zone* .... *State* ....

Canada & Foreign—$2.50 with order

AMAZING!

10 DAY FREE TRIAL! CHRONOGRAPH

The 4-in-1 Wonder Watch

Try to beat this bargain **ANYWHERE** in America! 4-in-1 imported Stop Swiss **CHRONOGRAPH** and Wrist Watch combined! Best of all, you can try it for 10 full days at **OUR RISK!**

11 — WONDER FEATURES — 11

It's a tachometer, telemeter, **DOUBLE** Push Button **STOP** watch. It measures **SPEED** as well as **DISTANCES** of horse and auto races, sports, airplanes, boats, moving objects. Actually has **SPLIT-SECOND** calibration, unbreakable crystal, sweep-second hand, luminous numerals and hands, sturdy **SHOCK RESIST** case. Everyone wants one, students, soldiers, sailors, race fans, sportsmen, photographers, engineers, aviators, and all active men. It's a wonderful timekeeper!

UNLIMITED GUARANTEE

EXCLUSIVE OF PARTS! Never a charge for skilled labor. **FULL INSTRUCTIONS** and gift case with each watch. **SEND NO MONEY.** Pay postman 6.95 plus 10% tax, or send only 7.65 and **SAVE** postage. Try at **OUR** risk for 10 full days. Price back **QUICK** if not thrilled. Order now—while they last!

U. S. DIAMOND HOUSE, Dept. 24L-236
127 West 33rd Street, New York 1, N. Y.

HA-HA...! NOW WHO IS THE DUMMY...?
NO! NO...IT CAN'T BE...!
THE VENTRILOQUIST PETER MORDANN FOUND THAT IN AN ARGUMENT, A MURDERED MAN CAN HAVE...
THE LAST WORD
PETER MORDANN, A LITTLE KNOWN VENTRILOQUIST, WATCHES ENVIOUSLY AS THE WORLD FAMOUS JACQUE TERCELLE PERFORMS WITH HIS EQUALLY FAMOUS DUMMY, PIERRE!
IF ONLY I COULD AFFORD A DUMMY LIKE HIS! I WOULD BE THE GREATEST VENTRILOQUIST IN THE WORLD!
WITH THE APPLAUSE FOR TERCELLE STILL RINGING IN HIS EARS, MORDANN RETURNS TO HIS APARTMENT, DETERMINED TO BECOME GREATER THAN THE MAN HE HAS JUST SEEN!
BAH...! WHAT IS THE USE OF REHEARSING...? WITH THIS MISERABLE DUMMY, I CAN DO NOTHING RIGHT!
1

I AM A GREAT ART! !BUT WITH YOU, I AM NOTHING!

THE NEXT DAY, MORDANN RETURNS TO THE THEATER AND WATCHES RAPTLY AS TERCELLE PERFORMS! AFTER THE SHOW, HE SNEAKS BACK-STAGE ...
NO ONE IS AROUND! I MUST LOOK AT HIM MORE CLOSELY!

YOU ARE A WORK OF ART! WITH YOU, I CAN DO ANYTHING...! ANYTHING!

WHAT ARE YOU DOING HERE? GIVE HIM TO ME! IMMEDIATELY!
NO...! I- I MUST HAVE HIM! I MUST!

YOU CANNOT HAVE HIM.... HE MUST BE MINE!
AAAAGGGRRR!

YOU--PERHAPS YOU'VE KILLED ME...! BUT...MY DUMMY... WILL REVENGE ME! HE WILL... REVENGE... ME...
HA-HA-HA...! NOW WE SHALL SEE WHO IS THE GREATEST VENTRILOQUIST IN THE WORLD!

WITH TERCELLE'S DUMMY, MORDANN SOON ESTABLISHES A REPUTATION AMONG THE SOCIETY ELEMENT OF THE CITY AND IS CALLED UPON TO ENTERTAIN AT MANY SOCIAL GATHERINGS!
HA-HA! THEY DO NOT RECOGNIZE YOU, PHILIP, WITH YOUR NEW NAME AND NEW HAIR! THEY WERE ENTHRALLED WITH OUR PERFORMANCE!

BUT WE MUST NOT BE CONTENT WITH THESE SMALL PERFORMANCES! THE WHOLE WORLD MUST SEE US! AND FOR THAT WE SHALL NEED MORE MONEY...!

WE WILL ONLY TAKE THE RING, PHILIP! IT WON'T BE MISSED!
MR. MORDANN! WHAT ARE YOU DOING...!

KILL HER...! KILL HER...!
WHAT--! YES...YOU'RE RIGHT! SHE MUST BE KILLED! NO ONE CAN STAND IN OUR WAY...!
AAAGGRRR!

I THOUGHT YOU SPOKE, PHILIP...! BUT KILLING HER WAS MY IDEA! SHE WOULD HAVE SPOILED EVERYTHING!

THE CRAFTY KILLER RETURNS TO HIS AUDIENCE IN ORDER TO COMPLETE HIS PERFORMANCE...AND TO AVOID AROUSING SUSPICION AS TO THE WHEREABOUTS OF THE MURDERED WOMAN!
WHA--?
I SAID, HOW CAN YOU TOLERATE THE IDIOTS SEATED BEFORE US...?

THE WOMAN'S BODY WAS FOUND BUT MORDANN NEVER WAS SUSPECTED. NOW, WHILE HE AWAITS A SUMMONS TO PERFORM AT ANOTHER PARTY, HE SATISFIES THE AVARICIOUS LUST OF HIS GREEDY BRAIN!

DIAMOND CUFF-LINKS! HA-HA! SINCE YOU'VE BEEN WITH ME, PHILIP, WE'VE DONE QUITE WELL! YOU'VE HELPED ME CONSIDERABLY...!

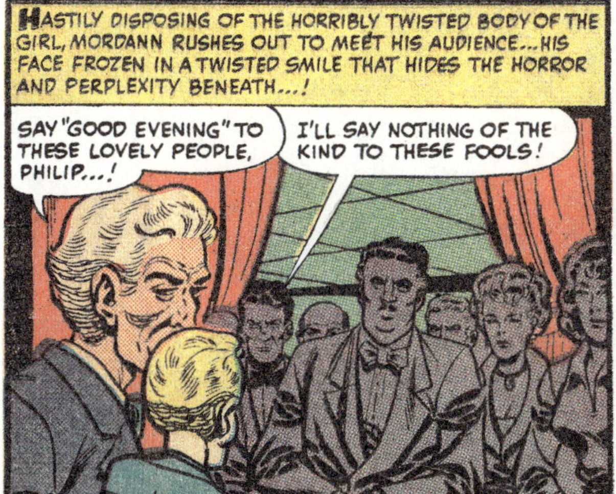
HASTILY DISPOSING OF THE HORRIBLY TWISTED BODY OF THE GIRL, MORDANN RUSHES OUT TO MEET HIS AUDIENCE...HIS FACE FROZEN IN A TWISTED SMILE THAT HIDES THE HORROR AND PERPLEXITY BENEATH...!
SAY "GOOD EVENING" TO THESE LOVELY PEOPLE, PHILIP...!
I'LL SAY NOTHING OF THE KIND TO THESE FOOLS!

HOW DARE HE!
I-I THINK YOU SHOULD APOLOGIZE, PHILIP...!
GO TO THE DEVIL!

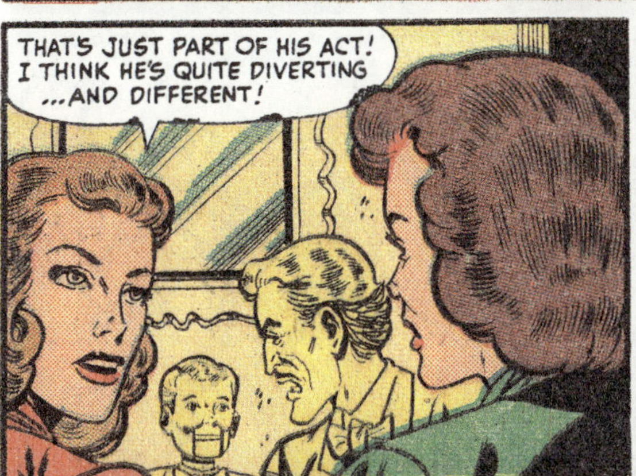
THAT'S JUST PART OF HIS ACT! I THINK HE'S QUITE DIVERTING ...AND DIFFERENT!

MORDANN, BAFFLED AND TERROR-STRICKEN, MANAGES TO BRING HIS ACT TO A CONCLUSION... THEN, IN THE PRIVACY OF HIS ROOM, MORDANN RAGES AT THE LIFELESS DOLL!
DID YOU SPEAK...! TELL ME...!! TELL ME!

YOU ARE NOTHING BUT PAINTED WOOD AND SAWDUST! IT WAS MY IMAGINATION...! THE WORDS I PUT INTO YOUR MOUTH...!

REMEMBER...I CAN KILL YOU AS I DID TERCELLE...AND THE OTHERS! NOTHING WILL STAND IN MY WAY...! NOTHING!
5

THE FOLLOWING MONTHS, HOWEVER, FIND MORDANN GROWING IN POPULARITY AND STATURE... THE POINT HAS COME WHERE HE IS SIGNED TO APPEAR IN THE CITY'S MOST EXCLUSIVE NIGHTCLUB AS THE FEATURE ATTRACTION!
I AM A SUCCESS, MY STUPID LITTLE DUMMY...! NO LONGER DOES MY IMAGINATION PLAY TRICKS ON ME!

IT GIVES ME GREAT PLEASURE TO PRESENT THE FABULOUS PETER MORDANN... AND PHILIP!

I- I CAN'T SPEAK...!
HA-HA! CAT GOT YOUR TONGUE?

I- I'M RUINED...!
HA! HA HA! HA HA HA HA! HA HA HA HA HA!

THE CRAZED MORDANN LURCHES HYSTERICALLY TO HIS ROOM, AND ONCE THERE TURNS HIS FEAR-RIDDEN, INSANE RAGE UPON THE LIFELESS DUMMY...!
I'M RUINED...! THE WORDS STUCK IN MY THROAT...! I-- I COULDN'T SPEAK!

YOU FOOL! YOU HAD NOTHING TO DO WITH IT! I DIDN'T SPEAK!
6

NO! NO...! YOU CAN'T BE...!

YOU ARE FINISHED, MORDANN... HA-HA-HA...!

NO! NO! I'LL KILL YOU... KILL YOU...! JUST AS I DID TERCELLE...!

THERE IS NOTHING LEFT FOR YOU, MORDANN, BUT DEATH! GET THE KNIFE FROM THE DESK...!
DEATH...? THE KNIFE...? HE-HE-HAAAA...!

YOU HAVE WON, TERCELLE...! YOU HAVE KILLED ME...! AAHHGGGRRRAAA...!

TERCELLE'S MURDERER LIES DEAD BY HIS OWN HAND...! OR WAS IT BY THE HAND OF AN UNKNOWN POWER TOO TERRIBLE TO COMPREHEND...? WHO AMONG YOU CAN TRUTHFULLY SAY WHAT IS IMAGINED AND WHAT IS REAL? MORDANN COULDN'T!!!
The End
7

NO PLACE TO HIDE!

They were coming from every nook of the countryside! They were pouring out of homes, sweeping in from the fields, stamping through the forest!

Torches seared the air sending up a message of warning . . . THEY WERE COMING!

He looked out and couldn't believe it! Yes, they were coming to get him. "But it's not my fault! It's not my fault!" he told himself again and again. But it was impossible to convince *them!*

On they came! Now the hounds took over. Loud and bloody growls tore into the night as the powerful dogs rushed ahead . . . straight to the tower . . . the tower in which he was hiding!

"He must be in there!"

"They've got his scent!"

"We've got him now!"

Loud voices, rough voices, horrible voices shouted it out. Yes, he was there!

"What now?" he said to himself. "What possibly can I do now? I can't even speak their language . . . how could I ever tell my story?"

They were only yards away. They began to spread out now, surrounding the tower.

"We've got you up there!"

"We'll burn you down!"

BANG! BANG! BANG!

Rifle fire shot out from their ranks towards the top of the tower!

He ducked low into the corner, scraping the dirt on the ground. Bullets crashed overhead, and now he was frightened.

"Why can't they understand me? Why does it have to end this way?"

Wild chants came from below. They were all there—men, women, children. They were shouting "Victory at last! The end has come!"

They made a picture of horror. Hundreds of people in a mad frenzy obsessed with murder!

Now they were throwing the torches! This had to be his finish!

Terror gripped him and held him firm in its grasp. His eyes bulged out and seemed to scream for help!

"Burn, you flames!"

"We'll burn you to the ground!"

A torch fell through the window! He pulled away, but the flames quickly moved along, spreading its chain of evil.

Now he was wild with fear. He dashed to the stairway and groped his way down. The flames leapt high and it was almost impossible to see.

Round and round the circular stairway he went. The mad screams continued outside in a hideous chorus!

"Why, oh why, do they torture me like this?"

The place was bursting with fire. Soon it would all crumble into ashes.

"He's coming down . . . I can hear him!"

"Get those rifles ready!"

"We'll toss more fire at him!"

He couldn't hear what they were saying. But he knew his final doom was near. There was no place to go . . . his life was quickly burning out!

"There he is now!"

"He's in the doorway!"

"That's it, throw the torch at him!"

They surrounded him and pounded him with their torches!

"AGGGGHHHHHHHH!!"

He was on fire, but they didn't stop. It would be endless torture till the end!

He was nothing but flames . . . and he finally fell to the ground.

The people wildly danced round him, singing in uncontrollable glee. They spat at the dreadful, flame-withered mass that had been . . . the Frankenstein Monster!

THE CRYPT OF DEATH

THE WEIRD EVENTS STARTED THAT DAY WHEN PROF. JOHN WILSON, EMINENT ARCHEOLOGIST, WENT CRAZY WITH FEAR AND TRIED TO COMMIT SUICIDE...

NO--STOP, YOU FOOLS! DON'T YOU SEE? I-I'LL BE HELPLESS NOW! DON'T--DON'T! THE CURSE WILL OVER-COME ME!

THIS IS A LITTLE SEDATIVE TO QUIET YOUR NERVES. YOU'VE BEEN UNDER A TREMENDOUS STRAIN. THERE!

KA WILL...FIND ME...HE'LL FIND ME! FIRST IT WAS COREY--THEN NIGEL...THEN IT WAS ANDERSON AND TALBOT--NOW ME! THE CURSE... OHHH...
WHAT DO YOU MAKE OF IT, JIM?
THESE WEIRD ACCIDENTS THAT KILLED OFF HIS COLLEAGUES MUST HAVE SHOCKED HIS MIND!
THE DOCTORS HAD REASON FOR PUZZLEMENT. PROF. JOHN WILSON, HEAD OF THE EXPEDITION THAT HAD UNCOVERED AND ENTERED THE TOMB OF KA, GREAT PHAROAH OF EGYPT MANY EONS AGO, WAS THE ONLY ONE ALIVE THREE MONTHS AFTERWARDS, THE REST DYING STRANGELY IN UNEXPLAINED DEATHS. BUT THAT NIGHT...
URRRGHH... GASP... GASP... URRGHH...
ARRRRGH! I HAVE COME FOR YOU! YOU CANNOT ESCAPE!!
N-NO! I..I DON'T WANT TO DIE! PLEASE--LISTEN TO ME! I--I ENTERED YOUR TOMB FOR THE SAKE OF SCIENCE! NO! DON'T TOUCH ME!!
YOU CANNOT ESCAPE! AAARRGH!
COME! YOU MUST STAY WITH ME AS THE CURSE DEMANDS--FOR YOU ARE THE LAST!

AS SWIFTLY AS IT HAD COME, THE GIANT MONSTER DISAPPEARED STEALTHILY INTO THE NIGHT.
A PEDESTRIAN REPORTED A STRANGE MONSTER MAKING ITS WAY TO THE MUSEUM. COME ON! WHATEVER IT IS--IT HAS PROF. WILSON!
THIS IS AN EMERGENCY ALERT! SEND UNITS TO SCIENCE MUSEUM AT 4TH AND VINE!
HOSPITAL
POLICE
AND MINUTES LATER...
PROF. WILSON MENTIONED SOMETHING ABOUT A CURSE--THAT WHOEVER ENTERS KA'S TOMB, DIES BY THE HAND OF KA--BUT--BUT ITS PREPOSTEROUS!
NEVERTHELESS, MR. PARKINS. WE'RE TAKING A LOOK AT THIS EGYPTIAN ROOM!
EEEEEEEEEEEEEEEEEE
W-WHAT WAS THAT?
I CAN GUESS! COME ON! HURRY!!
GOOD LORD! LOOK AT IT!
THERE'S PROF. WILSON! HE'S BEEN PUT ON A RACK!
AHHARRRRR
WATCH IT, BOYS! GET BACK! IT'S COMING TOWARDS US! OPEN FIRE!!

NOW THE NIGHTMARE CREATURE SPRANG AT THE GROUP OF DETERMINED MEN AND LIFTED ONE OF THEM HIGH IN THE AIR, ITS TERRIBLE SINEWS CRACKLING WITH UNNATURAL STRENGTH!
USE THE IBSIS! OVER THERE--QUICKLY! IT--IT'S CALLED THE WAND OF LIFE!
BUT THE MONSTER ADVANCED ON THE YOUNG DOCTOR, GIANT HANDS TIGHTENED ON HIS THROAT--SQUEEZING--SQUEEZING.
THE IBSIS! USE THE IBSIS! HOLD IT IN FRONT OF KA!
IF THIS IS WHAT THE OLD MAN'S TALKING ABOUT, I HOPE IT WORKS!!
ARRGH!
NOW--YOU SHALL DIE! YOU SHALL KNOW THE POWER OF KA, WHOM YOU DEFY!
GET BACK! GET BACK, YOU MONSTER! GET BACK BEFORE I FLING THIS IN YOUR FACE!
AAARRRRR
NO! TAKE IT AWAY FROM MY SIGHT! AAAGHH!
ARRRGGHHH--TAKE IT AWAY! I--I CANNOT FIGHT THE POWER OF LIFE!!
AAAIIIIIIEEEEEEEEE
IT--IT'S SHRIVELING UP! GREAT SCOTT! WHAT'LL HAPPEN NEXT IN THIS CRYPT OF DEATH!
ARRRGHHH! THE CURSE... CURSE... CURSE... AHHHH!
THE CURSE OF KA CAME TRUE AT LAST--FOR HIM! WILL ANYONE EVER BELIEVE US?
THE END

NOW YOU CAN FLY A REAL JET PLANE!

JETEX JAVELIN

SPECIAL OFFER

If bought in the store, the JETEX #50 engine alone would cost $1.95; the JETEX JAVELIN, $.75, a total cost of $2.70. Rush the coupon and you get both the JETEX JAVELIN and the JETEX #50 jet engine for only $1.98! (plus postage and handling charges, C.O.D.).

$1.98

Includes fuel supply.

Guaranteed to give you Fun-filled Flights!

You'll thrill and amaze your friends, be the envy of your neighborhood with this real JET airplane. The JETEX JAVELIN is a colorful, sleek-looking 14 inches of greased lightning. It will fly 1,000 feet! Go at a scale speed of 600 miles per hour! It takes off under its own power, loops, circles, stunts and then goes into a long glide and comes to a beautiful landing.

The JETEX JAVELIN is a cinch to build. Comes complete with the famous JETEX #50 jet engine and all parts already cut out. Nothing more to buy! Just follow the easy instructions, glue the parts together and you're ready for thrills! This amazing jet airplane uses the modern stressed skin construction which gives more strength and durability for its weight than any other type of construction. With ordinary care, it will make hundreds of fun filled flights.

It's fun to assemble, thrilling to fly. So don't delay—SEND NO MONEY—rush your order today to be sure of prompt delivery.

Designed by Commander Wallis Rigby

Yes, Commander Rigby, world famous designer, is the inventor of the JETEX JAVELIN. The Commander says, "I have created thousands of models, but the JETEX JAVELIN is the finest thing I have ever done"!

GUARANTEED TO FLY!

The JETEX JAVELIN is unconditionally guaranteed to fly if all instructions have been faithfully followed. If the JETEX JAVELIN does not fly, return the plane and the JETEX #50 engine within 10 days and your money will be refunded.

AMAZING JETEX #50 JET ENGINE

The world's smallest jet engine and the most powerful engine of its size ever sold! It runs on solid fuel, starts every time, completely reliable.

NO MOVING PARTS TO BREAK OR WEAR OUT. Can be used to power model airplanes, racing cars and boats.

JETEX JAVELIN Box 429 Huntington, N. Y.

MAIL THIS COUPON NOW!

JETEX JAVELIN DEPT. C-5 **RUSH!**

Box 429 Huntington, N. Y.

Please rush the JETEX JAVELIN and JETEX #50 jet engine. I will pay postman only $1.98 plus C.O.D. charges on arrival.

Name..

(*please print*)

Address..

City.............................Zone.......State..................

☐ I enclose $2.00 in cash, check or money order to save on C.O.D. charges. If the airplane does not fly, I may return it in 10 days for full refund of purchase price.

"THE WATCH OF THE ATOMIC AGE"

NOW YOURS at an unbelievable LOW PRICE — the timepiece of the Atomic Age! The SUBMARINE watch actually DEFIES BREAKAGE! A special SHOCK ABSORBER invention protects the balance staff or "heart" of your watch against shocks, rough handling, dropping! It even runs UNDER WATER. Unlike old fashioned watches, the case is SCREWED TIGHT and special GASKET helps keep out water, grime and dust. The accurate JEWELLED movement is PRECISION-MADE by Swiss Artisans. So handsome and THIN — yet so rugged! Why waste your money in an ugly, inferior and poorly made watch that breaks down easily? For only a few cents more than the CHEAPEST wrist watches you can be the proud owner of a SUBMARINE wrist watch — if you act QUICK!.

YOURS to try . . . at OUR risk!

Enjoy this wonderful timepiece without risk or obligation for you! Wear it for 10 days. See for yourself how attractive it looks! Observe its many QUALITY features, such as: Red Sweep-Second Hand, Split-Second calibrations, Unbreakable Crystal! See how the numbers and hands seem to "LIGHT UP" at night! Swim with it if you like! Drop it! Test it for accuracy! You can spend many times as much and not get ALL these great features! Yes, try it, test it, compare it —without risk! You be the judge! Full price back QUICK if not delighted! You just can't lose!

SEND NO MONEY!

Pay postman only 10.87 on arrival! NO EXTRAS! This price includes ALL tax and mailing costs! FREE! of extra cost — "U.S." FLEX METAL BAND and our UNLIMITED GUARANTEE Certificate exclusive of parts. Never one cent for skilled labor service! RUSH order now! Rising costs may force us to withdraw this sensational offer. You have NOTHING to lose and everything to gain!

ANYONE CAN USE IT!

BOYS! GIRLS! Now you can own your very own PORTABLE TYPEWRITER at a really CHEAP PRICE! You can type your own letters, homework, bulletins, etc., with this GREAT INVENTION! Imagine the fun you'll have doing it! It's so easy! ANYONE can learn to use it. Letters look just like REAL TYPING and are so neat! Your friends and teachers will praise and admire you! Besides this machine is so light you can carry it with you to school or on trips everywhere. Because it's made of strong metals and materials, it is hard to break and lasts a long time.

NEW "SPHERE" POINT PEN GIVEN

We offer this wonderful SPHERE POINT pen at $1.95, but if you buy a PORTABLE TYPEWRITER, we charge you NOTHING extra for it. After you type, sign your letters with this NEW SPHERE POINT pen! Writing just rolls on to the paper. It never scratches. It always writes smooth as silk. By the way, this wonderful pen writes UNDER WATER also, as well as in AIRPLANES. You can write with it lying down and upside down. It writes sharp and clear and dries quick on the paper. The SPHERE POINT pen also writes on LEATHER, METALS, GLASS. Now we don't ask you ONE PENNY EXTRA for this attractive, useful pen. It's yours FREE of extra cost with your typewriter, but please RUSH your order NOW! Send no money. Pay postman only 2.95 plus postage when he delivers your typewriter and sphere pen. Try them and enjoy them for 10 days at our risk! Full price back quick if you are not thrilled.

2.95

Item No.
158

10 DAY TRIAL - GIFT COUPON

Tear out and mail right away to:

U. S. DIAMOND HOUSE, 125 P

127 West 33rd St., New York 1, N. Y.

BUY NOW! SAVE UP TO 1/2

Write NUMBER, name & price of articles. Pay price to postman on delivery. No extras for tax! Satisfaction GUARANTEED or full price back quick! Send thin paper strip to show ring size.

NUMBER	ARTICLE	PRICE

YOUR NAME ____________________

ADDRESS ____________________

TOWN ____________________ STATE __________

☐ SAVE MORE . . . get more — by sending cash or money order with this coupon! We pay ALL fees and you get 2 GIFTS instead of only one!

You Can WIN
This 15" tall
SILVER TROPHY
JUST AS I DID IN
10 MINUTES
OF FUN
A DAY!
I GAINED
53 LBS. OF SHAPELY POWER-PACKED
MUSCLES!
Which of these
2 ME'S
is YOU ?
THAT 112 LB.-6 FT.
SPINDLE-ARMED SISSY below WAS ME
A FEW SHORT WEEKS AGO
THIS MAY BE
YOUR LAST CHANCE
TO GET ALL 5 PICTURE PACKED COURSES FOR 10¢
MILLIONS HAVE BEEN SOLD FOR $1 AND MORE
When I enrolled I was a skinny, sick weakling. As you can see in my "Before" Photo I looked like a child... years younger than my age. I was ashamed to take a picture in bathing trunks as I do now. I was shy with girls because I had nothing to show off. A few weeks after starting the Jowett Course my body was the best in the neighborhood. Now I get respect and admiration from every fellow and girl I meet.
Roger D. Hirsch
NEW YORK
NOW
There's that skinny scarecrow ROGER. Let's pass him by!
Roger Hirsch before
NO! friend you don't have to be SKINNY any more just mail NOW the FREE coupon below as I did. Soon YOU can add
6½ inches to your CHEST
3 inches to each ARM
and the rest in proportion just as I did.
How to Build MIGHTY ARMS
How to Build A MIGHTY CHEST
How to Build MIGHTY LEGS
How to Build A MIGHTY BACK
How to Build A MIGHTY GRIP
FREE
PHOTO BOOK HOW to Achieve Nerves of Steel, Muscles of Iron
How to BECOME A MIGHTY HE-MAN
Come on, PAL, NOW YOU GIVE ME
10 PLEASANT MINUTES A DAY IN YOUR HOME... AND I'LL GIVE
YOU a NEW HE-MAN BODY
For Your OLD SKELETON FRAME.
says George F. Jowett World's Greatest Builder of HE-MEN
GEORGE F. JOWETT
"Champion of Champions"
4 times Winner Perfect Man Contest
ROGER HIRSCH
was a 112 lb. 6 ft. WEAKLING.
Look at him NOW—
A MOVIE-STAR HE-MAN
from Head to Toe
as YOU can be soon!
NO! I don't care how skinny or flabby you are; if you're a teen-ager, in your 20's or 30's or over; if you're short or tall, or what work you do. All I want is JUST 10 EXCITING MINUTES in your home to MAKE YOU OVER by the SAME METHOD I turned myself from a wreck to a Champion of Champions.
YES! You'll see INCH upon INCH of MIGHTY MUSCLE added to YOUR ARMS. Your CHEST deepened. Your BACK AND SHOULDERS broadened. From head to heels, you'll gain SOLIDITY, SIZE, POWER, SPEED! You'll become an ALL-Around, ALL-American HE-MAN, A WINNER in everything you tackle—or my Training won't cost you one solitary cent.
Develop YOUR 520 MUSCLES
Gain Pounds, INCHES, FAST!
Friend, I've traveled the world. Made a LIFETIME STUDY of every way known to develop your body. Then I devised the BEST by TEST, my "5-WAY PROGRESSIVE POWER" the only method that builds you 5-ways fast. You save YEARS, DOLLARS like movie star Tom Tyler did. Like champ Roger Hirsch did. Like MANY THOUSANDS like you did. SO Mail coupon NOW!
MAIL COUPON IN TIME FOR FREE OFFER!
BOTH FREE FOR QUICK ACTION!
1. Photo Book of STRONG MEN
2. MUSCLE METER
Dept. HS-27
"Jowett Courses greatest in World for Building All-Around HE-MEN" —R. F. Kelley Director Physical
JOWETT INSTITUTE OF PHYSICAL TRAINING
230 FIFTH AVENUE, NEW YORK 1, N. Y.
Dear George: Please mail to me FREE Jowett's Photo Book of Strong Men and a Muscle Meter, plus all 5 HE-MAN Building Courses: 1. How to Build a Mighty Chest. 2. How to Build a Mighty Arm. 3. How to Build a Mighty Grip. 4. How to Build a Mighty Back. 5. How to Build Mighty Legs—Now all in One Volume "How to become a Mighty HE-MAN." ENCLOSED FIND 10¢ FOR POSTAGE AND HANDLING (no C.O.D.'s).
NAME
AGE
ADDRESS
CITY
ZONE
STATE

An Amazing NEW HEALTH SUPPORTER BELT

DOES a bulging "bay window" make you look and feel years older than you really are? Then here, at last, is the answer to your problem! "Chevalier", the wonderful new adjustable health supporter belt is scientifically constructed to help you look and feel years younger!

POSTURE BAD? Got a 'Bay Window'?

The CHEVALIER

LIFTS AND FLATTENS YOUR BULGING "BAY WINDOW"

Why go on day after day with an "old-man's" mid-section bulge . . . or with a tired back that needs posture support? Just see how "Chevalier" brings you vital control where you need it most! "Chevalier" has a built-in strap. You adjust the belt the way you want. Presto! Your "bay-window" bulge is lifted in . . . flattened out—yet you feel wonderfully comfortable!

DO YOU ENVY MEN who can 'KEEP ON THEIR FEET'?

and then he got a "CHEVALIER" . . .

YOU NEED A "CHEVALIER"!

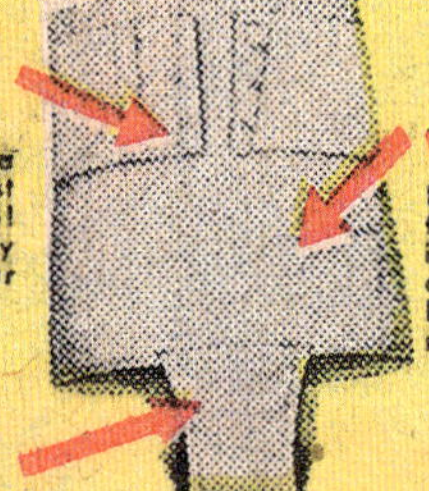

FRONT ADJUSTMENT
Works quick as a flash! Simply adjust the strap and presto! The belt is perfectly adjusted to your greatest comfort!

TWO-WAY S-T-R-E-T-C-H WONDER CLOTH
Firmly holds in your flabby abdomen; yet it s-t-r-e-t-c-h-e-s as you breathe, bend, stoop, after meals, etc.

DETACHABLE POUCH
Air-cooled! Scientifically designed and made to give wonderful support and protection!

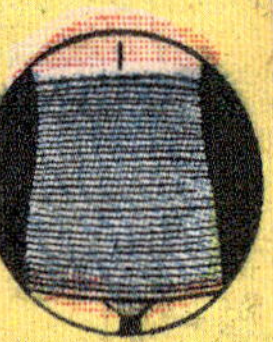

Rear View

FITS SNUG AT SMALL of BACK
Firm, comfortable support. Feels good!

Healthful, Enjoyable Abdominal Control

It's great! You can wear "Chevalier" all day long. Will not bind or make you feel constricted. That's because the two-way s-t-r-e-t-c-h cloth plus the front adjustment bring you *personalized* fit. The "Chevalier" is designed according to scientific facts of healthful posture control. It's made by experts to give you the comfort and healthful "lift" you want. Just see all the wonderful features below. And remember—you can get the "Chevalier" on FREE TRIAL. Mail the coupon *right now!*

FREE Extra Pouch. The Chevalier has a removable pouch made of a soft, comfortable fabric that absorbs perspiration. So that you can change it regularly we include an extra pouch. Limited offer. Order yours today.

FREE TRIAL OFFER

1. *You risk nothing!* Just mail coupon—be sure to give name and address, also waist measure, etc. — and mail TODAY!

2. Try on the "Chevalier". Adjust belt the way you want. See how your bulging "bay window" looks streamlined . . . how comfortable you feel. How good it is!

3. Wear the "Chevalier" for 10 whole days if you want to! Wear it to work, evenings, while bowling, etc. The "Chevalier" must help you look and feel "like a million" or you can send it back! See offer in coupon!

RONNIE SALES, INC., DEPT. YY11-E 487 Broadway, N. Y. 13, N. Y.

SEND NO MONEY: JUST MAIL COUPON

RONNIE SALES, INC. DEPT. YY11-E
487 BROADWAY NEW YORK 13, N.Y.

Send me for 10 days' FREE TRIAL a CHEVALIER HEALTH-SUPPORTER BELT. I will pay postman $3.98 (plus postage) with the understanding that includes my FREE pouch. In 10 days, I will either return CHEVALIER to you and you will return my money, or otherwise my payment will be a full and final purchase price.

My waist measure is __________
(Send string the size of your waist if no tape measure is handy)

Name __________

Address __________

City and Zone __________ State __________

☐ *Save 65c postage. We pay postage if you enclose payment now. Same Free Trial and refund privilege.*

TALES BEYOND BELIEF AND IMAGINATION!
TOMB OF TERROR
No.3
AUG.
TOMB OF ERROR
10¢
IN THIS ISSU
THE STORY BEHI
THE COVER –
CAVERN OF
THE DOOMED
THE FANTASTIC
CRYPT OF TOMORROW
THE TERRIFYING...
CRY OF SATAN
THE AMAZING...
DEATH PACT!

SOLDIERS
SAILORS
WACS
MORTARS
MARINES
PT BOATS
HOWITZERS
50 COMBAT ACTION PLASTIC TOYS
$1 POSTPAID
YOUR OWN TASK FORCE
Now you can be Commander in Chief of this complete task force. Have pitched battles, gunnery drills, deploy your troops for attack and defense. Here's a complete army . . . 50 pieces in all including soldiers, sailors, marines, PT boat, Howitzers, tanks, planes, and ships. You'll be thrilled and delighted with this complete task force. Nothing else like it!
LOOK WHAT YOU GET: SOLDIERS SAILORS • MARINES • WACS • TANKS JEEPS • PT BOATS • BATTLESHIPS • JET PLANES • BOMBERS • MACHINE GUNNERS HOWITZERS • TRUCKS • BAZOOKA MEN RIFLEMEN
Here's a great collection of military toys yours for just a single dollar bill. You'll have hours of fun and pleasure with this wonderful set. Every piece made of plastic in realistic scale. Precision formed of Styrene...nothing like it has ever been offered at this price. Rush your order now. 6" long die cut cannon that shoots harmless bombs included in your order NOW!
FREE 6" LONG DIE CUT SHOOTING CANNON!
Supplies Limited! Don't delay. Rush name and address and $1 for each set. Your complete 50-piece task force will be shipped by return mail. Sorry no COD's. Rush your dollar today.
FIGHTING FORCE Dept, HC
400 Madison Ave.
New York, N.Y.
I enclose ______ at $1 per set. Rush your 50-piece Fighting Force set prepaid.
Name ______
Address ______
City ______ State ______
MACHINE GUNS
BAZOOKAS
RIFLEMEN
JETS
TRUCKS
CANNONS
BOMBERS
TANKS
CRUISERS
BATTLESHIPS
PT BOATS
MARINES
WAVES
WACS
SAILORS
SOLDIERS
SOLDIERS
SAILORS
WACS
WAVES
MARINES
PT BOATS
BATTLESHIPS
CRUISERS
JETS
BOMBERS

TOMB OF TERROR

NO. 3
AUG.

CRYPT OF TOMORROW

CAVERN OF THE DOOMED

THE CRY OF SATAN

DEATH PACT

The aching arms of the gravestones thrust out to grab the fleeting wind. They twist it and turn it and force the night to cry out in agony!

Evil runs amock; the hordes of horrible beasts trample upon the sobbing sands of the graveyard; pain personified rides a headless horse of horror through the thick gloom of the night's fog!

And the road leads to the forbidden . . . to the horrible . . . to the ghastly . . . to the TOMB OF TERROR!!

Once caught on the road, the traveler can never again turn back. Or perhaps it is because he does not wish to turn back! Excitement, thrills, action, supernatural suspense wait at every turn!

The gruesome fingers shaped in the clouds overhead point straight ahead. The black cloak of night that seems to disappear for half a day lingers forever over the road ahead.

Witches that have stained history . . . monsters created in the evil corner of man's mind . . . vampires that drink human blood for nourishment . . . werewolves that howl a song of misery—all dwell in the site ahead!

Yes, twisted forms of the supernatural that have gone from the earth's four corners finally meet at the TOMB OF TERROR!

Now all is quiet; silence reigns in full splendor. And night hums a melody of anticipation.

Then all will suddenly break loose in a screeching, clanging turmoil of terror! The sky will be shattered in an explosion of evil! Satan will walk onto the scene . . . and rule! For this is the . . .

TOMB OF TERROR!

TOMB OF TERROR, AUGUST, 1952, Vol. 1, No. 3, is published monthly by HARVEY PUBLICATIONS, INC., at 420 DeSoto Avenue, St. Louis 7, Mo. Editorial, Advertising and Executive offices, 1860 Broadway, New York 23, N. Y. President, Alfred Harvey; Vice-President and Editor, Leon Harvey; Vice-President and Business Manager, Robert B. Harvey. Application for second-class entry pending at the Post Office at St. Louis, Mo. Single copies, 10c. Subscription rates, 10 issues for $1.00 in the U. S. and possessions, elsewhere, $1.50. All names in this periodical are entirely fictitious and no identification with actual persons is intended.

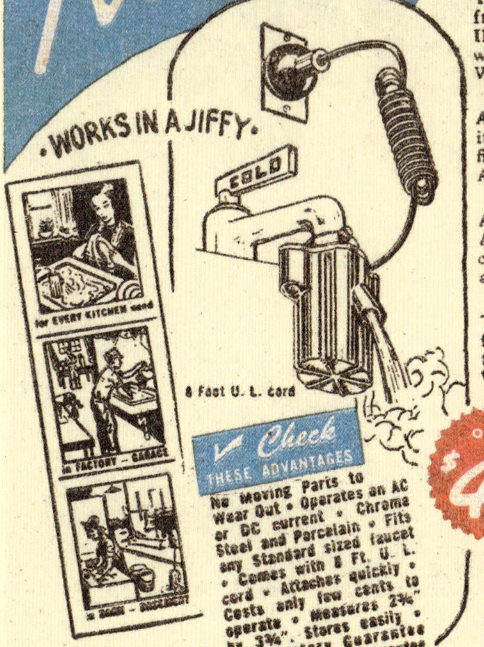

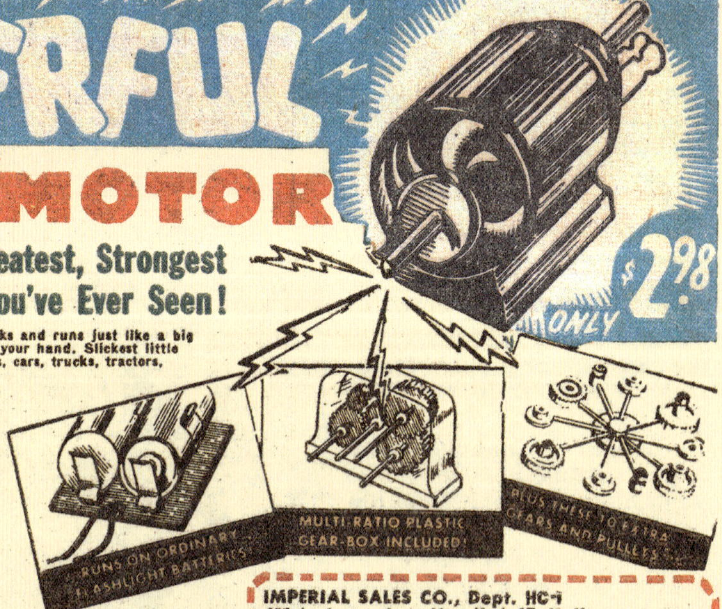

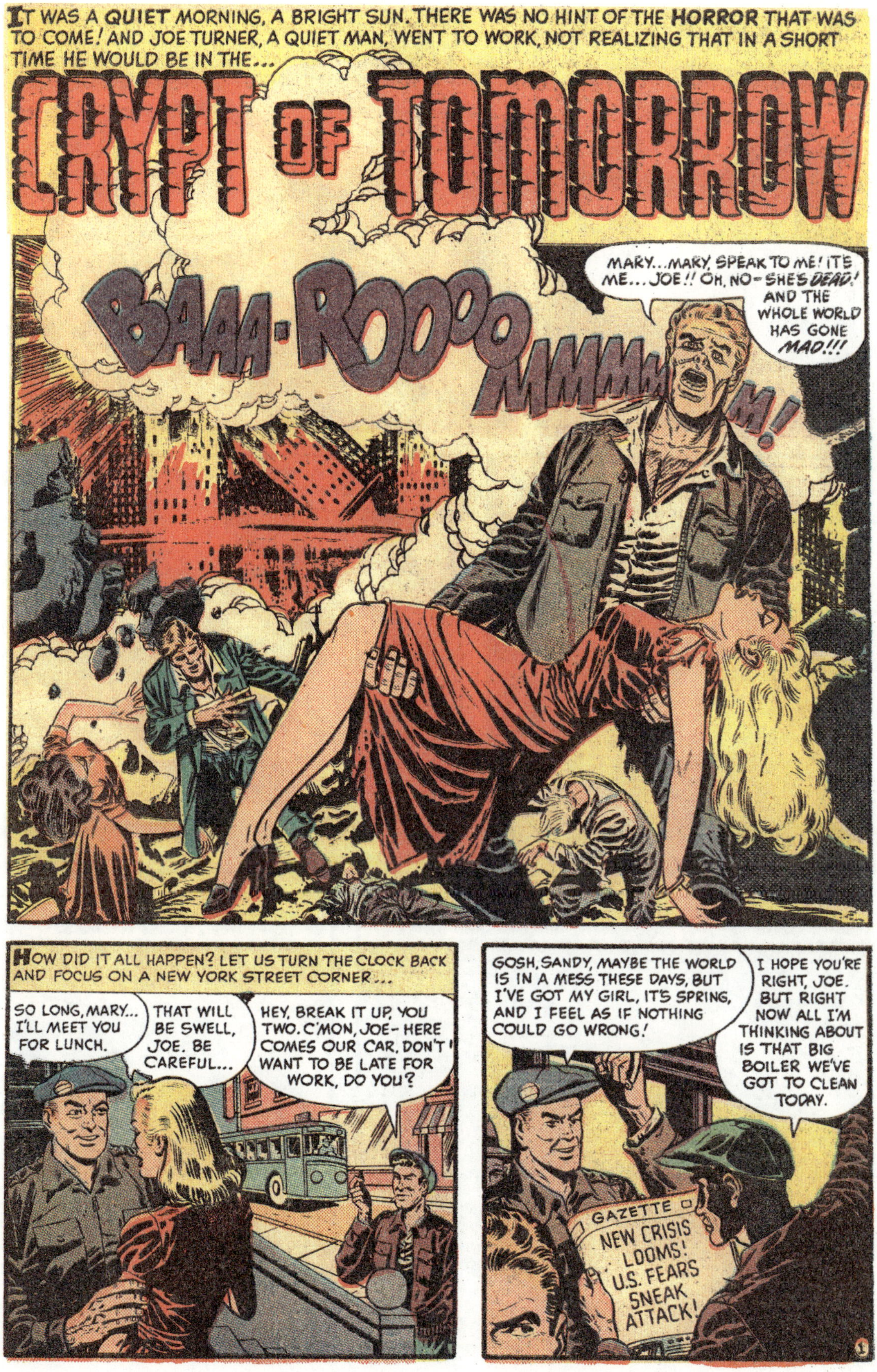

IT WAS A **QUIET** MORNING, A BRIGHT SUN. THERE WAS NO HINT OF THE **HORROR** THAT WAS TO COME! AND JOE TURNER, A QUIET MAN, WENT TO WORK, NOT REALIZING THAT IN A SHORT TIME HE WOULD BE IN THE...

CRYPT OF TOMORROW

BAAA-ROOOOMMMMM!

MARY... MARY, SPEAK TO ME! IT'S ME... JOE!! OH, NO—SHE'S *DEAD!* AND THE WHOLE WORLD HAS GONE *MAD!!!*

AND, AS JOE AND SANDY GO TO WORK AS THEY HAVE DONE FOR HUNDREDS OF OTHER MORNINGS, A PHONE RINGS ON A DESK IN WASHINGTON...
BRINNNNGGGG!

GENERAL, THE ATLANTIC RADAR NETWORK HAS PICKED UP A SQUAD OF UNIDENTIFIED AIRCRAFT HEADING TOWARD NEW YORK AT 900 MILES AN HOUR! BETTER COME DOWN HERE!
WHAT'S THAT!!? YES, CAPTAIN - I'LL BE THERE IMMEDIATELY!!

LOOK, GENERAL! AT THE RATE OF APPROACH THEY'LL BE OVER THE CITY IN LESS THAN AN HOUR!
SEND OUT OUR BEST WINGS TO INTERCEPT THEM IMMEDIATELY!

SQUAD LEADER JONES REPORTING IN. SHOULD ENGAGE ENEMY IN A FEW MINUTES. ROGER AND OUT!

AND IN A FEW MINUTES THE STRANGE, UNIDENTIFIED AIRCRAFT COME JETTING INTO SIGHT, TEARING THRU SPACE, LOOKING LIKE WEIRD, OMINOUS BIRDS OF DOOM!!
ZZZZ ZZZZ
ZZZ
ZZZZ

...THIS IS JONES REPORTING IN! THE AIRCRAFT ARE UNIDENTIFIABLE!! THERE IS NO INSIGNIA!! AND THEY LOOK AS IF THEY MIGHT HAVE COME FROM MARS - OR FROM HELL!!
3

...AND THE PLANES LOOK LIKE BATS! THEY'RE JET PROPELLED, BUT NO EARTHMAN HAS EVER CONSTRUCTED SUCH A MODEL!
GENERAL, COULD IT BE AN ENEMY FROM... FROM SPACE!!?
I DON'T KNOW! TELL JONES TO PRESS THE ATTACK!! WE'LL TAKE NO CHANCES!

ALL RIGHT, YOU HIDEOUS, BLACK DEVILS!! TAKE THIS--
TATATATATAT
TATATATATATATATATATA

AND AS THE HOT LEAD FROM SQUAD LEADER JONES' GUNS PIERCE THE BLACK ARMOR OF THE STRANGE CRAFT, THERE IS A TERRIBLE EXPLOSION WHICH SEEMS TO SPLIT THE VERY SKY, AND IT DESTROYS ALL THE PLANES IN THE AIR...
KAAAA-RRRROOOOOMMMMMMM

...EXCEPT ONE!!

...THERE MUST HAVE BEEN A TREMENDOUS EXPLOSION! IT WAS MORE POWERFUL THAN AN H-BOMB, GENERAL!! IT'S FROM ANOTHER WORLD!
ALL OUR PLANES WERE DESTROYED, GENERAL! ONE ENEMY AIRCRAFT STILL ALOFT-- AND HEADING FOR NEW YORK!
IN A FEW MINUTES HE'LL BE THERE-- AND NOTHING CAN STOP HIM! ALERT NEW YORK WHILE THERE'S TIME!
3

BUT THE BLACK PLANE, WITH A BURST OF SPEED, IS ALREADY OVER THE CITY...
SAY, LOOK AT *THAT!*
WHAT IS IT, A GAG?
LOOK! IT'S *DROPPING* SOMETHING!

MEANWHILE, IN A DEEP BASEMENT UNDERNEATH A NEW YORK OFFICE BUILDING, JOE TURNER WORKS ON THE INSIDE OF A HUGE BOILER, UNAWARESOF THE *BLACK MENACE* IN THE SKY...
GO AHEAD UP, SANDY! I'LL MEET YOU UPSTAIRS. I'LL BE DONE IN A FEW MINUTES!
OKAY, JOE- I COULD USE SOME FRESH AIR. BUT HURRY UP!

AND JUST AS SANDY REACHES THE STREET HE IS GREETED BY *DEATH* AND *DESTRUCTION!*
KAAAA-RRROOOMMM!
AHHHHH...!

MY GOD!! WHAT WAS *THAT!* EVERYTHING IS VIBRATING!! IT...IT MUST BE AN *EARTHQUAKE!!*

AND THEN, EVEN A LITTLE OF THE *NOXIOUS GASES* RELEASED BY THE *EARTH-SPLITTING EXPLOSION* SEEPS DOWN INTO JOE'S BOILER, STIFLING HIM- *BLACKING OUT* HIS SENSES!!
WHAT IS...(COUGH) THIS!! I..I CAN (COUGH-COUGH) H-HARDLY BREATHE!! OHOOO...

AND WHILE LIFE FLICKERS IN JOE TURNER, A HUGE, *POISONOUS* CLOUD OF GAS REACHES OVER THE WORLD, WIPING OUT LIFE WHEREVER IT GOES, CLUTCHING THE WORLD IN A *HUGE, BLACK HAND OF DEATH!!*
4

FOR HOURS A MYSTERIOUS MIST COVERS THE WORLD LIKE A SHROUD! AND, INDEED, IT IS A SHROUD, FOR ALL THAT LIES BENEATH IT SEEMS DEAD AND FOREVER SILENT!!

BUT SOME HOURS LATER, DEEP BENEATH THE RUBBLE THAT WAS ONCE THE GREATEST AND MIGHTIEST OF CITIES, ONE MAN MOVES...
OHOOO... HEAD FEELS LIKE ITS BEEN HIT BY A SLEDGE HAMMER!! WHERE AM I? OH-- REMEMBER NOW... EVERYTHING WAS SHAKING...

FUNNY... NOBODY AROUND...! GOT TO GET OUT... FIND MARY!

WHY, THAT LOOKS LIKE SANDY!! I'LL TURN HIM OVER AND SEE. MAYBE I CAN HELP HIM...

SLOWLY JOE TURNS HIS BEST FRIEND OVER, BUT WHAT HE SEES IS SOMETHING MORE HORRIFIC THAN EVER OCCURRED IN THE WILDEST NIGHTMARE OF A MADMAN...
MAYBE HE'S STILL ALI... AHHHHHH!!

THIS CAN'T BE TRUE!! I...I MUST BE HAVING A CRAZY NIGHTMARE! IN A MINUTE EVERYTHING WILL BE ALL RIGHT AGAIN... I'LL WAKE UP! OH, MARY... MARY... MARY!!!
5

SHE MUST BE IN HER OFFICE... I'LL FIND HER!!

AND JOE FINDS THE CORPSE THAT WAS HIS GOLDEN HAIRED GIRL EARLY THAT MORNING! HE STARES, BLANKLY, AND A GREAT, TERRIBLE QUESTION FORMS IN HIS BRAIN...
...MARY IS DEAD, TOO!

...A QUESTION WHICH HE FINALLY SPEAKS ALOUD, FOR OF ALL THE MILLIONS OF PEOPLE THAT LIVED IN THE CITY A FEW HOURS BEFORE, ONLY HE IS LEFT TO HEAR HIS OWN VOICE...
EVERYONE IS DEAD!! IS THERE NO ONE ELSE ALIVE ON ALL THIS EARTH!!?

AND IN THIS CITY OF THE DEAD, A LONE WAILING VOICE ECHOES THRU THE EMPTY STREETS AND BUILDINGS, AND FALLS UPON THE DEAF EARS OF THE GRISLY DEAD, THE MAD, WAILING VOICE OF JOE TURNER-ALONE IN THE UNIVERSE!!
HA-HA-HA-HA-HA!! I AM ALONE! ALONE! ALONE!!! HA-HA-HA-HA!

THIS IS MY CITY... MY WORLD!! HA-HA! THERE IS NOTHING I CAN'T HAVE!!

JEWELS WORTH MILLIONS - THEY ARE ALL MINE!!

CRAZED BY LONELINESS, JOE TURNER WANDERS THE CITY, FOR EVERY STORE, EVERY SAFE, EVERYTHING HE WANTS IS AVAILABLE TO HIM, EXCEPT A SINGLE HUMAN HAND THAT IS *ALIVE*...
I MUST SAY MY GUESTS AREN'T VERY TALKATIVE TONIGHT!! BUT THEY MUST BE ENJOYING THEMSELVES! SEE HOW THEY *GRIN*!!

COME ON!! SAY SOMETHING TO ME, BLAST YOU!! I HAVEN'T HEARD A HUMAN VOICE, A SOUND, IN MONTHS! TALK... TALK... *TALK*!!
RATTLE
RATTLE
RATTLE

FINALLY, JOE CAN STAND THE CITY NO LONGER, AND MAKES A DECISION...
I CAN'T BURY THEM ALL... AND THEY STARE AT ME SO ACCUSINGLY WITH THEIR *DEAD EYES*!! I'VE GOT TO LEAVE! MAYBE SOMEWHERE-SOMEHOW, THERE IS ANOTHER *STILL ALIVE*!!

FOR WEEKS THE THING THAT WAS ONCE JOE TURNER WANDERS THE COUNTRYSIDE LIKE A *LOST GHOST*, AND FINALLY- ONE MIDNIGHT, HE SEES...
...A LIGHT! CAN IT BE? HAVE I REALLY FOUND SOMEONE ELSE WHO LIVES ON THIS DEAD, BARREN EARTH??

BUT THE *LIFE* THAT JOE HAS FOUND RESEMBLES NOTHING HE HAD KNOWN IN THE PAST. THESE ARE THE *CREATURES* OF THE ATOMIC AGES THE *NEW FORMS OF LIFE* THAT HAVE ARISEN IN THE DEAD, RADIO-ACTIVE LAND...
NO... DON'T LOOK AT ME THAT WAY! LISTEN... I AM YOUR *FRIEND*! DO YOU HEAR? I AM A FRIEND!! SPEAK TO ME... SAY *SOMETHING*!!

BUT THE CREATURES DO NOT UNDERSTAND THE *LAST EARTHMAN* OF THE OLD AGE, AND THEY *DESTROY HIM* AS THE CAVEMEN OF ANOTHER ERA DESTROYED WILD BEASTS -WITH THEIR CLUBS!! AND THE LAST THING THAT JOE TURNER HEARS IS THE WEIRD LANGUAGE OF A *NEW* RACE...
The End

CAPTAIN BLACKETT NEEDED A HOME PORT FROM WHICH TO RUN HIS ILLEGAL TRADE IN DRUGS. HIS HEAVY JOWLS CREASED WITH SAVAGE JOY WHEN HE SAW THE ISLE OF FANGO IN THE CARIBEAN... A PERFECT BASE FOR...

THE CAPTAIN OF DEATH

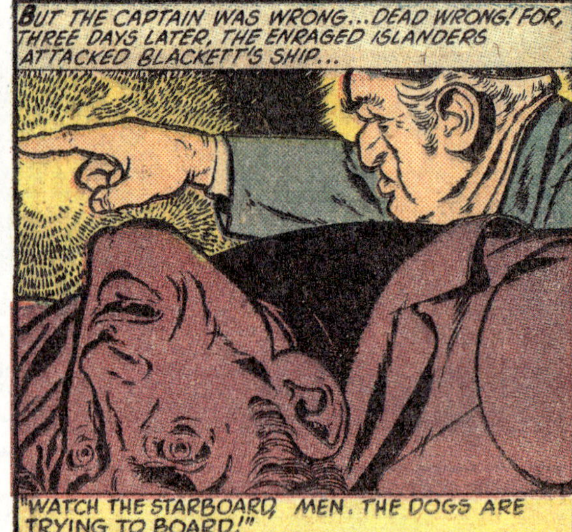

"THAT SCUM HAS FORCED US TO RETREAT. AYE, MATE, I CAN SEE THEM CHEERING. BUT I'LL BE BACK."

COUNTESS AURORA KARINE HAD SOLD HER SOUL TO THE DEVIL IN RETURN FOR MYSTERIOUS POWERS OVER LIFE! BUT LITTLE DID SHE KNOW SHE WAS TO ENTER THE...

CAVERN OF THE DOOMED

HEH, HEH... LET ME TELL YOU THE TALE OF ONE WHO WANTED POWER AND RICHES IN LIFE. SHE WAS YOUNG, BEAUTIFUL, CUNNING --THE *DEVIL'S OWN*--SO BEAUTIFUL THAT THE DEVIL HIMSELF CLAIMED HER FOR HIS QUEEN! HEH, HEH, HEH...

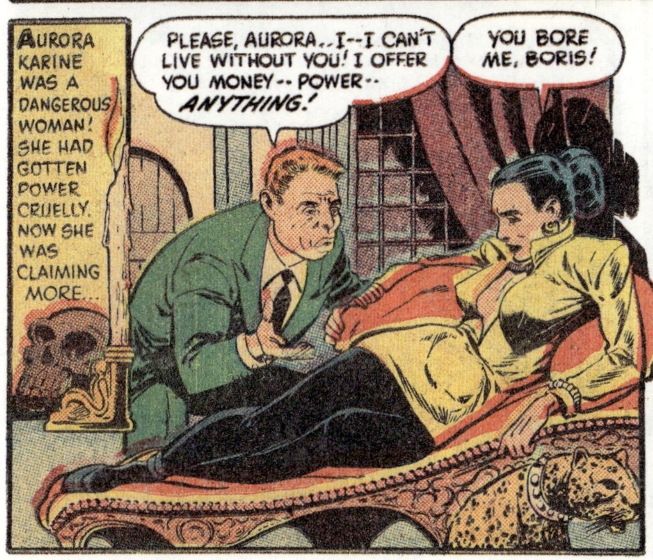

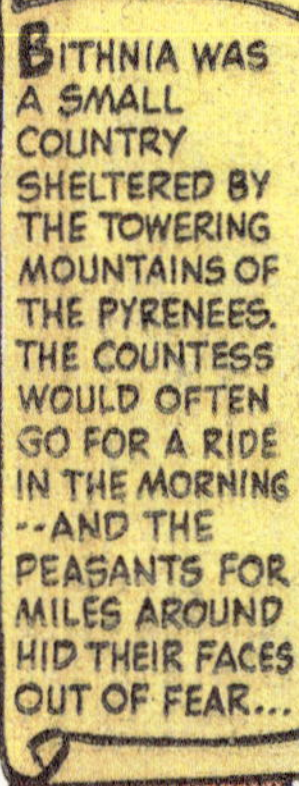

THE PEOPLE WERE SOON TO FIND OUT--FOR THEIR NATIONAL HERO--GENERAL MIGUEL ESTEBAN--WAS ALSO IN THE CLUTCHES OF THIS FEMALE HUMAN SPIDER...

AND ONE SHORT WEEK LATER, COUNTESS AURORA KARINE REAPED IN HER BLOOD-REWARD...

"--AND I LEAVE EVERYTHING TO COUNTESS KARINE WHO I AM TO MARRY SHORTLY, IN THE EVENT ANYTHING HAPPENS TO ME!" SIGNED MIGUEL ESTEBAN!

A TRAGIC LOSS MY DEAR! THE WEALTH HE LEFT YOU IS NO BALM FOR YOUR BROKEN HEART!

YES, YES... POOR ESTEBAN! WHY SHOULD HE DO SUCH A TERRIBLE THING--WHY?

GRADUALLY AND INEVITABLY THE COUNTESS GREW RICHER--MORE POWERFUL! HER SECRET? SHE HAD SOLD HER SOUL TO THE DEVIL IN RETURN FOR *WITCH'S POWERS!*

SOON SHE HAD TAKEN OVER THE REIGNS OF THE COUNTRY. INDEED SHE WAS NOW THE POWER BEHIND THE THRONE AND RULED WITH TREACHERY AND EVIL-- HER SEPULCHRE BEING DEATH!!

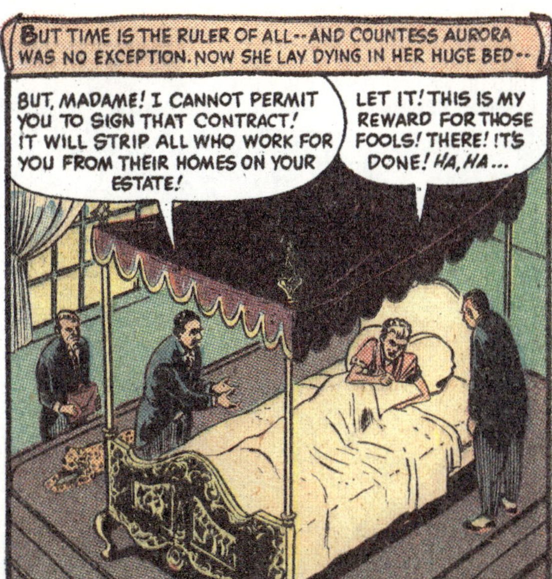
BUT TIME IS THE RULER OF ALL--AND COUNTESS AURORA WAS NO EXCEPTION. NOW SHE LAY DYING IN HER HUGE BED--
BUT, MADAME! I CANNOT PERMIT YOU TO SIGN THAT CONTRACT! IT WILL STRIP ALL WHO WORK FOR YOU FROM THEIR HOMES ON YOUR ESTATE!
LET IT! THIS IS MY REWARD FOR THOSE FOOLS! THERE! IT'S DONE! HA, HA...

THEY CURSED ME ALL MY LIFE--LET THEM NOW REALLY HAVE SOMETHING TO HATE ME ABOUT! HA, HA...AGHHHHHHH!
GENTLEMEN--EVERYONE--THE COUNTESS AURORA KARINE IS DEAD!

THEY BURIED HER IN THE FAMILY CRYPT AND FORGOT ABOUT HER. BUT THE WORLD OF THE DEAD NOW WAS TO CLAIM ITS DUE...
AURORA KARINE--AURORA--WAKEN! OPEN YOUR EYES!

W-WHA-T? W-WHERE AM I? OHH--I'M A YOUNG GIRL AGAIN! BUT YOU--YOU'RE ESTEBAN!
YES, AURORA! YOU ARE IN THE OTHER WORLD NOW! HERE, WE ARE NEVER DEAD! COME, DARLING! WE HAVE WAITED FOR YOU A LONG TIME!

AIIEE! YOU'VE SNAPPED CHAINS ABOUT MY NECK! L-LEAVE ME ALONE! I ONLY WANT PEACE NOW!
NO, AURORA! DESTINY HAS ORDAINED ANOTHER PATH FOR YOU! YOU SHALL NOT CHEAT US OF OUR REVENGE! HO, BROTHERS! GATHER ABOUT HER! SHE IS YOURS!
HA, HA, HA--HEH, HEH--AHA, HAH
3

TAKE HER TO THE CAVERN! HA, HA... THAT IS HER RIGHTFUL PLACE! MASTER TOLD US WE COULD SHOW HER HIS KINGDOM BEFORE HER PENALTY!
W-WHAT ARE YOU TALKING ABOUT? WHERE ARE YOU TAKING ME?

I WILL ANSWER ALL YOUR QUESTIONS, MY DARLING! IT IS MY TURN NOW TO HANDLE YOUR CHAIN! HA, HA, HA... YOU ARE ABOUT TO ENTER THE CAVERN OF THE DOOMED!
Y-YOU'RE BORIS!

YES, IT IS I, BORIS, THE ONE WHO BORED YOU!
EEEEEEE! SAVE ME FROM THEM! THEY ARE RIPPING ME TO PIECES! HELP!

DARLING! DARLING! DARLING! HA, HA, HA...
BORIS! I'LL MAKE IT UP TO YOU! ESTEBAN--HANS--YOU OTHERS--! PLEASE--! I'LL ATONE FOR MY SINS!

YOU CANNOT ATONE FOR YOUR SINS! YOU CAN ONLY SUFFER FOR THEM!
Y-YOU'RE TYING SOMETHING ABOUT ME! W-WHERE ARE YOU TAKING ME? WHY IS YOUR LAUGHTER LOUDER? TELL ME! TELL ME!

YOU'LL FIND OUT SOON ENOUGH, DARLING! HA, HA... WALLOW A BIT IN THE RIVER OF THE DAMNED... AND THEN WHEN YOUR HEART IS EATEN OUT BY THE FURRY CREATURES THAT SWIM IN IT, WE'LL PULL YOU OUT TO MEET--SATAN!
HA, HA... DARLING! DARLING! DARLING! HEH, HEH, HEH...
AAAAAAA!!IEEEEEE

SO COUNTESS AURORA KARINE MET HER MASTER! AND THE MORAL TO MY LITTLE TALE IS: IF YOU WANT FAME, POWER, AND MONEY, DON'T SELL YOUR SOUL TO THE DEVIL--OR YOU MAY MEET "OLD FRIENDS" AGAIN! HEH. HEH, HEH...
THE END
4

"John, she'll never walk again unless . . . unless . . ."

"Unless what, Dr. Martin? Tell me, please!"

"That fall Mary took yesterday severed nerve tissue at the base of the spine. As a result, the lower half of her body is paralyzed. Now, John, as you and Mary know, I have been performing certain experiments. And, because of what has happened, I will tell you what kind of experiments they are!"

The twilight shadows grew blacker as night came. The air became warm and still.

"What kind of experiments, Doctor?"

"Paralysis, John, paralysis!".

The young policeman bent forward. His eyes clawed at the aging features of the scientist's face.

"Paralysis?"

"Yes! If my experiments are right, such cases as Mary will need fear no longer. I think I have found a way of replacing the damaged nerve tissue with healthy tissue. After the operation, the patient could be on his feet in hours!"

"B-but..."

"I know what bothers you, John! Have I ever tried it on a human before? Can I be sure it'll work? No...only on animals and I'm not sure it'll work...on human beings!"

During the following minutes, hysterical with confused possibilities and realistic fears, the two men weighed the idea of submitting Mary to Dr. Martin's new discovery. They finally decided to tell everything to the girl and let her decide for herself.

Mary agreed!

The days passed slowly...painfully for both Dr. Martin and John. If the operation was a success, Martin would be hailed as the greatest scientist who ever lived. If the surgery was a failure, John would lose his wife.

Then, one night, a night buried under the wing of mystery, Dr. Martin raised his head from his notebooks. A wild thought pounded against the walls of his brain.

"The operation will have much more of a chance of succeeding if I have the nerve tissue from human specimens just killed. Of that I am sure. But that would mean murder!"

Candle light etched out crevices of debate on the man's face. If he could get the specimens, Mary's life might be saved and he would be recognized as the supreme genius. The man continued to think through the night.

Suddenly, the small town was clutched in the grasp of deadly horror. The experiments were forgotten. A monster was on the rampage ripping life from the screaming bodies of victims who curled in spasmodic fits of death. At police headquarters:

"An ape man, that's what it is! I saw him kill Mrs. Roberts! An ape man!"

John watched the witness squirm fearfully. He had been assigned to the case. That evening, he visited Doctor Martin.

"The ape man just disappears. He horribly mutilates the victims and just disappears."

"I've been reading about it in the papers. But, John, I do have something to tell you. By tomorrow, I will have completed the preparations for Mary's operations. It is unfortunate that this monster should be loose just when we must fully concentrate on Mary."

The policeman left Martin's house in a jumbled mental state. On the one hand, he had to battle a demon. On the other, he had to think about an operation which could end in the death of his wife. A walk! He needed to walk and think.

As John walked...

"AAAAAIIIEEEHHHH!"

A woman was screaming! He ran quickly in the direction of the shriek. As he turned a corner he saw...

THE APE MAN!

He tore out his gun. Fired! Fired! Fired! The ape man turned...staggered away...bleeding.

Seeing that the woman was all right, John madly pursued the monster. He saw it trying to climb the steps of Dr. Martin's house! It fell and, as it did, its fake head rolled from its shoulders revealing...

"Dr. Martin!"

"Y-yes, John! I've been the one. I-I had to k-kill! Take my notebooks to Dr. Tharp! He will save Mary. Tell h-him I have the necessary specimens. I-it was m-my one chance. I . . . I . . . ahhhhh . . ."

MANY PEOPLE THINK THAT THE EARTH HAS BEEN THOROUGHLY EXPLORED. BUT, UNKNOWN TO THEM, THIS PLANET STILL HARBORS PLACES OF MYSTERY... PLACES NO HUMAN HAS EVER SEEN OR WILL EVER SEE...

TUCKED AWAY IN THE SPRAWLING, SLIMY JUNGLES OF BRAZIL IS THE LAND THE DEMONS CALL *HALLA*... THE GROUND OF DEATH! IT IS THERE THAT THE DAMNED DEAD LIVE... AND SUFFER!

NUMEROUS ATTEMPTS HAVE BEEN MADE TO FIND *SHANGRILA* ALL HAVE FAILED. YET, *SHANGRILA* DOES EXIST... A LAND OF LIFE FOREVER. ITS STRANGE BEAUTY WILL BE ETERNALLY HIDDEN FROM MAN BY TOWERING MONSTERS... THE MOUNTAINS OF MYSTERIOUS TIBET.

SURROUNDED BY IMPENETRABLE WALLS OF VINES, TREES AND SWAMPS, THE LAND OF THE LOST AGES EXISTS. THERE, PREHISTORIC ANIMALS STILL LIVE AND *GROW* IN NUMBER. PERHAPS, WHEN THE TIME COMES, THEY WILL...

HAVE YOU EVER WONDERED WHAT REALLY IS DOWN AT THE BOTTOM OF THE OCEANS? DOWN IN THOSE MURKY DEPTHS OF DARKNESS AND DEVILNESS, ROAM MONSTERS WHICH WOULD RIP A MAN'S SANITY TO BITS. MORE THAN ONE SHIP HAS DISAPPEARED IN THE OCEANS' EXPANSES BECAUSE OF THE HORRIBLE ATTACKS OF THESE *THINGS*!!

HOW TO HYPNOTIZE
how to HYPNOTIZE
IT'S EASY TO HYPNOTIZE...
when you know how!
Want the thrill of imposing your will over someone? Of making someone do exactly what you order? Try hypnotism! This amazing technique gives full personal satisfaction. You'll find it entertaining and gratifying. HOW TO HYPNOTIZE shows all you need to know. It is put so simply, anyone can follow it. And there are 24 revealing photographs for your guidance.
SEND NO MONEY
FREE ten days' examination of this system is offered to you if you send the coupon today. We will ship you our copy by return mail, in plain wrapper. If not delighted with results, return it in 10 days and your money will be refunded. Stravon Publishers, Dept. H313, 113 West 57th St., New York 19, N. Y.
Mail Coupon Today
STRAVON PUBLISHERS, Dept. H313
113 West 57th St., N. Y. 19, N. Y.
Send HOW TO HYPNOTIZE in plain wrapper.
☐ Send C.O.D. I will pay postman $1.98 plus postage.
☐ I enclose $1.98. Send postpaid.
If not delighted, I may return it in 10 days and get my money back.
Name
Address
City Zone State
Canada & Foreign—$2.50 with order

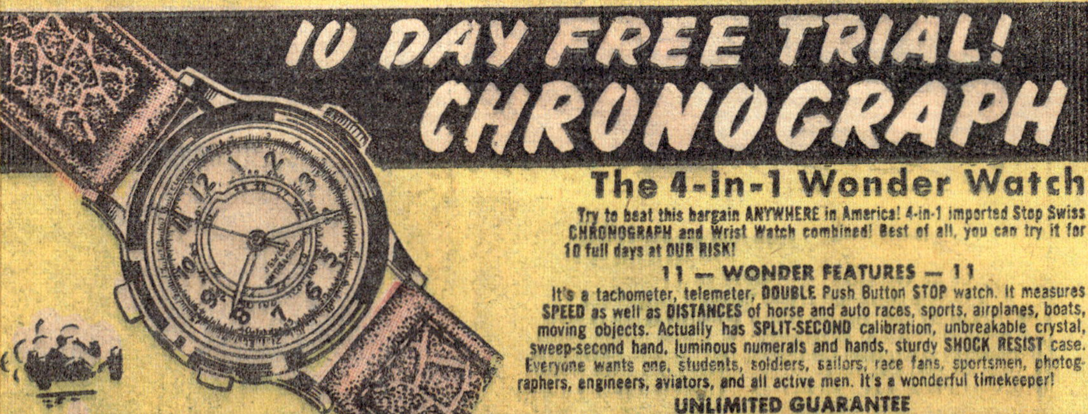
AMAZING!
10 DAY FREE TRIAL!
CHRONOGRAPH
The 4-in-1 Wonder Watch
Try to beat this bargain ANYWHERE in America! 4-in-1 imported Stop Swiss CHRONOGRAPH and Wrist Watch combined! Best of all, you can try it for 10 full days at OUR RISK!
11 — WONDER FEATURES — 11
It's a tachometer, telemeter, DOUBLE Push Button STOP watch. It measures SPEED as well as DISTANCES of horse and auto races, sports, airplanes, boats, moving objects. Actually has SPLIT-SECOND calibration, unbreakable crystal, sweep-second hand, luminous numerals and hands, sturdy SHOCK RESIST case. Everyone wants one, students, soldiers, sailors, race fans, sportsmen, photographers, engineers, aviators, and all active men. It's a wonderful timekeeper!
UNLIMITED GUARANTEE
EXCLUSIVE OF PARTS! Never a charge for skilled labor. FULL INSTRUCTIONS and gift case with each watch. SEND NO MONEY. Pay postman 6.95 plus 10% tax, or send only 7.65 and SAVE postage. Try at OUR risk for 10 full days. Price back QUICK if not thrilled. Order now—while they last!
U. S. DIAMOND HOUSE, Dept. 24L-239
127 West 33rd Street, New York 1, N. Y.

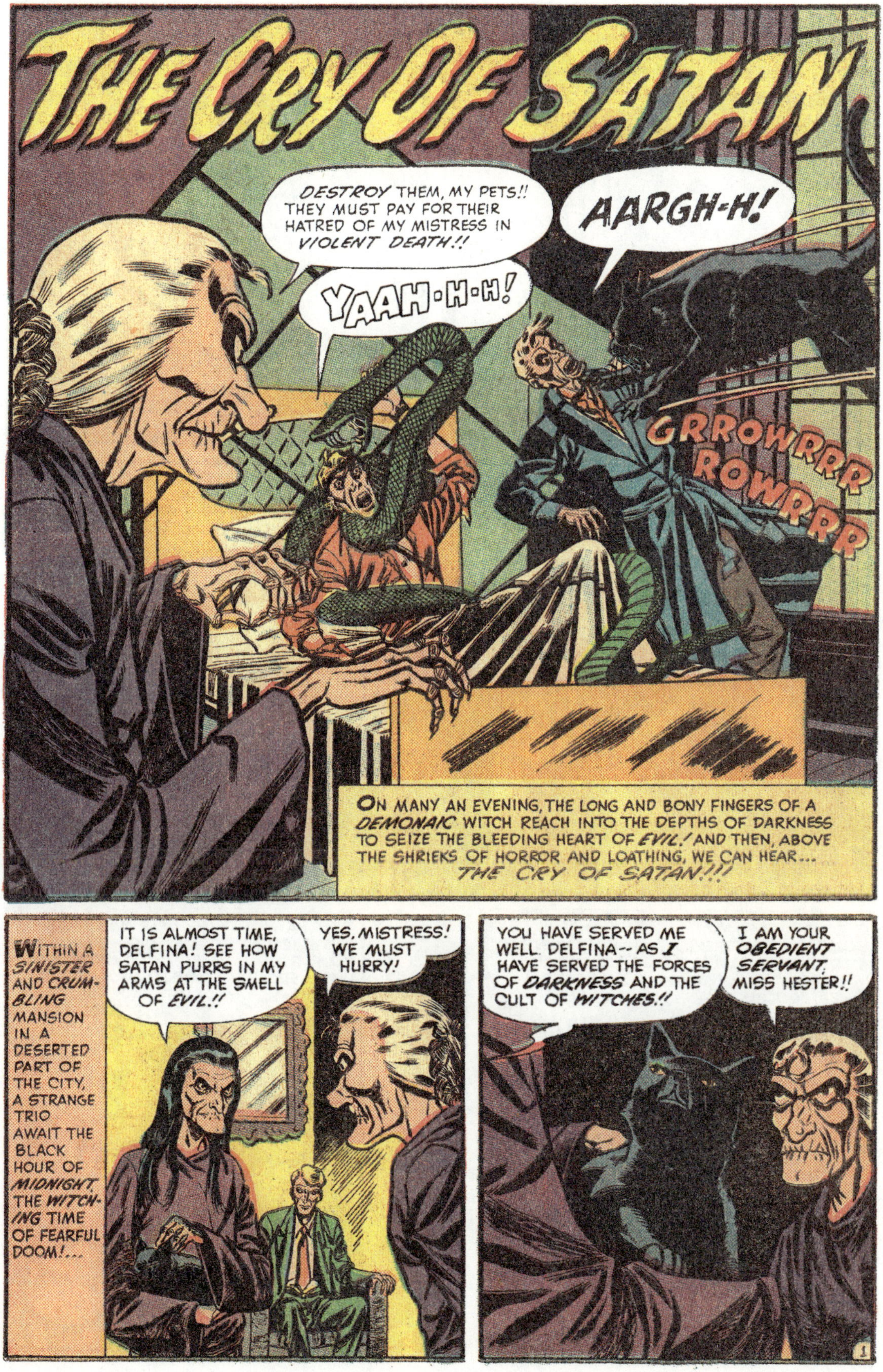

THE CRY OF SATAN

DESTROY THEM, MY PETS!! THEY MUST PAY FOR THEIR HATRED OF MY MISTRESS IN VIOLENT DEATH!!

AARGH-H!

YAAH-H-H!

GRROWRRR ROWRRR

ON MANY AN EVENING, THE LONG AND BONY FINGERS OF A *DEMONAIC* WITCH REACH INTO THE DEPTHS OF DARKNESS TO SEIZE THE BLEEDING HEART OF *EVIL!* AND THEN, ABOVE THE SHRIEKS OF HORROR AND LOATHING, WE CAN HEAR... *THE CRY OF SATAN!!!*

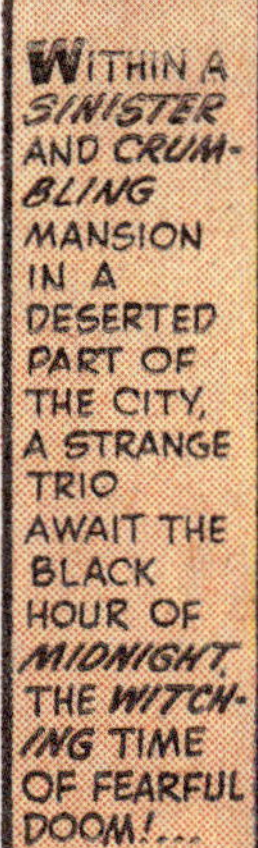

BUT AS THE AUNT AND NEPHEW CONTINUED THEIR FRIENDLY TALK, A LIGHT FLARES IN THE YOUNG MAN'S EYES LIKE A BRIEF AND TERRIBLE WARNING OF IMPENDING DOOM!...

BUT IN THAT DREADFUL HOUSE, HATE THRIVES LIKE SOME POISONOUS PLANT--AND LATE THAT EVENING, THE WITCH'S BROTHER SETS OUT ON A MURDEROUS MISSION!!...
AFTER TONIGHT, SHE'LL GLOAT NO LONGER!! HOW PROUD SHE IS OF HER LUSTROUS HAIR...SYMBOL OF HER POWER! THAT POWER WILL SOON BE--ENDED!!

SHE SLEEPS SO SOUNDLY! HER LAST SLEEP!! FOR ALL I MUST DO IS TAKE THIS SCISSOR AND--

---DESTROY HER BEAUTIFUL HAIR FOREVER---
WH-- EDGAR!! WHAT ARE YOU DOING? NO! NO! DON'T!!

---AND NOW ALL THAT IS POSSIBLE IS FOR THE POWERLESS WITCH TO--
EDGAR!! YOU MUSTN'T!! NOW I AM AS MORTAL AS YOU!! WE COULD...

---DIE!!
AAAARGH-H-H!

THAT MORNING, THE CLEAR LIGHT OF DAY GIVES UP THE MURDERED BODY OF HESTER TO THE SHOCKED VIEW OF HER SERVANT, AND THE CRIES OF SATAN SOUND WEIRDLY THROUGH THE HOUSE...
O MY MISTRESS!! MY MISTRESS!!
IT MUST HAVE BEEN SOME PROWLER!!

I WONDER WHY HE CAME--AND WHY HE IS LOOKING AT ME SO STRANGELY!
ODD THAT SHE SHOULD BE KILLED BEFORE I...BUT I'M GLAD SHE'S DEAD!
3

AS THE DAYS PASS, THE UNCLE AND THE NEPHEW, SENSING THEIR MUTUAL HATRED, ARE DRAWN CLOSER TOGETHER. AND IN THE SHADOWS, A GROTESQUE SERVANT--AND A CAT--MOURN AND WAIT...AND LISTEN...

SWIFTLY, THE CAT OF THE DEVIL LEAPS UPON HIS MISTRESS' BED--UPON THE SHINING MASS OF HAIR THAT ONCE ADORNED HER HEAD!...

THE HAIR! HER HAIR! PERHAPS THE POWER REMAINS--THE WITCH'S POWER TO DESTROY!! I'LL WEAVE IT INTO A BRAID AT ONCE!!

HER STRANGE TASK COMPLETED, DELFINA STEALS SILENTLY TO DAVID'S ROOM AND WITH A FIENDISH PURPOSE IN MIND...

HEAR ME, MISS HESTER! YOUR PRECIOUS HAIR IS IN MY HANDS! I ASK YOU TO CHANGE IT INTO A LOATHESOME SNAKE WITH WHICH TO KILL YOUR UNDUTIFUL NEPHEW!!

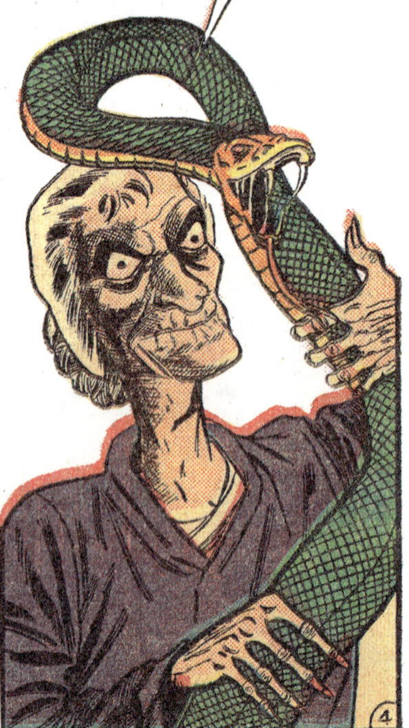

STRIKE POISON INTO HIS HATEFUL HEART, MY PET! YOU ARE THE SPIRIT OF MISS HESTER, COME TO DESTROY HER ENEMIES!!
WH--YAAH-H-H!! TAKE IT AWAY! TAKE IT AWAY!!

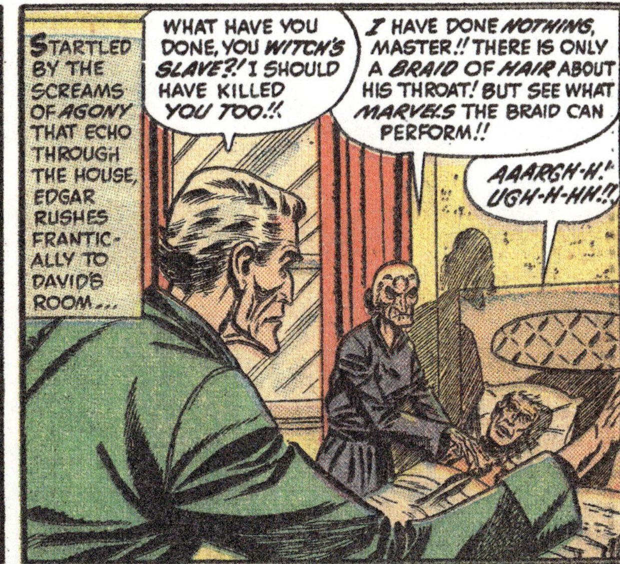
STARTLED BY THE SCREAMS OF AGONY THAT ECHO THROUGH THE HOUSE, EDGAR RUSHES FRANTICALLY TO DAVID'S ROOM...
WHAT HAVE YOU DONE, YOU WITCH'S SLAVE?! I SHOULD HAVE KILLED YOU TOO!!
I HAVE DONE NOTHING, MASTER!! THERE IS ONLY A BRAID OF HAIR ABOUT HIS THROAT! BUT SEE WHAT MARVELS THE BRAID CAN PERFORM!!
AAARGH-H! UGH-H-HN!!

I HAVE ONLY TO STROKE IT THUS... AND SATAN BECOMES A BEAST... A CREATURE OF THE DEVIL THAT MISS HESTER WORSHIPPED!!

DELFINA! YOU'RE INSANE!! SATAN WILL KILL US BOTH!!
NOT WHILE HE OBEYS ME!! HIS FURY IS FOR THE MURDERER OF HIS MISTRESS!! HE SHALL KILL ONLY...
SUDDENLY THE WITCH'S CAT BECOMES A BLACK MONSTER... A VICIOUS AND SNARLING INCARNATION OF BRUTE EVIL!!...

...YOU!!
GROWR-R-R
AARGH!

BUT AS THE UNEARTHLY ROAR OF SATAN BLASTS THE AIR, A FIGURE APPEARS FROM THE BEYOND LIKE A COLD AND SLIMY MIST FROM A FETID SWAMP!...
MY MISTRESS!!
DELFINA, YOU HAVE SERVED ME EVEN IN DEATH! BUT I MUST ASK YOU TO GIVE ME BACK MY PRECIOUS HAIR! I CANNOT SURVIVE IN THE BEYOND WITHOUT IT!!

I SHALL ALWAYS BE YOUR OBEDIENT SERVANT, MISS HESTER!! MAY YOU FIND PEACE WITH THIS BRAID OF HAIR!!
GOODBYE, DELFINA... GOOD... BYE...

AS THE WITCH'S SPIRIT FADES INTO DARKNESS, THE CAT OF THE DEVIL NOW TURNS ON THE POWERLESS SERVANT, THE LUST TO KILL GLEAMING LIKE A FIERY TORCH IN HIS TERRIBLE EYES!!...

THE BRAID!! I CANNOT CONTROL SATAN WITHOUT IT! MISS HESTER! COME BACK!! COME BACK!! NO!! N...

YAIEE-E-E-E-E!!
GRROWR-R

YAAGH-H-H!!
LISTEN!! SOUNDS LIKE SOMETHING HORRIBLE IS GOING ON IN THAT OLD HOUSE!!...
C'MON!

GOOD LORD!! LOOKS LIKE A MASSACRE IN HERE! UGH-H-H!!
I COULD HAVE SWORN I ONLY HEARD ONE PERSON SCREAMING!

AND AMIDST THE BLOODY SCENE OF VIOLENCE, A BLACK CAT PURRS CALMLY AND CONTENTEDLY, ITS GENTLE MEWING SO DIFFERENT FROM THE WILD... CRY OF SATAN!...
POOR CAT! YOU MUST HAVE SEEN SOME PRETTY AWFUL THINGS!
MEOW-W!
MEOWWW
THE END

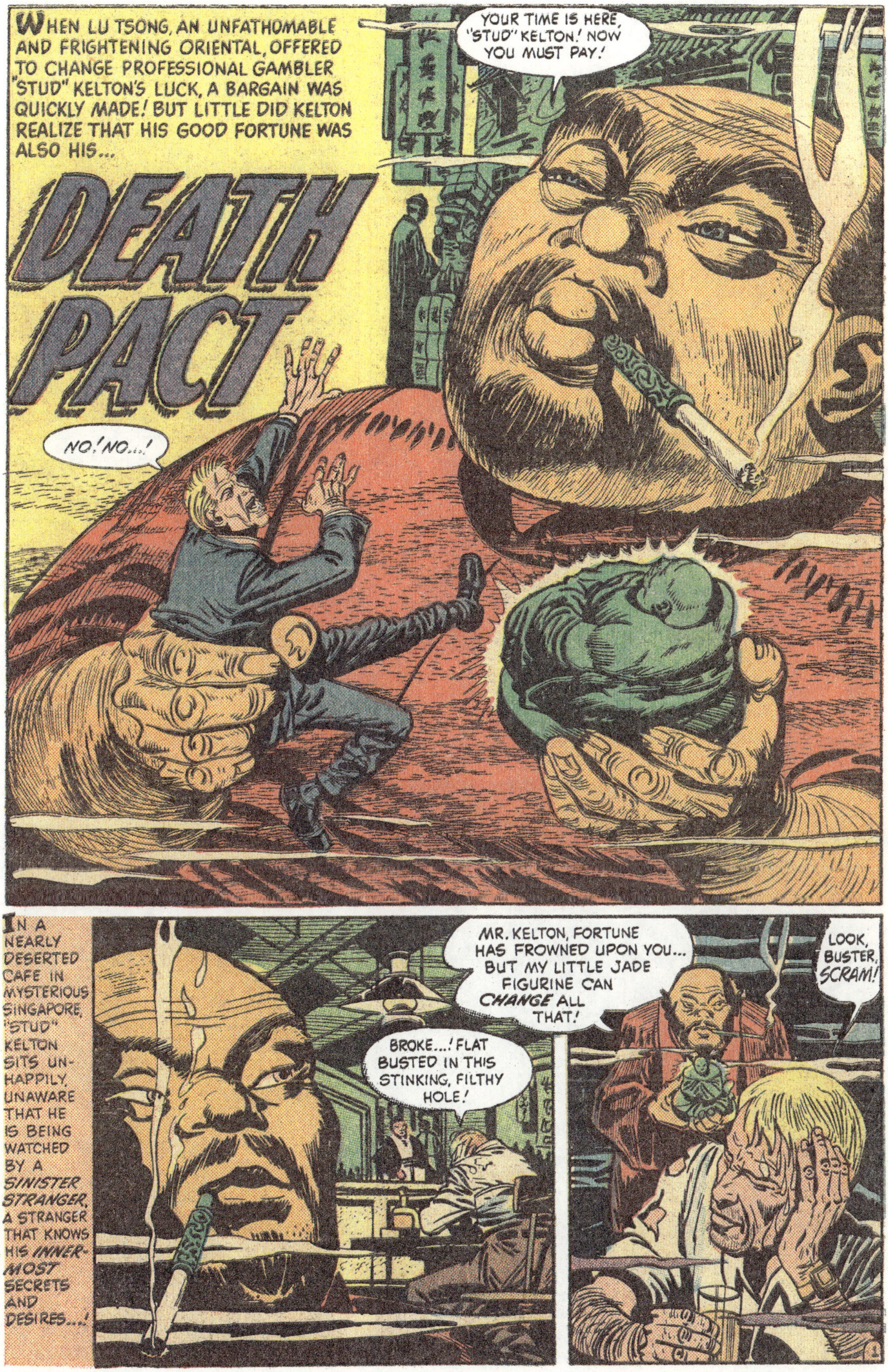

WHEN LU TSONG, AN UNFATHOMABLE AND FRIGHTENING ORIENTAL, OFFERED TO CHANGE PROFESSIONAL GAMBLER "STUD" KELTON'S LUCK, A BARGAIN WAS QUICKLY MADE! BUT LITTLE DID KELTON REALIZE THAT HIS GOOD FORTUNE WAS ALSO HIS...

YOUR TIME IS HERE, "STUD" KELTON! NOW YOU MUST PAY!

DEATH PACT

NO! NO...!

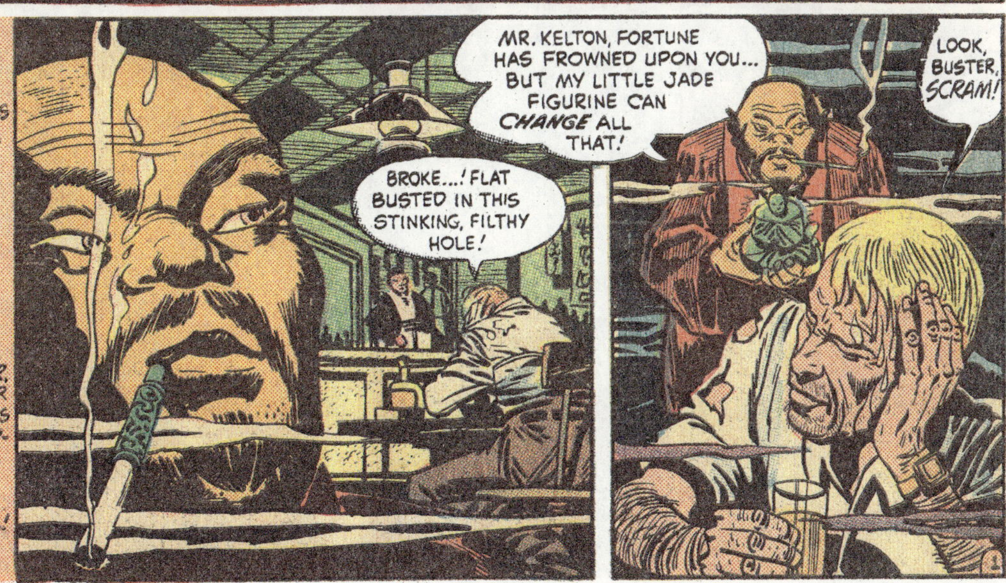

DURING THE NEXT FEW MONTHS...
SEVENTEEN BLACK!
THIS IS HIS FOURTH NIGHT HERE AND HE'S WON A FORTUNE EVERY NIGHT!

IN HIS APARTMENT, KELTON WILDLY EXTOLS THE *UN-BELIEVABLE* POWERS OF THE JADE FIGURINE... THE DOLL RESPONSIBLE FOR HIS FORTUNE... AND HIS *LIFE!*

TRYING TO KILL ME FOR MY MONEY! BUT MY JADE DOLL PROTECTS ME...!

AAARGH!!

THE PASSING OF A YEAR FINDS KELTON IN RENO... NO LONGER A DESTITUTE TRAMP IN SINGAPORE, BUT A FABULOUSLY WEALTHY MAN READY TO STRIKE A HARD BARGAIN!

BUT SLADE'S GRUESOME DEATH FAILS TO PERTURB KELTON, AND HE MAKES THE ROUNDS OF THE GAMBLING CASINOS...UNAWARE THAT HIS ACTIONS ARE BEING WATCHED CLOSELY...!
MY LUCK...! WHAT'S HAPPENED TO IT...? I'VE LOST FIFTY THOUSAND BUCKS...!
YOUR YEAR IS UP, MR. KELTON! THE DAY OF RECKONING IS HERE...! HA-HA...!
BLASTED! CAN IT BE TRUE? IS MY LUCK UP AT THE END OF THE YEAR...? IT'S NOT POSSIBLE! IT -- WHA---? IT'S LU TSONG!
I'VE GIVEN HIM THE SLIP... BUT I'VE GOT TO GET AWAY... FAR AWAY...! I CAN'T PAY HIM! I'VE GOT TO GET MORE MONEY!
FLEEING TERROR-STRICKEN FROM CITY TO CITY, THE FEAR-RIDDEN KELTON WILDLY ATTEMPTS TO CHANGE HIS LUCK! BUT ONCE THE DOWNHILL FLIGHT HAS BEGUN, IT IS IMPOSSIBLE TO CHECK ITS ONRUSHING MOMENTUM...!
THAT'S ALL FOR YOU, KELTON! YOU'RE EIGHT HUNDRED IN THE HOLE NOW!
I'LL PLAY FOR MY CUFF LINKS---! WHA...? LU TSONG!
THE DEVIL! HE'S EVERYWHERE...! WHAT DOES HE WANT--? I CAN'T PAY HIM...! I'VE GOT TO GET AWAY!
SAFE...! HE DIDN'T SEE--! WHAT... WHAT'S THAT...! FOOTSTEPS...! HE'S COME FOR ME...!
4

HIS HEART BEATING WILDLY, THE FEAR-CRAZED KELTON VENTS HIS IRE UPON THE JADE IMAGE... AS THE DREADED FOOTSTEPS POUND MADDENINGLY IN HIS FEVERED BRAIN...!
YOU ARE THE CAUSE OF THIS...YOU DEVIL DOLL...!
CRACK

STAY OUT...! DON'T--! I'LL... I'LL KILL YOU...! NO...!
BANG

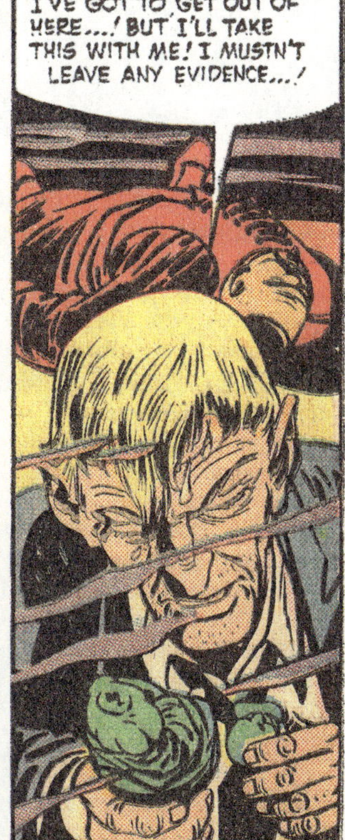
I'VE GOT TO GET OUT OF HERE...! BUT I'LL TAKE THIS WITH ME! I MUSTN'T LEAVE ANY EVIDENCE...!

FLEEING, AS IF FROM SOME HORRIBLE, UNKNOWN FATE, THE MADDENED MAN RACES RECKLESSLY AWAY FROM THE BLOOD-DRENCHED BODY OF THE MAN HE HAS JUST MURDERED...!
I'VE KILLED HIM... KILLED HIM...! HA-HA! HE'LL NEVER FOLLOW ME AGAIN--! THE CAR! IT'S OUT OF CONTROL!!

AIIIIIIIEEEE
CRASH

DRIVER'S DEAD...HEAD CUT RIGHT OFF! NO IDENTIFICATION... BUT WE DID FIND THIS JADE FIGURINE IN HIS POCKET!
THE END
5

BIRTH OF A VAMPIRE

Wearily, Marcia Hunt answered her telephone. She'd had a hard day at the laboratory, and she was tired.

"Come right over!" sounded her employer's voice over the wire. "I've got it at last, Marcia! I've *solved* the riddle I've been working on! And I need you—immediately!"

"But, Dr. Black..." Marcia protested. The click of the receiver at the other end was her only answer. Her boss had hung up. Sighing, Marcia went to the closet for her hat and coat. She was used to Dr. Jason Black's eccentric ways by now... and she needed the job.

"I am a man of science, Miss Hunt!" he'd told her the very first day she'd started to work for him. "Many strange and secret experiments are conducted in this laboratory... conducted as *I* see fit! I shall expect you to do as you're told, to ask no questions and demand no answers! Do you understand?"

"Yes, of course, Doctor!" she'd agreed.

Only it was easier said than done. It was very *hard* to keep silent when—as had happened so often in the past few months—she'd look up from her notes to find the scientist staring at her with such fearful intensity that his dark eyes seemed to be literally blazing out of their sockets, like the eyes of some evil creature of the night. At these times his face would be stark white, and his normally pleasant features would be contorted into the most terrible expression of malevolence that Marcia had ever seen! But before she could catch her breath to speak, he'd always turn back to his work with a slight laugh. "I *do* get quite lost in concentration, don't I?" he'd say. "Didn't mean to startle you, Marcia."

That was the kind of man Dr. Jason Black was, Marcia reflected, as she tapped lightly on the laboratory door. "And so, here *I* am!" she thought ruefully. "Going back to work at the stroke of *midnight!*"

"Come in, come in, my dear!" her employer greeted her cordially. He thrust a glass into her hand. "Here—first you must have a drink—to celebrate my triumph!"

The foaming brew in the glass had a dreadful odor, but, to please him, Marcia drained it all in one quick swallow. "Now, tell me!" she smiled. "What is this great discovery you've made, sir? This time you've *given* me the right to ask!"

"I certainly have, my dear!" retorted the Doctor, his eyes gleaming with suppressed laughter. There was something almost maniacal in his excitement, and for the first time, Marcia began to feel a bit uneasy.

"I," he continued, before she could speak, "have discovered the secret of one of the *blackest mysteries* of the supernatural! I HAVE FOUND THE WAY TO CREATE HUMAN VAMPIRES!!"

"Wh—what?" gasped Marcia, staggering to her feet. "You—you must be *mad!* I'm getting out of here..." Her knees buckled and she fell back into her chair, her whole body racked with tearing, agonizing stabs of pain!

"Oh, no you're not, my dear!" smiled the scientist. "I told you I *needed* you! You see, *you* have the honor to be the *first* of the race of human vampires I intend to create! That potion you just drank will take effect any minute now ... and I shall behold the success of my work *in the flesh!*"

Again the girl tried to scream, but no sound came. Instead, her body arched wildly as the pains tore at her insides. Her face turned blue, the lips parted, baring razor-edged, yellowed fangs of teeth. Her arms thickened and bulged until they resembled the dark wings of a bat. Her legs stretched longer and longer, until she towered fantastically tall and thin above her creator.

"Ah, my beauty—I've done it!" shouted the Doctor hysterically. "You are my *masterpiece!* I'll send you out into the night to kill and kill, until the *whole world* is mine! You *must* have human blood now! And you'll *kill* for it!"

Deep in its throat, the creature made a strange sound. Then . . . "BLOOD—BLOOD—I MUST HAVE HUMAN BLOOD!" And it leaped—straight for the throat of Dr. Jason Black!

"NO! AAAARRRGH!" screamed the terrified man. "NO! YOU CAN'T . . . " Suddenly, he screamed no more. Suddenly, the only sound to be heard was the sucking, gurgling enjoyment of the monster, as it greedily lapped up the fresh, warm blood that spurted from its dead master's throat!

Guaranteed to give you Fun-filled Flights!

You'll thrill and amaze your friends, be the envy of your neighborhood with this real JET airplane. The JETEX JAVELIN is a colorful, sleek-looking 14 inches of greased lightning. It will fly 1,000 feet! Go at a scale speed of 600 miles per hour! It takes off under its own power, loops, circles, stunts and then goes into a long glide and comes to a beautiful landing.

The JETEX JAVELIN is a cinch to build. Comes complete with the famous JETEX #50 jet engine and all parts already cut out. Nothing more to buy! Just follow the easy instructions, glue the parts together and you're ready for thrills! This amazing jet airplane uses the modern stressed skin construction which gives more strength and durability for its weight than any other type of construction. With ordinary care, it will make hundreds of fun filled flights.

It's fun to assemble, thrilling to fly. So don't delay—SEND NO MONEY—rush your order today to be sure of prompt delivery.

Designed by Commander Wallis Rigby

Yes, Commander Rigby, world famous designer, is the inventor of the JETEX JAVELIN. The Commander says, "I have created thousands of models, but the JETEX JAVELIN is the finest thing I have ever done"!

GUARANTEED TO FLY!

The JETEX JAVELIN is unconditionally guaranteed to fly if all instructions have been faithfully followed. If the JETEX JAVELIN does not fly, return the plane and the JETEX #50 engine within 10 days and your money will be refunded.

AMAZING JETEX #50 JET ENGINE

The world's smallest jet engine and the most powerful engine of its size ever sold! It runs on solid fuel, starts every time, completely reliable. NO MOVING PARTS TO BREAK OR WEAR OUT. Can be used to power model airplanes, racing cars and boats.

JETEX JAVELIN Box 429 Huntington, N. Y.

MAIL THIS COUPON NOW!

JETEX JAVELIN DEPT. C-5 **RUSH!**
Box 429 Huntington, N. Y.

Please rush the JETEX JAVELIN and JETEX #50 jet engine. I will pay postman only $1.98 plus C.O.D. charges on arrival.

Name..
(*please print*)

Address..

City.............................Zone.........State.......................

☐ I enclose $2.00 in cash, check or money order to save on C.O.D. charges. If the airplane does not fly, I may return it in 10 days for full refund of purchase price.

You Can WIN
This 15" tall SILVER TROPHY JUST AS I DID IN 10 MINUTES OF FUN A DAY!
I GAINED 53 LBS. OF SHAPELY POWER-PACKED MUSCLES!
Which of these 2 ME'S is YOU ?
THAT 112 LB.-6 FT. SPINDLE-ARMED SISSY below WAS ME A FEW SHORT WEEKS AGO
THIS MAY BE YOUR LAST CHANCE TO GET ALL 5 PICTURE PACKED COURSES FOR 10¢ MILLIONS HAVE BEEN SOLD FOR $1 AND MORE
When I enrolled I was a skinny, sick weakling. As you can see in my "Before" Photo I looked like a child... years younger than my age. I was ashamed to take a picture in bathing trunks as I do now. I was shy with girls because I had nothing to show off. A few weeks after starting the Jowett Course my body was the best in the neighborhood. Now I get respect and admiration from every fellow and girl I meet.
Roger D. Hirsch
NEW YORK
NOW
There's that skinny scarecrow ROGER. Let's pass him by!
Roger Hirsch before
NO! friend you don't have to be SKINNY any more just mail NOW the FREE coupon below as I did. Soon YOU can add 6½ inches to your CHEST 3 inches to each ARM and the rest in proportion just as I did.
How to Build MIGHTY ARMS
How to Build A MIGHTY CHEST
How to Build MIGHTY LEGS
How to Build A MIGHTY BACK
How to Build A MIGHTY GRIP
FREE
PHOTO BOOK HOW to Achieve Nerves of Steel, Muscles of Iron
How to BECOME A MIGHTY HE-MAN
ROGER HIRSCH was a 112 lb. 6 ft. WEAKLING. Look at him NOW— A MOVIE-STAR HE-MAN from Head to Toe
as YOU can be soon!
Come on, PAL, NOW YOU GIVE ME 10 PLEASANT MINUTES A DAY IN YOUR HOME... AND I'LL GIVE YOU a NEW HE-MAN BODY For Your OLD SKELETON FRAME.
says George F. Jowett World's Greatest Builder of HE-MEN
GEORGE F. JOWETT "Champion of Champions" 4 times Winner Perfect Man Contest
NO! I don't care how skinny or flabby you are; if you're a teen-ager, in your 20's or 30's or over; if you're short or tall, or what work you do. All I want is JUST 10 EXCITING MINUTES in your home to MAKE YOU OVER by the SAME METHOD I turned myself from a wreck to a Champion of Champions.
YES! You'll see INCH upon INCH of MIGHTY MUSCLE added to YOUR ARMS. Your CHEST deepened. Your BACK AND SHOULDERS broadened. From head to heels, you'll gain SOLIDITY, SIZE, POWER, SPEED! Everything you'll become an ALL-Around, ALL-American HE-MAN, A WINNER in everything you tackle—or my Training won't cost you one solitary cent.
Develop YOUR 520 MUSCLES Gain Pounds, INCHES, FAST!
Friend, I've traveled the world. Made a LIFETIME STUDY of every way known to develop your body. Then I devised the BEST by TEST, my "5-WAY PROGRESSIVE POWER" the only method that builds you 5-ways fast. You save YEARS, DOLLARS like movie star Tom Tyler did. Like champ Roger Hirsch did. Like MANY THOUSANDS like you did. SO Mail coupon NOW!
MAIL COUPON IN TIME FOR FREE OFFER!
BOTH FREE FOR QUICK ACTION!
1. Photo Book of STRONG MEN
2. MUSCLE METER
Dept. HS-27
"Jowett Courses greatest in World for Building All-Around HE-MEN" —R. F. Kelley Director Physical
JOWETT INSTITUTE OF PHYSICAL TRAINING
230 FIFTH AVENUE, NEW YORK 1, N. Y.
Dear George: Please mail to me FREE Jowett's Photo Book of Strong Men and a Muscle Meter, plus all 5 HE-MAN Building Courses: 1. How to Build a Mighty Chest. 2. How to Build a Mighty Arm. 3. How to Build a Mighty Grip. 4. How to Build a Mighty Back. 5. How to Build Mighty Legs—Now all in One Volume "How to become a Mighty HE-MAN." ENCLOSED FIND 10¢ FOR POSTAGE AND HANDLING (no C.O.D.'s).
NAME AGE
ADDRESS
CITY ZONE STATE

An Amazing NEW HEALTH SUPPORTER BELT

For men in their 30's, 40's, 50's who want to

LOOK SLIMMER and FEEL YOUNGER

POSTURE BAD? Got a 'Bay Window'?

DO YOU ENVY MEN who can 'KEEP ON THEIR FEET'?

and then he got a "CHEVALIER" . . .

YOU NEED A "CHEVALIER"!

DOES a bulging "bay window" make you look and feel years older than you really are? Then here, at last, is the answer to your problem! "Chevalier", the wonderful new adjustable health supporter belt is scientifically constructed to help you look and feel years younger!

The CHEVALIER

LIFTS AND FLATTENS YOUR BULGING "BAY WINDOW"

Why go on day after day with an "old-man's" mid-section bulge . . . or with a tired back that needs posture support? Just see how "Chevalier" brings you vital control where you need it most! "Chevalier" has a built-in strap. You adjust the belt the way you want. Presto! Your "bay-window" bulge is lifted in . . . flattened out—yet you feel wonderfully comfortable!

FRONT ADJUSTMENT

Works quick as a flash! Simply adjust the strap and presto! The belt is perfectly adjusted to your greatest comfort!

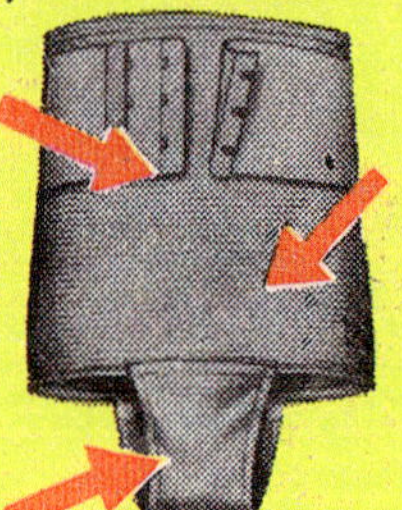

TWO-WAY S-T-R-E-T-C-H WONDER CLOTH

Firmly holds in your flabby abdomen; yet it s-t-r-e-t-c-h-e-s as you breathe, bend, stoop, after meals, etc.

DETACHABLE POUCH

Air-cooled! Scientifically designed and made to give wonderful support and protection!

Healthful, Enjoyable Abdominal Control

It's great! You can wear "Chevalier" all day long. Will not bind or make you feel constricted. That's because the two-way s-t-r-e-t-c-h cloth plus the front adjustment bring you *personalized* fit. The "Chevalier" is designed according to scientific facts of healthful posture control. It's made by experts to give you the comfort and healthful "lift" you want. Just see all the wonderful features below. And remember—you can get the "Chevalier" on FREE TRIAL. Mail the coupon *right now!*

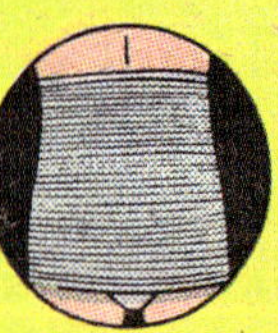

Rear View

FITS SNUG AT SMALL of BACK

Firm, comfortable support. Feels good!

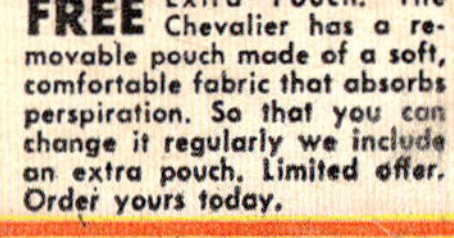

FREE Extra Pouch. The Chevalier has a removable pouch made of a soft, comfortable fabric that absorbs perspiration. So that you can change it regularly we include an extra pouch. Limited offer. Order yours today.

FREE TRIAL OFFER

1. *You risk nothing!* Just mail coupon—be sure to give name and address, also waist measure, etc. — and mail TODAY!

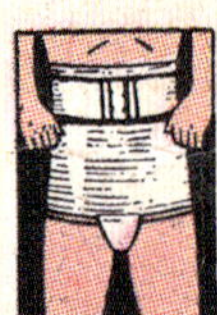

2. Try on the "Chevalier". Adjust belt the way you want. See how your bulging "bay window" looks streamlined . . . how comfortable you feel. How good it is!

3. Wear the "Chevalier" for 10 whole days if you want to! Wear it to work, evenings, while bowling, etc. The "Chevalier" must help you look and feel "like a million" or you can send it back! See offer in coupon!

RONNIE SALES, INC., Dept. YY05-E, 487 Broadway, N. Y. 13, N. Y.

SEND NO MONEY: JUST MAIL COUPON

RONNIE SALES, INC. Dept. YY05-E
487 Broadway, New York 13, N. Y.

Send me for 10 days' FREE TRIAL a CHEVALIER HEALTH-SUPPORTER BELT. I will pay postman $3.98 (plus postage) with the understanding that includes my FREE pouch. In 10 days, I will either return CHEVALIER to you and you will return my money, or otherwise my payment will be a full and final purchase price.

My waist measure is..................
(Send string the size of your waist if no tape measure is handy)

Name ....
Address ....
City and Zone..............................State............

☐ *Save 65¢ postage. We pay postage if you enclose payment now. Same Free Trial and refund privilege.*

TALES BEYOND BELIEF AND IMAGINATION!
TOMB OF TERROR
No.4
SEPT.
TOMB OF TERROR
PDC
10¢
"YOU BURIED ME IN HERE! YOU DID THIS TO ME I'M GOING TO KILL YOU!"
FOR THE FIRST TIME ! THE HORROR SPECTACLE NO ONE ELSE DARED TO PRINT ! .....
THE GLACIER BEAST !

TOMB OF TERROR

No.4 SEPT.

DIRT OF DEATH!

GRAVEYARD MONSTERS!

VINCENT ZARN FOUND A FOOLPROOF METHOD FOR ELIMINATING HIS BROTHER. BUT WHAT HE DIDN'T KNOW WAS THAT THE BEYOND SINGLED HIM OUT TO BE–

HIS BROTHER'S KEEPER

GLACIER BEAST

The tomb is open! Eyes are cast down upon the most horrendous figures, the most misshapen forms, the most ghastly of ghouls in an endless stream of terror!

The TOMB OF TERROR is open, and wild mobs fight for places in the auditorium of the unknown! A babel of voices reaches a piercing pitch as the weird creatures of the forbidden parade forth in panic-filled scenes!

Unbelieving eyes see for themselves the evil that lurks in man and takes shape in the dripping slime of horror. Jungles that live and breathe violence, murder, suspense and action form background. Then, too, the ghastly terrors of the Sahara, the swamps, the unknowns of India take the stage!

And above all is the icy hand of Satan that twists in hideous contortions as the world groans a loathesome gloom . . . the rotting hand of Satan that stretches from the . . . TOMB OF TERROR!

The home of horror has been found! The resting place of witches, ghouls, monsters, ghosts, spirits, mummies, werewolves and the whole congregation of evil has been opened!

The strangest stories ever told . . . the weirdest tales ever lived . . . the most grotesque adventures ever imagined are here in the TOMB OF TERROR!

Aching shrieks, cries of doom, shouts from Bedlam, songs of misery, mad voices dripping with agony chime in the . . .

TOMB OF TERROR!

TOMB OF TERROR, SEPTEMBER, 1952, Vol. 1, No. 4, is published monthly by HARVEY PUBLICATIONS, INC., at 420 DeSoto Avenue, St. Louis 7, Mo. Editorial, Advertising and Executive offices, 1860 Broadway, New York 23, N. Y. President, Alfred Harvey; Vice-President and Editor, Leon Harvey; Vice-President and Business Manager, Robert B. Harvey. Application for second-class entry pending at the Post Office at St. Louis, Mo. Single copies, 10c. Subscription rates, 10 issues for $1.00 in the U. S. and possessions, elsewhere, $1.50.

You Can Be a Bombshell In Any Tough Spot!
NOW . . . A Rugged Fighting-Man Shows You How To Explode Your Hidden-Powers In Self-Defense
AMERICAN COMBAT JUDO
AMERICAN COMBAT JUDO
FREE 7-DAY TRIAL! Mail Coupon
No true American wants to be a tough! But YOU, and every red-blooded man and boy wants to be always ready and able to get out of any tough spot . . . no matter what the odds. You want to have the real know-how of skillfully defending yourself . . . of fearlessly protecting your property, or your dear ones . . . against Bullies, Hoodlums, Roughnecks and the like. And, if in service, or going in, you've got to be ready to fight rough and tough, for your very life may depend on it in hand-to-hand combat.
Here's where a rugged, two-fisted fighting-man tells you . . . and shows you . . . the secrets of using every power-packed trick in the bag. You get it straight from "Barney" Cosneck, in AMERICAN COMBAT JUDO . . . training-manual for Troopers, Police, Boxers, Wrestlers, Commandos, Rangers and Armed Forces. What a man! He's dynamite from head to toes! Twice, he was Big 10 Wrestling Champ, and during World War II was Personal Combat Instructor to the U. S. Coast Guard. "Barney" has devoted most of his life to developing, perfecting, teaching rough, tough fighting tactics. He gives YOU all the angles in easy-to-follow steps. Mastery of his skills and tactics will give even a little guy the blasting-power of a bombshell . . . to knock the steam out of a bruiser twice his size.
"Barney" keeps no secrets in AMERICAN COMBAT JUDO! He tells all . . . shows all! He gives you the real lowdown on when and how to use each power-packed Blow, Hold, Lock, Jab, Throw and Trip, that will make YOU the "Boss" in any tough spot. You'll be thrilled and amazed when you see what YOU can do with your bare hands . . . even if you are light and small. For, the real secret of "Barney's" super-tactics is in using the other fellow's muscle and brawn against him . . . as if it were your own . . . to make him helpless and defenseless.
200 Dynamic-Action, Start-To-Finish photos show you what to do . . . how to do . . . the skillful fighting tactics that will make you slippery as an eel . . . fast as lightning . . . with striking-power like a panther . . . with a K.O. punch in both hands. What's more, you'll learn the secrets of using every ounce of your weight . . . every inch of your size . . . to give you giant-power . . . crushing-power . . . that will keep you on your feet when the other guy's down. Best of all, you'll be surprised how easy it is. Your friends, too, will be surprised when they see your speed, skill and power.
Send for your copy of AMERICAN COMBAT JUDO right now! Keep it for 7 days, and if you don't think it's the best buck you ever spent, return it and get your money back. But, don't wait — you don't know when you may have to do your stuff.
WHAT A BOOK!
It's super-charged with the know-all and do-all of every winning-trick in JUDO . . . WRESTLING BOXING . . . POLICE TACTICS. Actually, 4 Dynamic-Action Books in 1. Loaded with 200 Start-To-Finish Photos. All for ONLY $1.00.
PARTIAL CONTENTS
Disabling Blows . . . Chart of Disabling Blows . . . Hacks . . . Jabs . . . Holds . . . Locks . . . Breaks . . . Releases . . . Throws . . . Trips . . . Arm Drag . . . Full Nelson . . . Shoulder Throw . . . Hip Throw . . . Pile Driver . . . Fighting Two Men At Once . . . Disarming Assailant . . . and many others
4 DYNAMIC-ACTION BOOKS IN 1
ONLY $1.00 POST PAID
SPORTSMAN'S POST, 26 East 46th St. New York 17, N. Y.
Dept. HC9
FREE TRIAL COUPON ....Mail Today!
SPORTSMAN'S POST, Dept. HC9
26 East 46th St.,
New York 17, N. Y.
Gentlemen:
You've got something! Rush me my copy of AMERICAN COMBAT JUDO on 7 Days' Free Trial. I have checked how I am ordering:
☐ Here's my $1.00 in ___cash ___money order ___ check. Send postpaid.
NAME
ADDRESS
CITY ZONE STATE
WARNING! If you are a Merchant, Guard, Taxi-Driver, Trucker, Farmer, Cashier, Gas-Station Operator, Serviceman, Nightworker, or in some other occupation where, due to location or circumstances, you are often alone, or go through dark, lonely places, AMERICAN COMBAT JUDO is a must for you. Women and girls, too, should know how to defend and protect themselves when alone or unescorted. MAIL THIS COUPON NOW!

REVENGE DROVE SIMON LORENS TO HELL'S MOST HORRIBLE SCHEME! HIS ENEMIES WERE ALL DEAD... BUT HE BROUGHT THEM BACK TO LIFE AS THE...

GRAVEYARD MONSTERS!

NO! STAY AWAY FROM ME! YAAAAAAH!
YOU CAN'T ESCAPE, SIMON! I HAVE NO BRAIN, BUT I CAN THINK!
I HAVE NO HANDS, BUT I CAN CHOKE!
I HAVE NO EYES, BUT I CAN SEE!
AND I HAVE NO HEART-- BUT I CAN FEEL TRIUMPH!

SOON GRETA AND CARL WERE MARRIED AND SIMON TURNED TO DR. RATNER AND HIS PLASTIC SURGERY FOR HELP...
REMEMBER, SIMON. I HAVEN'T SAID I CAN CHANGE YOU! BUT YOU OWE ME NOTHING NO MATTER HOW YOU LOOK!
STOP YOUR CHATTER, RATNER! REMOVE THE BANDAGES--HURRY!
DR. RATNER M.D.

I DON'T WANT YOU TO BE DISAPPOINTED ...YOUR TISSUES WERE VERY DIFFICULT TO CUT... I HAVE NEVER SEEN ANYTHING LIKE IT!
HURRY! HURRY! IT'S COMING OFF! QUICK!

AIIIEEEE! MY FACE--LOOK AT MY FACE! I'M EVEN MORE UGLY THAN BEFORE! YOU'VE RUINED ME! AIEEE!

PLEASE, SIMON! CALM YOURSELF! I WARNED YOU OF WHAT MIGHT HAPPEN!
NO! YOU DID IT DELIBERATELY! BUT I'LL PAY YOU FOR IT... I'LL PAY YOU BACK!

SIMON THEN CHANCED HIS LUCK ON A DRUG AND HERB STORE IN THE VILLAGE...
HO, SIMON! SO YOU NOW WANT TO BE A BUSINESSMAN, EH? WELL--I WARN YOU--YOU'LL HAVE PLENTY OF COMPETITION!
BAH! STAY OUT OF MY AFFAIRS, VILANO, IF YOU KNOW WHAT'S GOOD FOR YOU!
DRUGS HERBS

WELL, SIMON! WE CAN'T ALL BE GOOD BUSINESS-MEN! HA, HA...
YOU HAVE DELIBERATELY STOLEN MY CUSTOMERS AWAY FROM ME! WAIT! WAIT! I'LL FIX YOU!
2

DAYS LATER, HE WENT TO SEE MARLIN, THE BANKER, FOR A LOAN.
NO! I REFUSE, SIMON! IN MY OPINION, YOU'LL NEVER BE A BUSINESSMAN!
PLEASE! I'LL PAY IT BACK TO YOU WITHIN A MONTH! PLEASE!

YOU DIDN'T MAKE ONE CENT PROFIT IN YOUR BUSINESS, SIMON. I CAN'T TAKE THE RISK! GO TO SOMEONE ELSE!
YOU PENNY-PINCHING MISER! KEEP YOUR GOLD-- WALLOW IN IT! BUT THERE WILL COME MY DAY WHEN I SHALL LAUGH AT YOU ALL!

SIMON SOON GOT A SUITABLE JOB... THAT OF CARETAKER AND EMBALMER FOR THE DEAD! THIS GAVE HIS EVIL MIND A CHANCE TO SPAWN A LOATHESOME SCHEME THAT WAS HATCHED AT THE VILLAGE CARNIVAL...
LET'S SEE WHETHER GRETA LOVES YOU NOW, CARL... DRINK IT DOWN! YOU'LL ENJOY IT! HA, HA...

...AND NOW LET'S MAKE A TOAST TO OUR YOUNG SWEETHEARTS! MAY THEY HAVE A LONG AND HAPPY LIFE TOGETHER!
I'LL DRINK TO THAT! HA, HA...
GOOD! NO ONE WILL EVER FIND THE POISON IN YOUR SYSTEM! IT IS UNTRACEABLE!

THAT NEXT MORNING, CARL DIED FROM A "HEART-ATTACK" ACCORDING TO DOCTOR RATNER. BUT COINCIDENCE PLAYED A GHASTLY TRICK. THE OLD DOCTOR ALSO SUCCUMBED TO THE GRIM REAPER... AND SIMON WAS THERE TO THE VERY END...
HE WAS A GOOD MAN!
TWO OF MY ENEMIES ARE ELIMINATED! NOW FOR THE REMAINING TWO!

THE VERY NEXT DAY AT EARLY DAWN, A SHAPELESS FIGURE MADE HIS WAY TO THE HIGH BRIDGE OVER A RAGING TORRENT.
THERE! LET VILANO COME!
3

VILANO WAS ALWAYS THE FIRST ONE OVER THE BRIDGE... HIS PROMPTNESS COST HIM HIS LIFE!
NOW ONLY MARLIN REMAINS!
CRRRRUNNCHH
YA-A-A-A-AH!

HOURS LATER, SIMON RETAINED THE BODY OF VILANO AND MADE HIS WAY DOWN THE NARROW WINDING MOUNTAIN-PATH TO THE CEMETERY.
GET OUT OF THE WAY, DOLT! YOU'RE FRIGHTENING MY HORSES WITH YOUR FACE!
BUT OF COURSE, MR. MARLIN!

BE CAREFUL, FOOL! YOU'RE DRIVING ME OFF THE ROAD; I'LL FALL! AAAAIIIEEEE!
CRACK! CRACK!
NEEEEE-EE-EIGH!

TOO BAD, MARLIN! NOW YOU'LL JUST HAVE TO JOIN OUR OTHER FRIENDS! HA, HA, HA, HA...

THE FOUR DEATHS AROUSED THE TOWNSFOLK, BUT IT WAS BLAMED ON COINCIDENCE. A FEW NIGHTS LATER, SIMON LORENS LOOKED AT HIS ENEMIES, AND LAUGHED LOUD AND LONG!
THERE YOU ARE, MY FRIENDS! HA, HA, HA... I TOLD YOU I'D HAVE MY REVENGE! BUT YOU HAVEN'T ESCAPED ME THAT EASILY! NO! I HAVE MORE IN STORE FOR YOU!

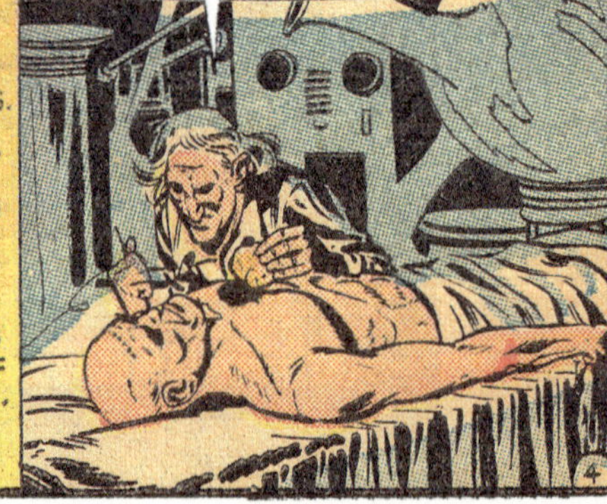
SIMON HAD SAVED THE CORPSE OF A GIANT MAN LONG DEAD AND ROTTING. TO THE DECAYED BONES, HE NOW BEGAN TO SEW ON VARIOUS BITS OF FLESH...
FOR YOUR BRAIN, I'LL GIVE YOU THAT OF THE BUSINESSMAN, VILANO'S! YOUR HANDS SHALL BE DOCTOR RATNER'S HANDS! FOR YOUR EYES, YOU'LL HAVE BANKER MARLIN'S ORBS, THOSE THAT DARED TO LOOK AT ME SO CONTEMPTUOUSLY--AND LAST--I'LL GIVE YOU THE HEART OF CARL. HE LOVED SO BEAUTIFULLY! HA, HA...

DAY AFTER DAY, SIMON LORENS WORKED ON THE ROTTED CORPSE, MAKING IT A COMPOSITE OF ALL HIS ENEMIES, AND IT SLOWLY FORMED INTO THE IMAGE OF FOUR MEN...
HA, HA ... WE'LL SEE SOON! HA, HA...

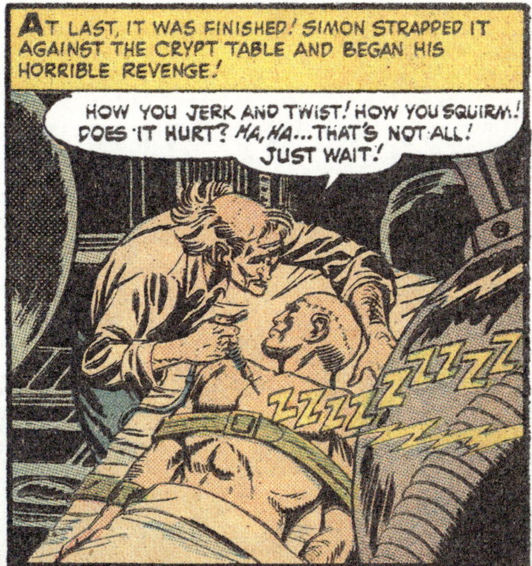
AT LAST, IT WAS FINISHED! SIMON STRAPPED IT AGAINST THE CRYPT TABLE AND BEGAN HIS HORRIBLE REVENGE!
HOW YOU JERK AND TWIST! HOW YOU SQUIRM! DOES IT HURT? HA, HA... THAT'S NOT ALL! JUST WAIT!
ZZZZZZZZZ

FASTER, FASTER! SPIN, YOU DYNAMOS! WHIRL, YOU ELECTRICAL BOBBLES! LET IT TRY TO GET AWAY FROM ME NOW! THIS IS REVENGE! THIS IS WHAT I HAVE DREAMED ABOUT!
WEEEEEEEEEZZZNNNNNN

AS THAT HORRIBLE ELECTRICAL WHINING PENETRATED THE SILENCE OF NIGHT, SOMETHING STIRRED IN THE GRAVEYARD OF THE DEAD. THE FULL-MOON HAD REACHED ITS PEAK IN THE SKY... AND NOW THE SCRAPING INCREASED TO A RUMBLE!
R.I.P.
IN MEMORY OF
CCRUUNNNCCH

THERE, BROTHERS! THE ONE WE SEEK IS IN THERE!

SIMON!
I'LL RAISE THE JUICE UP SOME MORE! I'LL--AIAAIAIAIIEE!

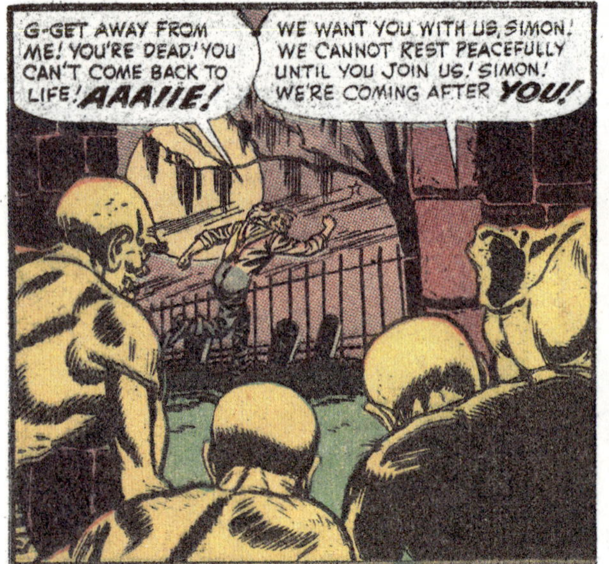
G-GET AWAY FROM ME! YOU'RE DEAD! YOU CAN'T COME BACK TO LIFE! AAAIIE!
WE WANT YOU WITH US, SIMON! WE CANNOT REST PEACEFULLY UNTIL YOU JOIN US! SIMON! WE'RE COMING AFTER YOU!

I'LL RUN TOWARDS THE SWAMPS! THEY'LL NEVER CATCH ME THERE! I KNOW MY WAY AROUND THAT PLACE! I'VE GOT TO RUN--RUN!

YOU CAN'T EVER DECEIVE US AGAIN, SIMON! THE DEAD SEE EVERYTHING! WE WANT YOU, SIMON!
OH, MY GOD! THEY'RE COMING CLOSER--CLOSER. I'VE GOT TO THINK OF SOMETHING!

I CAN'T SEE YOU, SIMON! BUT I CAN HOLD YOU IN MY ARMS!
I CAN'T CATCH YOU, SIMON! BUT I CAN SEE YOU!
JUST TRY IT! I'LL ESCAPE BOTH OF YOU! HA, HA... YOU'RE DEAD THINGS--DEAD! AND I'M ALIVE! HA, HA...

I HAVE NO HEAD, SIMON! BUT I STILL HAVE HANDS AND FEET!
YES...YOU HAVE HANDS AND FEET--BUT NO BRAIN! YOU'RE WITLESS--AND I'LL ALWAYS OUTSMART YOU LIKE I'M DOING NOW! HA, HA...

AND AS FOR YOU, I'LL PUSH YOU INTO THE QUICKSAND! DIE! DIE--HA, HA... DIE, AGAIN... AGAIN, AGAIN! HA, HA, HA ...A CORPSE WITH NO HEART CAN APPRECIATE MY JOKE! HA, HA...
ARRRGHHHH!
6

THE CARETAKER NOW STUMBLED BACK TO HIS CRYPT-HOUSE. LAUGHTER BUBBLED FROM HIS HEAVING CHEST, A LAUGHTER OF A REPRIEVED SOUL... A MAN WHO HAD OUTWITTED THE DEAD!
I WAS TOO CUNNING FOR THEM! I'LL ALWAYS BE TOO CUNNING! HA, HA...THEY'RE GONE--GONE! THEY'RE LOST HOPELESSLY IN THOSE SWAMPS! HA, HA...

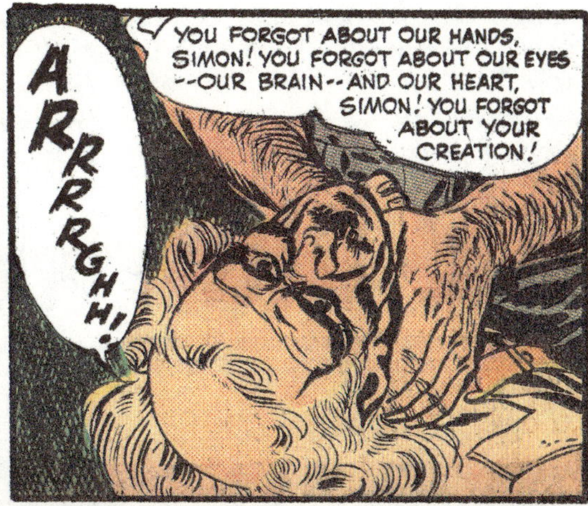
YOU FORGOT ABOUT OUR HANDS, SIMON! YOU FORGOT ABOUT OUR EYES --OUR BRAIN--AND OUR HEART, SIMON! YOU FORGOT ABOUT YOUR CREATION!
ARRRRGHH!

N-NO! YOU'LL NOT GET ME! I'LL ESCAPE FROM YOU YET! HA, HA... YOU'LL NOT GET ME!
RUN, PUNY MAN! RUN AS FAST AS YOUR LEGS CAN CARRY! THERE IS NO ESCAPE!

THROUGH GROTTO AFTER GROTTO, LABYRINTH AFTER LABYRINTH HE FLED. AND ALWAYS THAT OMINOUS SOUND OF FOOTSTEPS BEHIND HIM. NOW THERE WAS NOWHERE TO RUN. IT WAS THE LAST CHAMBER OF THE CRYPT!
I CAN SEE IN THE DARK WITH MY EYES, SIMON!
I'LL GET FREE YET! IT'S TOO CLUMSY! I'LL DODGE AND TWIST MY WAY OUT BACK WHERE I CAME FROM!

YOU FORGOT MY ARMS, SIMON! I CAN GRAB YOU AND HOLD! YOU HAVE LOST!
Y-A-A-A-A-A-A-A-A-A-AH!

THE NIGHT MERGED INTO DAWN AND DAWN BROUGHT THE TOWNS-PEOPLE. THEY FOUND SIMON LORENS...AND THEY FOUND THE UNIDEN-TIFIED, MYSTERIOUS CORPSE NEXT TO HIM. BOTH DEAD!

BUT--WHO--WHAT COULD HAVE HAPPENED HERE? HOW DID SIMON DIE?
I--I DON'T KNOW! BUT LOOK--UPON MY IMMORTAL SOUL--LOOK! LOOK AT HIS HEART!

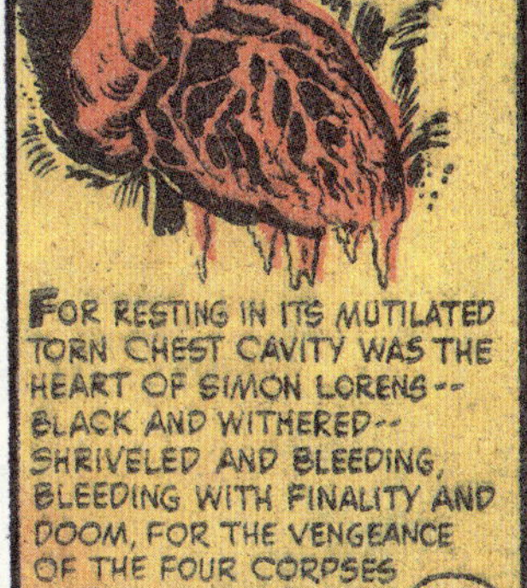
FOR RESTING IN ITS MUTILATED TORN CHEST CAVITY WAS THE HEART OF SIMON LORENS--BLACK AND WITHERED--SHRIVELED AND BLEEDING, BLEEDING WITH FINALITY AND DOOM, FOR THE VENGEANCE OF THE FOUR CORPSES HAD BEEN COMPLETE!
THE END.

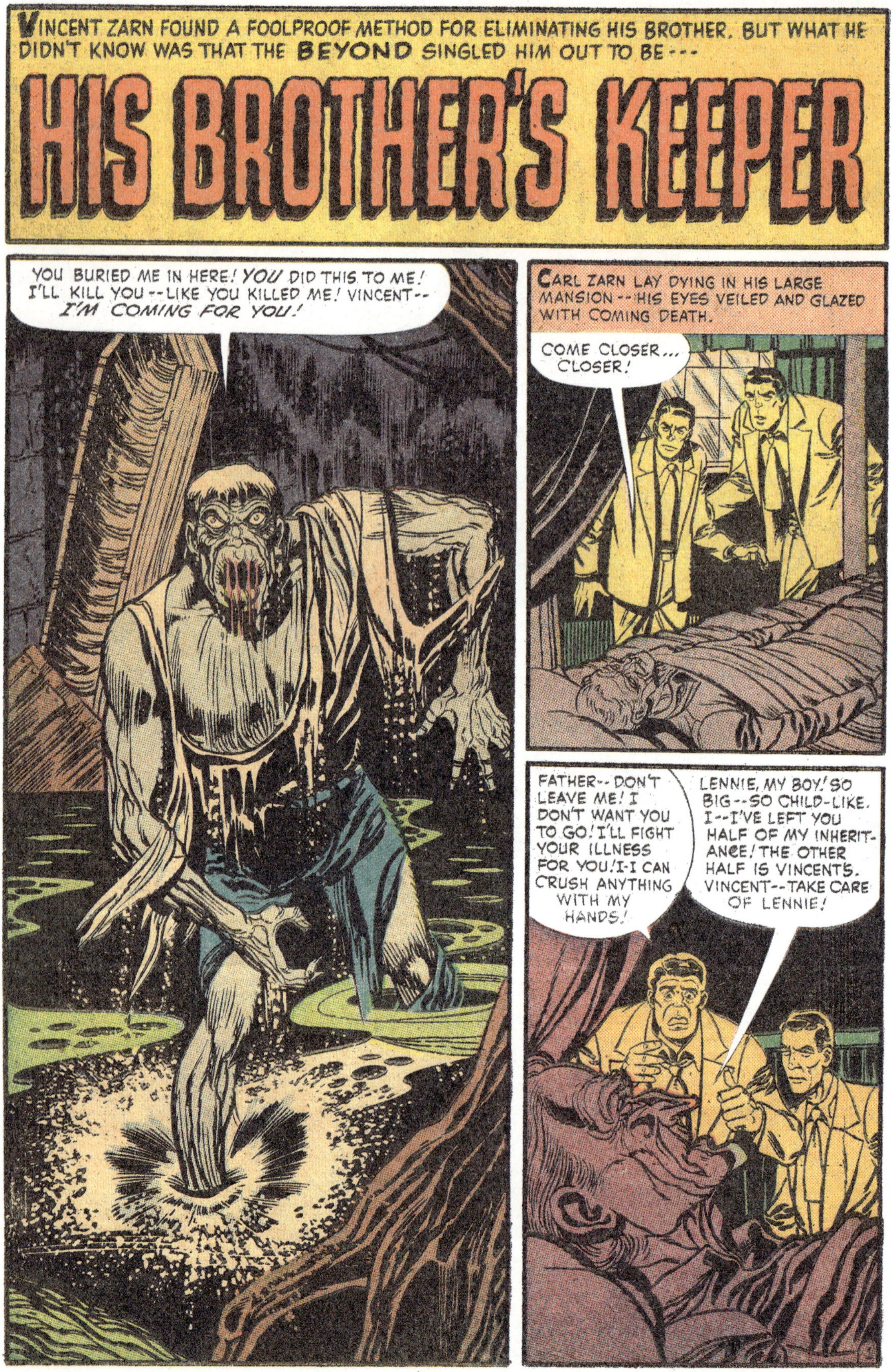

VINCENT ZARN FOUND A FOOLPROOF METHOD FOR ELIMINATING HIS BROTHER. BUT WHAT HE DIDN'T KNOW WAS THAT THE **BEYOND** SINGLED HIM OUT TO BE---

HIS BROTHER'S KEEPER

YOU BURIED ME IN HERE! *YOU* DID THIS TO ME! I'LL KILL YOU--LIKE YOU KILLED ME! VINCENT-- *I'M COMING FOR YOU!*

CARL ZARN LAY DYING IN HIS LARGE MANSION--HIS EYES VEILED AND GLAZED WITH COMING DEATH.

COME CLOSER... CLOSER!

BUT CARL ZARN DID NOT DIE SO SWIFTLY! HE WHEEZED AND COUGHED AND RANTED FOR HOURS. THEN NIGHT CAME AND WENT. AND LENNIE KEPT WATCH WITH VINCENT...

B-BUT WHO'S GONNA TAKE CARE OF ME WHEN I GET THE SHAKES? YOU KNOW I GET THE SHAKES, VINCENT! I HAD IT SINCE I WAS A KID! WHO'S GONNA GIVE ME THEM PILLS?

I'LL GIVE THEM TO YOU, LENNIE. THAT'S A GOOD BOY, NOW GO TO BED!

"TABLETS FOR EPILEPTIC SEIZURES"--HMMM--SUPPOSE LENNIE HAD ONE OF HIS FITS--AND SUPPOSE I FORGOT TO GIVE HIM HIS PILLS? THE FAMILY CRYPT IS IN THE CELLAR. YES...THAT'S IT!

ONCE AGAIN THE GREY SWAMP DAY CAME ON THE ZARN ESTATE SET IN THE LOUISIANA SWAMP LAND.

I--I FEEL FAINT! I'M GONNA START SHAKING AGAIN! HELP ME-- VINCENT!
I'M HERE, LENNIE! CAN YOU MOVE?

NO! I--I'M PASSING OUT! GET ME THE PILLS, VINCENT--THE PILLS!
SORRY, LENNIE! SPEAK LOUDER! I CAN'T HEAR YOU! WHAT DID YOU SAY? HA, HA...

LENNIE ZARN LAPSED INTO UNCONSCIOUSNESS--HIS GIANT FRAME TWITCHING OCCASIONALLY FROM THE MALADY THAT SEIZED HIM. THEN...
SO LONG, LENNIE! YOU LIKED TO BE WITH DAD SO MUCH, YOU CAN JOIN HIM! HA, HA... YOU'RE AS GOOD AS DEAD RIGHT NOW!

JUST A FEW MORE NAILS--AND--W-WHAT WAS THAT? I HEAR VOICES UPSTAIRS!
THUD! THUD!

DROPPING EVERYTHING, VINCENT LOCKED SHUT THE CRYPT-DOOR AND RUSHED OUT, JUST IN TIME TO GREET THE SHERIFF AND HIS DEPUTY...
I HEARD YOUR POP WAS SICK, MR. ZARN! HOW IS HE?
SHERIFF--HE--HE--PASSED AWAY A FEW MINUTES AGO. HE DIDN'T LAST OUT THE NIGHT!

TOO BAD, BOY! A GOOD MAN! WHERE'S LENNIE?
UH--HE WENT INTO THE SWAMPS ON ONE OF HIS CRAZY MISSIONS. I SUPPOSE, YOU KNOW HOW HE IS, SHERIFF--HE WAS BROKEN UP OVER DAD'S DEATH!

WELL--IF THERE'S ANYTHING WE CAN DO, JUST CALL ON US! SO LONG!
I WILL, SHERIFF--GOODBYE!
HA-HA! YOU'LL NEVER SEE ME AGAIN, FOOL!
3

TWO DAYS PASSED--PRECIOUS DAYS WHICH VINCENT USED TO TEAR THE HOUSE APART TO FIND THE MONEY HIS FATHER HAD BURIED BY THE BUSHELFUL. AND IN THE CRYPT, A DEAD LENNIE, NOW SUFFOCATED, LAY QUIET AND OMINOUS. BUT...

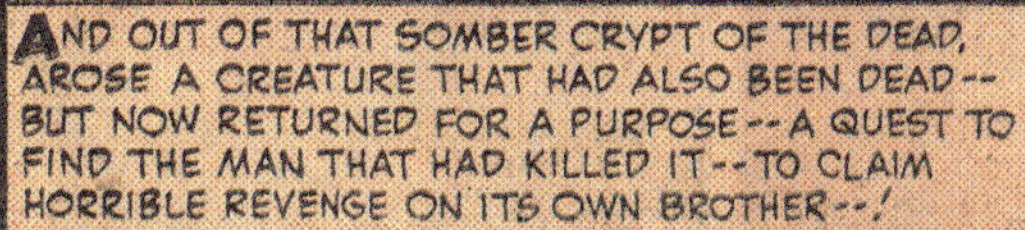

LIKE A CAT STALKING A RAT, THE HUGE BEHEMOTH OF DOOM MOVED SILENTLY THROUGH THE GLOOMY CORRIDORS OF THE MANSION--UNTIL IT FOUND ITS VICTIM!

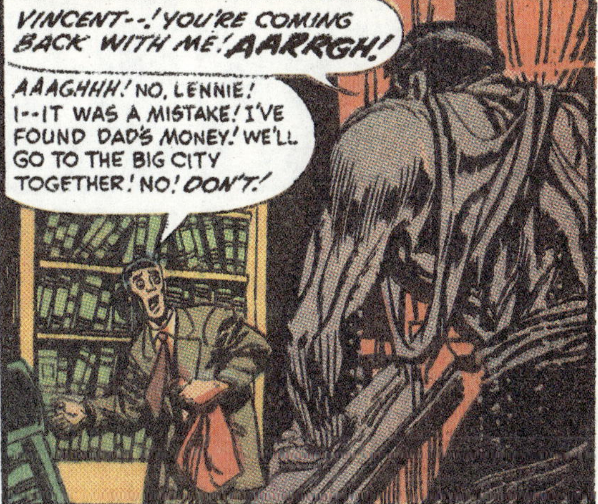

WITH ONE MIGHTY SWOOP, THE ROTTED CADAVER, ALIVE WITH TERRIBLE STRENGTH, SNATCHED THE SCREAMING BROTHER UNDER HIS ARM!

PLEASE, LENNIE-- PLEASE...
GOODBYE, VINCENT! GOODBYE!
BANG! BANG!

MOMENTS LATER, THE GLOOM OF EVENING WAS BROKEN BY A GIANT FIGURE STUMBLING OUT OF THE CRYPT AND INTO THE SWAMP-LANDS CARRYING A DISTORTED WOODEN SHAPE--THE COFFIN OF VINCENT ZARN-- BURIED ALIVE!
I'M TAKING YOU INTO THE SWAMP, VINCENT! I'M GONNA THROW YOU INTO QUICKSAND! I--

AAAAAAGHH!
THUD!

BUT CHANCE HAD PULLED ONE OF ITS QUIRKS AGAIN. THE THING FROM THE BEYOND, STEPPING ON A SOFT POCKET OF SAND, HAD FALLEN INTO THE QUAGMIRE ITSELF!
AAARRGHH!

YAAAAAAH

GLUG..GLUG..GLUG
GURGLE..
SECONDS LATER, A YELLOWISH BUBBLE MARKED THE SCUMMY SURFACE. THE BROTHERS--SO APART FROM EACH OTHER IN LIFE --HAD AT LAST BEEN UNITED IN--DEATH!!
THE END
5

SOLDIERS
SAILORS
WACS
MORTARS
MARINES
PT BOATS
HOWITZERS
TRUCKS
CANNONS
BOMBERS
TANKS
CRUISERS
BATTLESHIPS
PT BOATS
MARINES
WAVES
WACS
SAILORS
SOLDIERS
SOLDIERS
SAILORS
WACS
WAVES
MARINES
PT BOATS
BATTLESHIPS
CRUISERS
JETS
MACHINE GUNS
BAZOOKAS
RIFLEMEN
50 COMBAT ACTION PLASTIC TOYS
$1 POSTPAID
Your Own TASK FORCE
Now you can be Commander in Chief of this complete task force. Have pitched battles, gunnery drills, deploy your troops for attack and defense. Here's a complete army 50 pieces in all including soldiers, sailors, marines, PT boat, Howitzers, tanks, planes, and ships. You'll be thrilled and delighted with this complete task force. Nothing else like it!
LOOK WHAT YOU GET. SOLDIERS • SAILORS • MARINES • WACS • TANKS • JEEPS • PT BOATS • BATTLESHIPS • JET PLANES • BOMBERS • MACHINE GUNNERS • HOWITZERS • TRUCKS • BAZOOKA MEN • RIFLEMEN
Here's a great collection of military toys yours for just a single dollar bill. You'll have hours of fun and pleasure with this wonderful set. Every piece made of plastic in realistic scale. Precision formed of Styrene...nothing like it has ever been offered at this price. Rush your order now. 6" long die cut cannon that shoots harmless bombs included in your order NOW!
FREE 6" LONG DIE CUT SHOOTING CANNON!
Supplies Limited! Don't delay. Rush name and address and $1 for each set. Your complete 50-piece task force will be shipped by return mail. Sorry no COD's. Rush your dollar today.
FIGHTING FORCE Dept. 11
1860 Broadway
New York 23, N.Y.
I enclose ________ at $1 per set.
Rush your 50-piece Fighting Force set prepaid.
Name ________ Age ___
Address ________
City ________ State ________

SHANGRILA!

Once Shangrila has been entered, it can never be left. No one must ever return to the outside world to tell the story of the land's mysteries... for if he does, he will change into an old dying man!

B-but, I've been a doll-maker all my life, sir!" quavered the old man. "I—I don't know anything about any other trade! I'll starve . . ."

"Now, now, Wilkins!" interrupted Frederick Finch, owner of the Finch Doll Factory, waving his cigar carelessly in Horace Wilkins' face. "I'm sure you won't starve! You'll find some other—uh—employment, some other job that requires skilled hands like yours! You're an excellent craftsman, Wilkins—I have no fault to find with your work. It's just that these new machines can do your job better, faster and cheaper than you—or any other man, for that matter—can do it! That's why I have to let you go . . ."

"You'll be sorry, Mr. Finch!" sobbed Horace Wilkins. His voice rose higher, almost to a shriek. "You'll be sorry for this!"

* * *

In the crude little workshop he'd built for himself, the old doll-maker worked far into the night. His gnarled but skilled hands moved swiftly and surely.

"So he wants machines, does he?" he muttered aloud. "Machines are better than men, are they? Very well, Mr. Frederick Finch, you shall have your machine . . . *you certainly shall have it!"*

On and on he labored, carving each limb until the proportions were exactly right, fitting each wire until it worked perfectly, making each tiny adjustment over and over until there was no flaw whatever in the mechanism. And then at last it was done. The huge doll stood in the middle of the workshop floor—almost as tall as a ten-year-old child—a diabolic instrument of death and destruction!

Painstakingly, Horace Wilkins tested every switch on the tiny control board. The doll responded perfectly! All his years in the trade had served Wilkins well. He had indeed created a masterpiece . . . and vengeance would soon be his!

* * *

Frederick Finch sat alone in his office, poring over the account books that showed his company's steadily-increasing profits. A smile played around Finch's mouth, a smile of satisfaction. He didn't see the door to his office slowly opening. He didn't see the grotesque figure gliding towards his desk until it stood squarely before him . . . waiting for the command from Horace Wilkins' control board.

Frederick Finch never had a chance. Before he could so much as scream, the doll's hands reached him . . . slowly, methodically, breaking every bone in the doomed man's body . . . crushing the bones to a fine, gray powder . . .

* * *

In the hall outside the office, Horace Wilkins thrilled to each savage crunch of sound from within. His eyes blazed with unholy joy as he visualized the hideous vengeance his doll-monster was wreaking. His hands trembled so, that the control board slipped from his nerveless fingers and crashed to the floor.

Immediately, there was stark silence inside the office. Evidently some of the fine mechanism had been damaged in the fall. But no matter . . . the doll had done its work well . . . the controls could be easily repaired . . .

A towering shadow fell across Horace Wilkins' stooped figure as he bent to pick up the board.

"Aaaaargh!" The scream gurgled in the old man's throat like rushing blood. "Wh—what's happened? *No!* Stand back! I am your master! I created you . . . !"

"Yes!" the doll rumbled hoarsely. "You created me, and I have obeyed your orders! You ordered death—and death is what you got—and what you *will* get! You have invoked the spirit of evil, the spectre of death! Very well, old man . . . I AM DEATH!"

Slowly, the monster moved forward. No longer was it a doll. The face was twisted into a mask of pure evil . . . the limbs had lost their artificial stiffness . . . they swung freely now, like human limbs . . . the eyes glowed with a weird, all-seeing light . . . the stabbing light of the *Demon of Darkness!*

Long, bony fingers reached for Horace Wilkins—fingers that were no longer made of wood.

"Aieeeeeee! Agh! No . . . have mercy . . ."

Fine gray powder dribbled through the fingers . . . The Devil-Doll laughed—once . . .

Then all was still. And on the floor of the Finch Doll Factory lay a broken wooden doll—about the size of a ten-year-old child—and a little mound of fine gray dust!

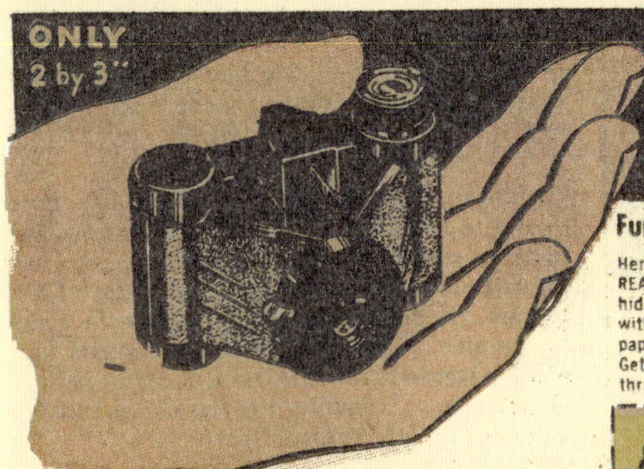

TINY MIDGET CAMERA

TAKES SECRET PICTURES

1.39

Fun and Thrills Galore for You!

Here's a real, honest-to-goodness camera that takes REAL, CLEAR pictures – yet it's so SMALL you can hide it in the palm of your hand! Take SECRET pictures without being seen, of friends or enemies – like F.B.I. men or newspaper reporters. So EASY – anybody can use it! Just AIM and CLICK! Get YOURS now – bargain price only 1.39. GUARANTEED to satisfy and thrill you or MONEY BACK. Send COUPON below.

Fits in palm of hand!

- EVEN A CHILD CAN USE IT!
- TAKES DANDY, CLEAR PICTURES!
- POCKET SIZE — ONLY 2 BY 3 INCHES!
- TAKES REAL ACTION PHOTOS!
- QUALITY GROUND LENS!

Here's one of the world's SMALLEST cameras. Just the same you get beautiful, jumbo 2 x 3 enlarged photos from standard, low cost 828 film. Also – Kodak COLOR pictures – real, NATURAL looking pictures of friends and family that live on in your memory for years and years. Takes ACTION shots of sports events, school affairs, races, accidents, boats, nature scenes, etc. EASY – just AIM AND CLICK! Nothing complicated! GUARANTEED to satisfy you or full price back. SEND NO MONEY – pay postman only 1.39, plus postage on arrival. SAVE MORE – Send only 1.39 with order and get a NICE GIFT in your package besides! RUSH COUPON NOW – Don't miss this GUARANTEED BARGAIN!

CONSUMERS MART, Dept. 35-G-32
131 West 33rd Street New York 1, N. Y.

TRIAL COUPON

CONSUMERS MART, Dept. 35-G-32
131 West 33rd Street New York 1, N. Y.

GENTLEMEN: Send me the GUARANTEED MIDGET CAMERA that takes SECRET pictures. I will pay bargain price of only 1.39, plus postage, on delivery. If I am not thrilled and satisfied during a full week's trial you will send back my 1.39 without fail.

NAME____________________

ADDRESS____________________

TOWN__________ STATE__________

☐ SAVE MORE MONEY and receive a delightful GIFT free of extra charge! Just send 1.39 – not ONE PENNY extra – with this coupon. We will pay all postage charges. Same MONEY-BACK GUARANTEE, of course.

BOTH NOW ON SALE! BE SURE TO GET YOUR COPIES!

AS THEY BEGAN TO CLIMB THE MYSTERY MOUNTAIN IN SEARCH OF GOLD, AN OMINOUS HORROR SURROUNDED THEM AND, THEN, ATTACKED! IT WAS THE DREADED...

GLACIER BEAST

ARRRGHHHH!

T-THEY'RE COMING FOR US! I...I'LL KILL 'EM ALL! I...**AAAAGHHHH!**

MARIE NORET AND TWO TOUGH-LOOKING TOURISTS, IN REALITY AMERICAN GANGSTERS IN HIDING, RUSHED TO THE DOOR!
FATHER! WHERE HAVE YOU BEEN? WHAT'S WRONG?
QUICKLY...! CLOSE THE DOOR! IS AFTER ME! CLOSE IT! CLOSE IT! AIIEEE! THERE IT IS!

AAAARRRGH!

EEEEEEEEEE!
STAY AWAY...WHATEVER YOU ARE! ROCKY...DRILL HIM! HURRY!

LOOK, NICK! ITS RUNNING INTO THOSE WOODS!
HOLD IT, THEN! PUT THE GAT AWAY! WE DON'T WANT THESE YOKELS GETTING TOO CURIOUS ABOUT OUR CARRYING RODS!

OH...IT...IT WAS HORRIBLE! WH-WHAT WAS IT, PAPA? WHAT WAS IT THAT WANTED TO KILL US?
HEY...LOOK! THERE'S SOMETHING MADE OF ICE ON THE FLOOR!

UGHH! IT'S A HAND...A CLAWED LUMPY, HAND MADE OF ICE! I...I MUST HAVE BROKEN IT OFF WHEN I HIT IT WITH THAT POKER!
I-I NEVER HEARD O' SUCH THINGS LIKE THIS! NICK...SOMEONE'S TRYIN' TO PUT SOMETHIN' OVER ON US! T-THEY'RE TRYIN' TO SCARE US! THE OLD JERK'S GONNA EXPLAIN NOW OR I'LL...

NO--NO, MONSIEUR! I ASSURE YOU THAT WHAT YOU SAW WAS REAL... TERRIBLY REAL! I HAD JUST CLIMBED DOWN FROM THE WHITE MOUNTAIN. I SAW AN IDOL MADE OF GOLD UP THERE... AN IDOL BELONGING TO THESE GHASTLY MONSTERS THAT MUST LIVE THERE!
GOLD? WOULD YOU LEAD US BACK UP THERE?

NO, MONSIEUR NICK! THERE ARE LEGENDS CONCERNING THE WHITE MOUNTAIN... LEGENDS BETTER NOT PROVEN! YOU SAW THE HORROR WE FACED!
YEAH... BUT THINK OF THE GOLD, MARIE! WE'LL ALL BE RICH...

PERHAPS... BUT YOU DO NOT KNOW OF THE LOST RACE THAT DWELLS BEYOND THE REACH OF MAN..! NONE WHO ASCEND THE MOUNTAIN... EVER RETURN!
BALONEY! YOUR POP DID... AND SO WILL WE!

BUT, AS THE DAYS PASSED...
COME ON, MARIE! ALL WE GOTTA DO IS FIND THAT IDOL YOUR OLD MAN WAS TALKING ABOUT! THEN WE'LL BE RICH...I'LL BUY ALL THE THINGS YOU'VE WANTED! HOW ABOUT IT?
I...I DON'T KNOW! LET ME THINK!

MARIE WAS WON OVER, HER MIND DULLED BY THE BEAUTIFUL FUTURE NICK PAINTED SO GLIBLY. WEEKS LATER THEY STARTED ON THE JOURNEY TO THE TOP OF THE MOUNTAIN!!
FROM HERE ON... WE MUST ATTACH ROPES... THE CLIMB IS DANGEROUS!

OHH...I...I'M SLIPPING! HELP ME!
GOT YOU! BE CAREFUL!

YEAH...JUST BE CAREFUL UNTIL WE GET UP THAT MOUNTAIN. THEN YOU CAN DIVE OFF FOR ALL I CARE! THAT GOES FOR ROCKY AND THE OLD JERK AS WELL!

FOR HOURS, THE PARTY OF FOUR CLIMBED, CLUTCHED CLAWED THEIR WAY UP THE STEEP, CHILLED, ICY SIDES OF THAT OMINOUS MOUNTAIN...

THEN...
AGHH! THIS LOUSY SNOW BLINDS MY EYES!
NICK...I SEE SOMETHING OVER THERE!

ARRGHHH!
WE ARE LOST! THEY HAVE SEEN US!...THE MONSTERS OF THE MOUNTAIN! HELP!
STAY AWAY FROM US YA ©-※!#! SLOBS!

I'LL FIX YA ALL! YOU DON'T SCARE ME! BULLETS CAN KILL YOU JUST LIKE IT KILLS OTHERS!
ROCKY...YA DUMB NUT! NOW YOU'VE DONE IT! THEY'RE COMING FER US!
BANG! BANG!

ARRGHH! ARRGHH!
YAAAAH! NICK... HELP! HELP! THEY'RE BITING ME! YAAAAAH!
COME ON! W-WE GOTTA RUN UP TO THE TOP..! WE CAN'T GO DOWN IN THAT STORM! QUICK... BEFORE WE'RE TORN TO SHREDS.

HOLY SMOKE! IT'S...IT'S UNBELIEVABLE! I...I'M GOING BATS! I GOTTA BE!
GASP... GASP... THERE IS YOUR GOLD IDOL...THERE ...IN THE CENTER OF THAT...THAT FANTASTIC VILLAGE!

THE GANGSTER MANAGED TO ELUDE HIS PURSUERS AND HIDE IN ONE OF THE MANY GROTTOS RIMMING THE MOUNTAIN TOP. HOURS WENT BY, THE SILENCE BROKEN ONLY BY THE ETERNAL DRIPPING STALAGMITES INSIDE THE WEIRD LABYRINTH. THEN...

AHHRRRGHHH!

WHAT WAS THAT? IT SOUNDED LIKE OLD CARL'S VOICE! I...I'VE GOTTA TAKE MY CHANCE NOW... AN' SEE IF I CAN MAKE IT DOWN THE MOUNTAIN!

NICK CAUTIOUSLY LEFT THE CAVE OPENING, AND JUST AS CAUTIOUSLY PREPARED TO SNAKE DOWN THE MOUNTAINSIDE, FOR THE SNOW HAD NOW SUBSIDED, BUT THE ONE LAST LOOK HE CAST ON THE VILLAGE, TRANSFIXED HIM WITH HORROR!
AIIEE! S-SHE'S FROZEN SOLID... AND OLD CARL'S DEAD!

ARRGHH!
ARGGH!
THEY'VE SPOTTED ME! WELL... I'M NOT GONNA GET CAUGHT!
BANG!
BANG!

NICK RAN, STUMBLED, TWISTED, DODGED HIS EERIE PURSUERS, FIRING WILDLY, FRANTICALLY, AND DESPERATELY AS HE TRIED TO ESCAPE. SUDDENLY, AN OMINOUS RUMBLING INCREASED TO A ROAR! HIS PISTOL SHOTS HAD STARTED A SNOWSLIDE.
CRASH-H!

HA, HA, HA! WHAT LUCK! NOW YOU'LL NEVER GET ME, YOU SLIMEY RATS! GO AHEAD AND TRY... YOU'LL HAVE TO CROSS TEN YARDS OF THIN AIR FIRST! HA, HA, HA...

I SHOWED 'EM! HA, HA!... I'M GONNA BE RICH... RICH LIKE I NEVER WAS BEFORE! WHO SAID I'D NEVER COME BACK? I'LL... MY ARM!

IT... IT'S TURNING INTO SOLID ICE...! I... I'M GETTING FROZEN ALL OVER... LIKE THEM! NO! NO! AIIEEEEEEEEEEE!
THE END

WHAT CAUSED LARS STELPSEN'S GRASS TO SHOOT UP AS IT DID... EACH BLADE A GIANT, TWISTING, GREEN FINGER OF DEATH? WHAT HORRIBLE SECRET LAY BEHIND THE...
DIRT OF DEATH!
LARS STELPSEN'S LAWN WAS THE MAIN INTEREST IN HIS LIFE, AND ONE MORNING, AS HE COMPARED IT WITH HIS NEIGHBORS' LAWNS...
I DON'T UNDERSTAND. IT WAS DOING BEAUTIFULLY TILL I BOUGHT THAT BATCH OF FERTILIZER FROM OLD GARGAN TWO WEEKS AGO.
YOU THINK THE FERTILIZER RUINED IT?

OF COURSE IT DID! THAT FERTILIZER KILLED MY SOIL FOR GOOD! I'LL HAVE TO START MY LAWN ALL OVER AGAIN!

THAT MEANS ABOUT $500 FOR NEW TOPSOIL! WELL, I'M NOT PAYING FOR IT! GARGAN'S RESPONSIBLE... I'LL GET THE MONEY FROM HIM!
YOU HAVEN'T A CHANCE! GARGAN WOULD RATHER PART WITH HIS LIFE THAN $500!

IN AN ISOLATED SPOT AT THE EDGE OF TOWN, GARGAN SEPARATED BONES FROM ANIMAL CARCASSES, AND TOGETHER WITH OTHER ROTTING INGREDIENTS, GROUND AND BLENDED THEM INTO FERTILIZER!
THERE HE IS NOW! I'LL MAKE THE OLD FRAUD PAY EVEN IF IT'S HIS LAST CENT!

WHAT DO YOU WANT, STELPSEN? MORE FERTILIZER?
I'M NOT BUYING FERTILIZER FROM YOU AGAIN!
LS

YOUR LAST BATCH RUINED MY LAWN... AND I'M GOING TO MAKE YOU PAY FOR A NEW ONE!
YOU ARE, HUH? AND JUST HOW ARE YOU GONNA GO ABOUT DOING THAT LITTLE THING?
2

LIKE THIS, YOU OLD SWINDLER!
STELPSEN... AAGHH... STOP!

SURE I'LL STOP... WHEN YOU... WHEN YOU DECIDE TO PAY ME $500!
I... I'LL PAY... ONLY... AAGH... LET GO!

THE-THE MONEY'S INSIDE. YOU WAIT HERE... I'LL GET IT!
THAT'S BETTER. I KNOW YOU'VE GOT PLENTY, YOU OLD SKINFLINT!

STELPSEN WAITED... UNTIL SOME INNER PREMONITION WARNED HIM TO TURN AROUND...
COME HERE AND TRY TO BLACKMAIL ME, WILL YOU? I'LL FIX YOU!
WH-WHAT?

YOU OLD FOOL! A LITTLE WATER SHOULD COOL YOU OFF!
NO! NO! NOT IN THERE!

HELP ME! HELP! THE POOL... IT... IT'S...

OWWW! THAT WATER...IT...
IT BURNS LIKE FIRE!
AAAGHH!
SPLASH!

THE POOL...IT...IT'S QUICKLIME AND ACID...
FOR DISSOLVING THE FLESH FROM ANIMAL
CARCASSES! HIS BODY...IT..IT'S DISINTEGRATING
ALREADY!

THEY...THEY'LL KNOW I DID IT! I WAS A
FOOL FOR TELLING JONES THAT I WAS
COMING HERE! MUST DISPOSE OF THE
EVIDENCE...COMPLETELY... BUT HOW?

AND THEN, DESPERATION CARVED A CUNNING
PLAN IN STELPSEN'S FRANTIC BRAIN!
MUST GET THE HAND UNDER...MUST
DISSOLVE THE WHOLE BODY.

SOON...
NO BODY...NO CRIME! THEY CAN'T
ACCUSE ME OF MURDER IF THEY
CAN'T FIND THE CORPSE!
4

NEVER THOUGHT YOU'D BE FERTILIZER, EH, GARGAN?

SEE HOW EASY IT IS TO COLLECT ONE'S DEBT!

THAT NIGHT, LARS STELPSEN PUT A NEW FERTILIZER IN THE SCRAGGLY PARTS OF HIS LAWN...
I'LL BURY THE BONES AROUND MY GARDEN!

BUT STELPSEN WAS MISTAKEN... FOR HIS LAWN RESPONDED TO THAT NEW FERTILIZER... THE GRASS GREW HIGHER AND HIGHER... TILL BY EARLY DAWN...
MY ROOM... FULL OF GRASS! WH-WHAT'S HAPPENING?

NO... NO... GET AWAY! GET... AWAY... FROM... MY... THROAT!

AAARGHHHH
THE END

The plague had swooped down from the skies, had come up from the sewers, and was now twisting and turning the city in its ugly paws.

Bodies fell in the streets, in homes, in restaurants, in theatres—all giving way to the ghastly scars of the hideous curse.

The gates of the city were closed tight. None could be allowed exit . . . none would dare enter. It was a city alone, entrapped in the tentacles of the plague, with no sign of relief!

"The serum isn't working properly!"

"We need more serum!"

"Our cause is hopeless!"

Those were the voices of doctors in the hospital wards. Their eyes had seen man after woman after child fall prey to the sweeping disease. They had watched bodies rot to the bone . . . people cry out in the most hideous screams . . . agony reign in evil splendor!

"I've got to get out! I've got to get out!" Those were the voices of many, but few could make it. The guards were ordered to shoot at sight anyone who dared climb the gates.

Lew Oliver was one who dared make the climb.

But Lew Oliver wasn't that stupid to try to scale the walls outright, chancing his life on his physical capabilities. He considered himself a mental giant, and he worked on his escape with his mind . . . and his wallet.

It was difficult to get to a guard who would accept money for escape . . . their lives were at stake should they be discovered. But it was not impossible.

Lew Oliver found such a man.

"Well, how much do you offer me?"

"Five thousand is all I can give you. That's all I've . . ."

"Look, mister, your life is worth more than that! Don't tell me that's all you've got!"

"Eight thousand, that's all I can spare!"

"Ten thousand, and you've found your man!"

So Lew Oliver found his man.

"Tomorrow night, we'll try it. There's a full fifteen minutes when they change guards at the South Gate that n all alone. You be there at 11:30 SHARP! I'll have my back turned, and you'll dash through. From there on, you're on your own."

"I understand fully. I'll be there."

"Don't run away, sir. I'll take my money first!"

The next day moved like a turtle walking backwards. The clock sweated off the minutes, and Lew Oliver perspired profusely keeping time with the horrible hands of the clock.

Nine o'clock was curfew hour. The streets were cleared. Only policemen and sanitary patrols cleaning the dead from the streets pounded the pavement.

The clock swung round to eleven. Lew Oliver clutched what strength he had left, and stole into the streets. Stealthily he made his way in the blackness, fading into hallways and barns.

"Agghhhhh!"

He had almost tripped on a wasted body that lay strewn across the sidewalk.

After that, things went well. He reached the gate at 11:30. All was as the guard said.

"You're on time, my friend. My back is turned to you. Good luck!"

Lew Oliver didn't say a word. He mumbled some kind of recognition and hastened through the gates of freedom.

He rushed down the roadway, running as he never had before.

"I'm free! I'm free!" He shouted to himself, sang to himself, laughed to himself!

Suddenly he felt a pang in his leg.

"What's that? No . . . it can't be! It mustn't be!"

But there it was . . . a boil had popped up showing its loathesome face! And then he felt more and more!

His face, his body were growing hot. An inferno had started blazing from within him. But on he went, struggling with every step.

"There'll b-e-e-e-e a docto-o-o-or at the next city-y-y-y-y-y-y-y-y!"

He could see the next city now, pushing its hopeful form onto the horizon. But then all went blank and he fell to the dirt . . . dead.

The next morning, a group of young boys walked past the decaying body. They ran with horror . . . but not before they bent over the man and sucked in . . . the plague!

And so the *BLACK PLAGUE* began to spread over Europe!

THEY LAUGHED WHEN I STARTED TO TALK!

HA HA
HA HA - LOOK WHO'S TRYING TO TELL A JOKE

SOON AFTER.

TONIGHT'S MARY'S BIRTHDAY PARTY. I'LL REALLY SURPRISE THEM WITH MY SPECIAL LIST OF PARTY JOKES... THANKS TO THIS FREE BOOKLET!

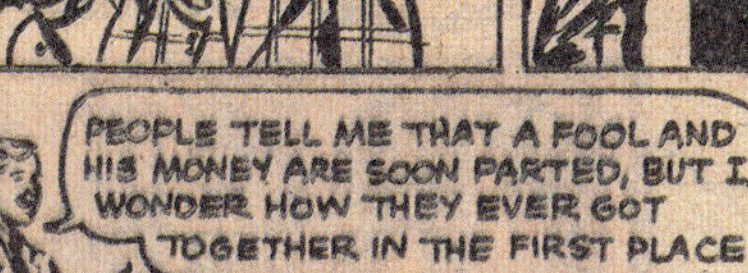

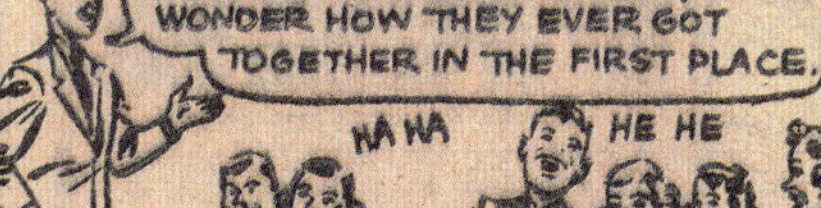

YOURS **FREE** WITH EACH ORDER OF "FUN PARADE ANNUAL" AND "HELLO BUDDIES ANNUAL"

NOW YOU TOO CAN TELL FUNNY JOKES

How often have you wished you could tell a funny joke and tell it the way the experts do? There are hundreds of times you can win a point by telling the right story at the right time in the right way. It's easy when you know HOW! The editors of FUN PARADE, one of the nation's funniest humor magazines, have written a simple guide titled "HOW TO TELL FUNNY JOKES." It is written in simple language and tells you completely HOW TO TELL FUNNY JOKES, where to find material, how to improvise, how to change a joke so that it fits your story and many other revealing secrets. Now for the first time offered anywhere.

FOR PUBLIC SPEAKERS
FOR TEACHERS
FOR WRITERS
FOR SCHOOL PLAYS, CLUB SKITS, ETC.

EACH VOLUME 192 PAGES

BOTH VOLUMES ONLY **$1.00** PLUS FREE "HOW TO TELL FUNNY JOKES"

CARTOONS BY AMERICA'S FAMOUS CARTOONISTS!

Here are only a few of America's leading cartoonists who illustrate some of the jokes appearing in "FUN PARADE ANNUAL," and "HELLO BUDDIES ANNUAL"—You'll recognize their signatures on cartoons in the leading humor magazines and in newspapers from coast to coast. DAN FLOWERS, AL ROSS, REAMER KELLER, ANGELO, DAVE BREGOR, DAN O. BROWN, E. SIMMS CAMPBELL, SWAN, LARIAR, KIRK STILES, HENRY BOLTINOFF, WENZEL, VIC HERMAN, SALO, MILOKINN, ALI, ATKINS, R. GUSTAFSON, JEFF KEATE, CHARLES STRAUS, CRAMER, SCOTT, LINDA & JERRY WALTERS, ERIC ERICSON *and many others.*

SEND FOR THIS WONDERFUL COMBINATION OFFER TODAY

MONEY BACK GUARANTEE

After you have examined these fun packed books and you are not entirely satisfied, you may return them to us, within 5 days in good condition and your dollar will be refunded. You may keep the booklet, "HOW TO TELL A FUNNY JOKE." Don't wait. You can't lose. Send your order today.

FUN PARADE INC. DEPT. WT
1860 BROADWAY NEW YORK 23, N.Y.

MAIL THIS ORDER TODAY!

FUN PARADE INC., DEPT. WT
1860 BROADWAY
NEW YORK 23, NEW YORK

Yes, please send me postpaid your free booklet "HOW TO TELL FUNNY JOKES." Here is my dollar for the TWO ANNUALS, FUN PARADE and HELLO BUDDIES, each 192 pages.

PRINT NAME ______________________

ADDRESS ______________________

CITY ____________ ZONE IF ANY ______ STATE ____________

SORRY, NO C.O.D.'S OR ORDER OUTSIDE U.S.A.

SEND NO MONEY — Try at our risk!

Here's a LIFETIME BARGAIN for you! Compare with domestic binoculars selling up to 10.00 for clarity, light weight and rugged construction! Just look thru them once and you'll be convinced of their quality. You will be thrilled with the GERMAN KLARO-VIS lens that give you TERRIFIC MAGNIFICATION POWER, a wide field of view and sharp, brilliant detail! Smooth SYNCHRONIZED centre focusing mechanism gives you quick, easy adjustments. Light weight — easy to carry with you — yet they are so STRONGLY made that it is virtually IMPOSSIBLE TO BREAK THEM in normal use! Yes, this is what you have always wanted - now yours at an unbelievably LOW PRICE — while they last!

BIG SIZE — BIG POWER — BIG VALUE

Please do not confuse the KLARO-VIS with crudely made Binoculars claiming 18 MILE RANGES! These are NEW and so DIFFERENT, made by GERMAN ARTISANS. You receive BIG POWER, BIG SIZE and a BIG, LIFETIME BARGAIN!

A LIFETIME OF THRILLS AWAITS YOU!

When you own this power-packed instrument, distances seem to melt away . . . you always have a "ringside" seat at boxing matches, races, baseball or football. You get an intimate view of nature, the sky at night, distant sunsets, birds and wild animals, distant boats, seashore scenes, etc. You see what your neighbors are doing (without being seen). Carry them with you on hunting trips too!

FREE TRIAL OFFER — ENJOY AT OUR RISK!

We want to send you a pair of these super-power glasses for you to examine and enjoy for ONE WHOLE WEEK — without obligation. You take no chances. Test them . . . use them as you like. Compare them for value and power with binoculars selling up to 10.00. Then YOU be the JUDGE! If you're not thrilled, then return and get your MONEY BACK! Don't send ONE PENNY — pay postman only 3.00 plus postage on arrival. Do it today — WHILE SUPPLY LASTS. Don't miss the fun and thrills another day. RUSH THE TRIAL COUPON RIGHT NOW.

MAIL COUPON FOR HOME TRIAL!

CONSUMERS MART, Dept. 35-G-134

131 West 33rd Street New York 1, N. Y.

GENTLEMEN: RUSH your guaranteed KLAROVIS Super Power Field Glasses for a whole week's home trial — FREE of obligation and your SURPRISE FRIENDSHIP GIFT. I will pay postman 3.00 plus postage on arrival. I shall enjoy them, and use them for a whole week and if not satisfied with this thrilling bargain, you are to send my 3.00 back. The surprise Friendship Gift is mine to KEEP even if I return the KLAROVIS!

NAME ____________________

ADDRESS ____________________

TOWN ____________ STATE ____________

☐ EXTRA SAVINGS FOR YOU! Send 3.00 cash, check or money order with this coupon and we pay ALL POSTAGE costs. SAME MONEY-BACK GUARANTEE!

YOU can WIN this big 15" Silver Trophy as Roger just did
When I enrolled I was a skinny, sick weakling. I was shy with girls because I had nothing to show off. A few weeks after starting the Jowett Course my body was the best in the neighborhood. Now I get respect and admiration from every fellow and girl I meet.
Roger D. Hirsch
ROGER HIRSCH was an 112 lb. 6 ft. weakling LOOK AT HIM NOW!
Aren't YOU as SICK and Tired as I was of being SKINNY
CHICKEN-CHESTED
SPINDLE-ARMED
NARROW-SHOULDERED
SHORT-WINDED
WEAK, HALF-ALIVE
JEERED, BULLIED
?
Then do as I did...
MAIL THE COUPON BELOW
There's that skinny scarecrow ROGER. Let's pass him by!
I gained 53 lbs. of mighty muscle
I added 6½ inches to my CHEST
3 inches to each ARM
And the rest in proportion — ALL IN A FEW SHORT WEEKS by using the JOWETT SYSTEM
for building Real HE-MEN
Come on, PAL, Now YOU give me 10 pleasant Minutes a Day in your own home . . . and I'll give YOU a NEW HE-MAN BODY for your OLD SKELETON FRAME.
says GEORGE F. JOWETT
World's Greatest Builder of HE-MEN
NO! I don't care how skinny or flabby you are; if you're a teen-ager, in your 20's or 30's or over; if you're short or tall, or what work you do. All I want is JUST 10 EXCITING MINUTES in your home to MAKE YOU OVER by the SAME METHOD I turned myself from a wreck to a Champion of Champions.
YES! You'll see INCH upon INCH of MIGHTY MUSCLE added to YOUR ARMS. Your CHEST deepened. Your BACK AND SHOULDERS broadened. From head to heels, you'll gain SOLIDITY, SIZE, POWER, SPEED! You'll become an ALL-Around, ALL-American HE-MAN, a WINNER in everything you tackle—or my Training won't cost you one solitary cent!
George F. Jowett Whom experts call "Champion of Champions"
• World's wrestling and wt. lifting champ
• World's Strongest Arms.
• 4 times "World's Perfect Body" Winner.
FREE!
If you mail coupon NOW
1 MUSCLE METER
2 JOWETT'S Photo Book of Famous Strong Men!
His amazing book, "Nerves of Steel, Muscles of Iron," has guided thousands of weaklings to muscular power. Packed with photos of miracle men of might and muscle who started perhaps weaker than you are. Read the thrilling adventures of Jowett in strength that inspired his pupils to follow him. They'll show you the best way to might and muscle. Send for FREE gift book of PHOTOS OF FAMOUS STRONG MEN
NOW LET ME MAKE YOU LIKE ROGER A WINNER IN EVERY WALK OF LIFE
WHAM
DARLING, THAT BULLY WON'T PICK ON YOU AGAIN.
JOE WALLOPED ANOTHER HOMER. HE'S SURE TO BE CAPTAIN NOW.
JOE YOUR NEW ENERGY AND APPEARANCE SURE DO A GOOD JOB. YOU EARNED YOUR PROMOTION.
JOES JOWETT HE-MAN STRENGTH AND BUILD WON HIM THOSE STRIPES
Develop YOUR 520 MUSCLES
Gain Pounds, INCHES, FAST!
Friend, I've traveled the world. Made a LIFETIME STUDY of every way known to develop your body. Then I devised the BEST by TEST, my "5-WAY PROGRESSIVE POWER" the only method that builds you 5-ways fast. You save YEARS, DOLLARS like movie star Tom Tyler did. Like Champ Roger Hirsch did. Like MANY THOUSANDS like you did. SO . . .
MAIL COUPON NOW and GET
This may be Your LAST chance to GET AMAZING NATIONAL EMERGENCY OFFER
All these 5 Picture Packed COURSES on He-Man Building for only while supply lasts!
10¢
MILLIONS have been sold for $1 and more
FREE Photo Book How you can Become an All-Around All-American HE-MAN
How to Build MIGHTY ARMS
How to Build A MIGHTY CHEST
How to Build A MIGHTY GRIP
How to Build A MIGHTY BACK
How to Build MIGHTY LEGS
How to BECOME A MUSCULAR HE-MAN
BOTH FREE!
1. Photo Book of STRONG MEN
2. MUSCLE METER
DEPT. HS-29
"Jowett Courses greatest in World for Building All-Around HE-MEN". —R.F. Kelley Physical Director
JOWETT INSTITUTE OF PHYSICAL TRAINING
230 FIFTH AVENUE, NEW YORK 1, N.Y.
Dear George: Please mail to me FREE Jowett's Photo Book of Strong Men and a Muscle Meter, plus all 5 HE-MAN Building Courses: 1. How to Build a Mighty Chest. 2. How to Build a Mighty Arm. 3. How to Build a Mighty Grip. 4. How to Build a Mighty Back. 5. How to Build Mighty Legs—Now all in One Volume "How to become a Muscular He-Man." ENCLOSED FIND 10c FOR POSTAGE AND HANDLING (No C.O.D's).
NAME ____ AGE ____
ADDRESS ____
CITY ____ ZONE ____ STATE ____

FOOT ITCH

ATHLETE'S FOOT

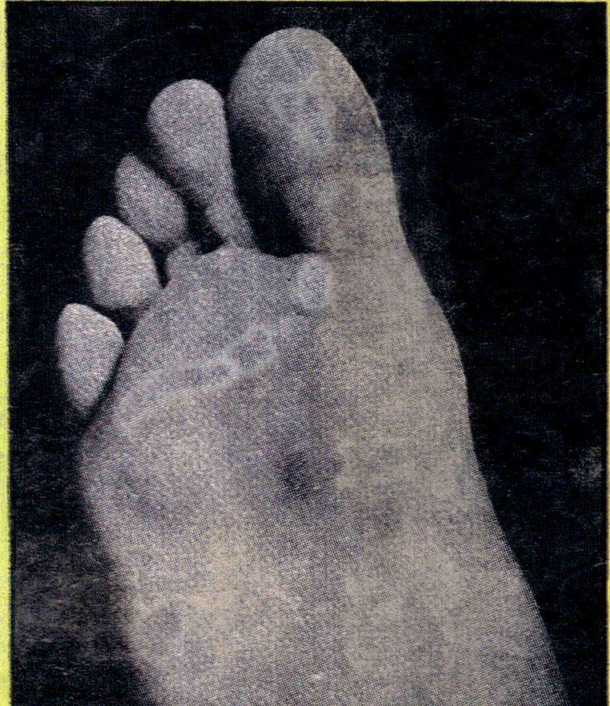

DISEASE OFTEN MISUNDERSTOOD

The cause of the disease is not a germ as so many people think, but a vegetable growth that becomes lodged in and immediately beneath the outer tissue of the skin.

To obtain relief the medicine to be used should first, gently remove the horny outer layer of skin and kill the vegetable growth.

This growth is so hard to kill that a test shows it takes 15 minutes of boiling to destroy it; however, laboratory tests also show that H. F. will kill it upon contact in 15 seconds.

DOUBLE ACTION NEEDED

Recently H. F. was developed solely for the purpose of relieving Athlete's Foot. It gently removes the horny outer layer of the skin, killing the vegetable growth, in and immediately under the skin, upon contact. Both actions are necessary for prompt relief.

H. F. is a liquid that doesn't stain. You just paint the infected parts nightly before going to bed. Often the terrible itching is relieved at once.

H. F. SENT ON FREE TRIAL

Sign and mail the coupon, and a bottle of H. F. will be mailed you immediately. Don't send any money and don't pay the postman any money; don't pay anything any time unless H. F. is helping you. If it does help you, we know you will be glad to send us $1 for the bottle at the end of ten days. That's how much faith we have in H. F. Read, sign and mail the coupon today.

PAY NOTHING TILL RELIEVED

Send Coupon

At least 50% of the adult population of the United States are being attacked by the disease known as Athlete's Foot.

Usually the disease starts between the toes. Little watery blisters form, and the skin cracks and peels. After a while, the itching becomes intense, and you feel as though you would like to scratch off all the skin.

BEWARE OF IT SPREADING

Often the disease travels all over the bottom of the feet. The soles of your feet become red and swollen. The skin also cracks and peels, and the itching becomes worse and worse.

Get relief from this disease as quickly as possible, because it is both contagious and infectious, and it may go to your hands or even to the under arm or crotch of the legs.

GORE PRODUCTS, Inc. Z

619 Girod St., New Orleans 12, La.

Please send me immediately a bottle of H. F. for foot trouble as described above. I agree to use it according to directions. If at the end of 10 days my feet are getting better, I will send you $1. If I am not entirely satisfied, I will return the unused portion of the bottle to you within 15 days from the time I receive it.

NAME ______________________

ADDRESS ______________________

CITY ______________ STATE ______________

TALES BEYOND BELIEF AND IMAGINATION!
TOMB
OF TERROR
No. 5
OCT.
TOMB OF TERROR
PDC
10¢
THEIR LOVE FOUGHT TIME! THEIR DETERMINATION ALLOWED MURDER HE CAME BACK TO JOIN HER IN...
THE MARRIAGE OF THE MONSTERS!
LEE ELIAS

IN THIS ISSUE

OCT.
NO. 5

TOMB OF TERROR

FOUR SAW THE LEGENDARY FACE OF UNUTTERABLE DOOM... AND EACH ONE MET A FATE TOO HORRIBLE TO DESCRIBE! BUT ONE AMONG THEM WAS THE TRUE GHOUL FROM THE **BEYOND!** WHO WAS IT? WHO ALONE OBEYED...

HEAD OF THE MEDUSA

MILLION YEARS AGO, WHEN THE EARTH WAS A STEAMING MIST, MANY STRANGE THINGS
VED... AND DISAPPEARED WITHOUT A TRACE. BUT SOME DIDN'T DISAPPEAR, AND STILL LURK IN
RK UNTRODDEN CORNERS OF THE WORLD. WHAT MERRILL DANE SAW DEEP IN THE EVERGLADES
OKED LIKE A SICK BLOTCH OF GREEN SLIME... BUT HE SOON FOUND OUT THAT IT WAS...

THE LIVING SLIME!

OVE CAN FRIGHTEN AS WELL
S SOOTHE—KILL AS WELL AS
RING HAPPINESS. THE LOVE
F CENTURIES COULD NOT BE
TIFLED—EVEN IF IT HAD TO
RAG ITSELF OUT OF ITS
OTTED TOMB TO FULFILL ITS
DESTINY!

MARRIAGE OF THE MONSTERS!

OUT OF MY WAY, MORTAL! NO POWER ON EARTH CAN STOP ME FROM CLAIMING MY LOVE! ARRRGHHH!

E HAD THE SOUL OF A
RAT, AND A GRISLY SERIES
F EVENTS GAVE HIM THE
ODY OF A RAT, TOO!
ND, UNTIL THAT LAST
RONIC DINNER, BENNY
NICKERED WITH EVIL
EE OVER THE STRANGE
VIST OF FATE THAT HAD
DE HIM...

THE RAT MAN

Welcome into this crypt of the unknown! Enter the world behind the forbidden shadows! Delve into the mysteries that live in this timeless sanctum! Read the TOMB OF TERROR!

Climb the wall of blackness and feel the terror . . . the thrills . . . the chills that dwell in the beyond! The wailing wind works its way through the gravestones and forces a groan of agony . . . The spirits come from yesterday to live again . . . to dance their Satan steps once more . . . to reign again in the TOMB OF TERROR!

Never before have such tales been told! Never before has such an asylum of horror been formed! Page after page . . . scene after scene . . . word after word of chilling suspense!

The horrible fate of evil . . . the loathesomeness that dwells in many mortals . . . the thrills of the supernatural all come together in the TOMB OF TERROR!

What is the ghastly meaning behind the "Marriage of the Monsters"? What is the endless horror that lives in "The Rat Man"? Why did a world go berserk when it faced the "Head of Medusa"? And what could stop the shrieking message of madness that was the "Living Slime"!

See it all! Watch a thousand monsters collide in an inferno of Satan! Catch your breath as you face the greatest host of suspense stories ever published!

Climb the weird wall that encloses the . . .

TOMB OF TERROR!

TOMB OF TERROR, OCTOBER, 1952, Vol. 1, No. 5, is published monthly by HARVEY PUBLICATIONS, INC., at 420 DeSoto Avenue, St. Louis 7, Mo. Editorial, Advertising and Executive offices, 1860 Broadway, New York 23, N. Y. President, Alfed Harvey; Vice-President and Editor, Leon Harvey; Vice-President and Business Manager, Robert B. Harvey. Application for second class entry pending at the Post Office at St. Louis, Mo. Single copies, 10c. Subscription rates, 10 issues for $1.00 and in the U. S. and possessions, elsewhere $1.50. All names in this periodical are entirely fictitious and no indentification with actual persons is intended.

You Can Be a Bombshell In Any Tough Spot!
NOW . . . A Rugged Fighting-Man Shows You How To Explode Your Hidden-Powers In Self-Defense
AMERICAN COMBAT JUDO
AMERICAN COMBAT JUDO
FREE 7-DAY TRIAL! Mail Coupon
No true American wants to be a tough! But YOU, and every red-blooded man and boy wants to be always ready and able to get out of any tough spot . . . no matter what the odds. You want to have the real know-how of skillfully defending yourself . . . of fearlessly protecting your property, or your dear ones . . . against Bullies, Hoodlums, Roughnecks and the like. And, if in service, or going in, you've got to be ready to fight rough and tough, for your very life may depend on it in hand-to-hand combat.
Here's where a rugged, two-fisted fighting-man tells you . . . and shows you . . . the secrets of using every power-packed trick in the bag. You get it straight from "Barney" Cosneck, in AMERICAN COMBAT JUDO . . . training-manual for Troopers, Police, Boxers, Wrestlers, Commandos, Rangers and Armed Forces. What a man! He's dynamite from head to toes! Twice, he was Big 10 Wrestling Champ, and during World War II was Personal Combat Instructor to the U. S. Coast Guard. "Barney" has devoted most of his life to developing, perfecting, teaching rough, tough fighting tactics. He gives YOU all the angles in easy-to-follow steps. Mastery of his skills and tactics will give even a little guy the blasting-power of a bombshell . . . to knock the steam out of a bruiser twice his size.
"Barney" keeps no secrets in AMERICAN COMBAT JUDO! He tells all . . . shows all! He gives you the real lowdown on when and how to use each power-packed Blow, Hold, Lock, Jab, Throw and Trip, that will make YOU the "Boss" in any tough spot. You'll be thrilled and amazed when you see what YOU can do with your bare hands . . . even if you are light and small. For, the real secret of "Barney's" super-tactics is in using the other fellow's muscle and brawn against him . . . as if it were your own . . . to make him helpless and defenseless.
200 Dynamic-Action, Start-To-Finish photos show you what to do . . . how to do . . . the skillful fighting tactics that will make you slippery as an eel . . . fast as lightning . . . with striking-power like a panther . . . with a K.O. punch in both hands. What's more, you'll learn the secrets of using every ounce of your weight . . . every inch of your size . . . to give you giant-power . . . crushing-power . . . that will keep you on your feet when the other guy's down. Best of all, you'll be surprised how easy it is. Your friends, too, will be surprised when they see your speed, skill and power.
Send for your copy of AMERICAN COMBAT JUDO right now! Keep it for 7 days, and if you don't think it's the best buck you ever spent, return it and get your money back. But, don't wait — you don't know when you may have to do your stuff.
WHAT A BOOK!
It's super-charged with the know-all and do-all of every winning-trick in JUDO . . . WRESTLING BOXING . . . POLICE TACTICS. Actually, 4 Dynamic-Action Books in 1. Loaded with 200 Start-To-Finish Photos. All for ONLY $1.00.
PARTIAL CONTENTS
Disabling Blows . . . Chart of Disabling Blows . . . Hacks . . . Jabs . . . Holds . . . Locks . . . Breaks . . . Releases . . . Throws . . . Trips . . . Arm Drag . . . Full Nelson . . . Shoulder Throw . . . Hip Throw . . . Pile Driver . . . Fighting Two Men At Once . . . Disarming Assailant . . . and many others
4 DYNAMIC-ACTION BOOKS IN 1
ONLY $1.00 POST PAID
SPORTSMAN'S POST, 26 East 46th St. New York 17, N. Y. Dept. HC9
FREE TRIAL COUPON ....Mail Today!
SPORTSMAN'S POST, Dept. HC9
26 East 46th St.,
New York 17, N. Y.
Gentlemen:
You've got something! Rush me my copy of AMERICAN COMBAT JUDO on 7 Days' Free Trial. I have checked how I am ordering:
☐ Here's my $1.00 in ___cash ___money order ___ check. Send postpaid.
NAME
ADDRESS
CITY ZONE STATE
WARNING! If you are a Merchant, Guard, Taxi-Driver, Trucker, Farmer, Cashier, Gas-Station Operator, Serviceman, Nightworker, or in some other occupation where, due to location or circumstances, you are often alone, or go through dark, lonely places, AMERICAN COMBAT JUDO is a must for you. Women and girls, too, should know how to defend and protect themselves when alone or unescorted. MAIL THIS COUPON NOW!

HE HAD THE SOUL OF A RAT, AND A GRISLY SERIES OF EVENTS GAVE HIM THE BODY OF A RAT, TOO! AND, UNTIL THAT LAST IRONIC DINNER, BENNY SNICKERED WITH EVIL GLEE OVER THE STRANGE TWIST OF FATE THAT HAD MADE HIM...
THE RAT MAN
BENNY THE RAT, A CHEAP WATERFRONT HOOD, WAS ON THE RUN AFTER CROSSING THE MOB...
NAILS HAS THE GUYS OUT LOOKING FOR ME. I'M FINISHED IF I DON'T GET CLEAR OF THE WATERFRONT!
THE AFRICAN BEAUTY IS DOCKING! I CAN MIX IN WITH THE CROWD TILL DARK AND THEN MAKE A BREAK FOR IT!
1

TOO BAD I'M NOT A REAL RAT LIKE HIM. I COULD SNEAK AWAY EASILY!

MEANWHILE, ON BOARD THE AFRICAN BEAUTY...
I'VE HEARD A LOT ABOUT YOUR RESEARCHES, PROFESSOR OGDEN. EXACTLY WHAT HAVE YOU BEEN DOING?
CAREFUL WITH THAT TRUNK, MEN. IT CONTAINS MY LIFE WORK.

I'VE DEVELOPED A FLUID THAT I'M SURE WILL BRING LIFE TO DEAD MATTER. CAREFUL THERE, CAREFUL!

AT THAT MOMENT, BELOW...
THERE'S NAILS! HE...HE'S SPOTTED ME...BUT HE WON'T DARE SHOOT WITH ALL THESE PEOPLE AROUND ME!

JUST THAT RAT'S LUCK TO BE WHERE I CAN'T GET A GOOD SHOT AT HIM! HMMM... I WONDER...MAYBE I CAN GET HIM AT THAT!

IF I CATCH THAT ROPE JUST RIGHT, I CAN SEND THE TRUNK CRASHING DOWN ON HIS HEAD!

MEANWHILE, LIQUID FROM THE PROFESSOR'S SHATTERED TRUNK SLOWLY FILTERED OUT, DRIPPING OVER THE TWO BODIES GRUESOMELY INTERMINGLED IN ONE GORY SPLASH OF BLOOD AND FLESH AND CRACKED BONE!

AT THAT MOMENT, A FEW HUNDRED YARDS AWAY...
I'M ALIVE... AFTER THAT TERRIBLE ACCIDENT... AND I'M WALKING ON ALL FOURS LIKE AN ANIMAL! WH-WHAT'S HAPPENED TO ME? I MUST LOOK IN THE WATER... SEE MY REFLECTION!

I--I'VE CHANGED! SOMEHOW, MY BODY, AND THE BODY OF THAT RAT HAVE BECOME ONE!

I'LL GET NAILS AFTER WHAT HE DID! I'LL GET THEM ALL... WITH TOOTH AND CLAW!

A LITTLE LATER, INSIDE A WATERFRONT DIVE...
HEY! WH-WHAT'S THAT? L-LOOKS LIKE A GIANT RAT!
AWW... JUST YOUR IMAGINATION! WHADDYE THINK-- BENNY'S COMING BACK TO HAUNT US?

DIDN'T EXPECT ME BACK, DID YOU, BOYS?
IT.. IT IS BENNY! HE--HE'S CHANGED INTO A REAL RAT!

YOU'RE NEXT, NAILS!
AAAAAHHH! NO! LEMME OUT!
4

WITH FANGED TEETH RIPPING, AND SHARP CLAWS SLASHING, BENNY DEALT OUT VICIOUS DEATH!
NAILS GOT AWAY, BUT THE REST OF YOU WON'T!
BENNY! NO! NO! AGGGH!
SPECIAL

I SEE NAILS LEFT YOU TO SAVE HIS OWN HIDE! I DIDN'T GET HIM, BUT I'LL GET REVENGE ON HIM THROUGH YOU!
BENNY... PLEASE... DON'T TOUCH ME!

HER BLOOD CHILLED WITH TERROR, THOSE FEW MOMENTS OF UN-SPEAK-ABLE HORROR TRANS-FORMED THE PRETTY GIRL IN-TO A GIBBER-ING OLD WOMAN!
IT.. IT'S ONLY A RAT... A BIG, BIG RAT... CAN'T HURT!
WHEN NAILS GETS A LOOK AT YOU, HE'LL KNOW I CAN HURT. I'LL LEAVE YOU HERE... TILL HE GETS BACK!

NOW TO BURROW A HOLE NEAR THE RUINS OF THAT OLD TENEMENT, AND HIDE OUT. COME ON, RED. I... CAN... USE... YOU.
BAR

SOME TIME LATER...
WE'RE ALL TOGETHER AGAIN, BOYS. NICE AND COZY DOWN HERE, ISN'T IT? HOW DOES IT FEEL TO BE THE GUESTS OF BENNY THE RAT?

FOR THE NEXT FEW DAYS, THE WHOLE CITY SENSED A SICKENING WAVE OF TERROR AS THE RAT-MAN STRUCK... AGAIN AND AGAIN!

A GUY CAN REALLY GET PLACES WITH FOUR FEET.

EEEHHH! HELP!

NEVER EXPECTED VISITORS UP HERE ON THE FIFTEENTH FLOOR, DID YOU?

LUCKY I FOUND THAT OLD DRAIN-PIPE LEADING UNDER THE BANK. WITH THESE CLAWS I CAN DIG MY WAY UP THROUGH ANYTHING!

I CAN'T BUY ANY-THING THAT'LL DO ME ANY GOOD... BUT I CAN USE THIS STUFF TO GET POWER... REAL POWER OVER THE WHOLE CITY!

TERROR STRICKEN CITY HELPLESS AGAINST RAT

ONE EVENING...
NAILS! WH-WHAT ARE YOU DOING HERE?
IT'S OKAY, CHUM! I JUST THOUGHT OUT A WAY WE CAN HELP EACH OTHER...A LOT!

I GOT IN TOUCH WITH ALL THE MOBS ...AND WE WANT YOU TO TAKE OVER. WE'LL PLAN THE JOBS...AND YOU CARRY THEM OUT.
HMMM...I WAS KIND OF THINK-ING OF THAT MY-SELF...BUT WHAT GOOD IS MONEY TO ME?

IT ISN'T THE DOUGH ...BUT YOU'LL BE THE BIG WHEEL IN THE CITY.. IN CHARGE OF EVERY OPERATION WE PULL, AND BESIDES, THERE'S THIS...
WAIT! WHAT YOU GOT IN THERE?

DON'T YOU SEE? YOU CAN'T WALK INTO A RESTAURANT...OR INTO A STORE...BUT WE CAN BRING YOU EVERYTHING... TELEVISION SETS...ANY KIND OF FOOD YOU WANT ...LIKE THIS STEAK AND FRENCH FRIES I BOUGHT.

IT'S A DEAL! YOU GUYS ARE SMART.
SURE.. I KNEW THAT CHOW WOULD MAKE YOU SEE IT RIGHT. STEAK AND FRENCH FRIES WAS ALWAYS YOUR FAVORITE, WASN'T THEY?

YEH I ALWAYS... OWWW... WHAT... WHAT DID YOU PUT IN THIS? YOU...YOU.. DIDN'T...?

YEAH, BENNY, I DID! YOU JUST DOWNED ENOUGH RAT POISON TO KILL A WHOLE ARMY OF RATS!
THE END
7

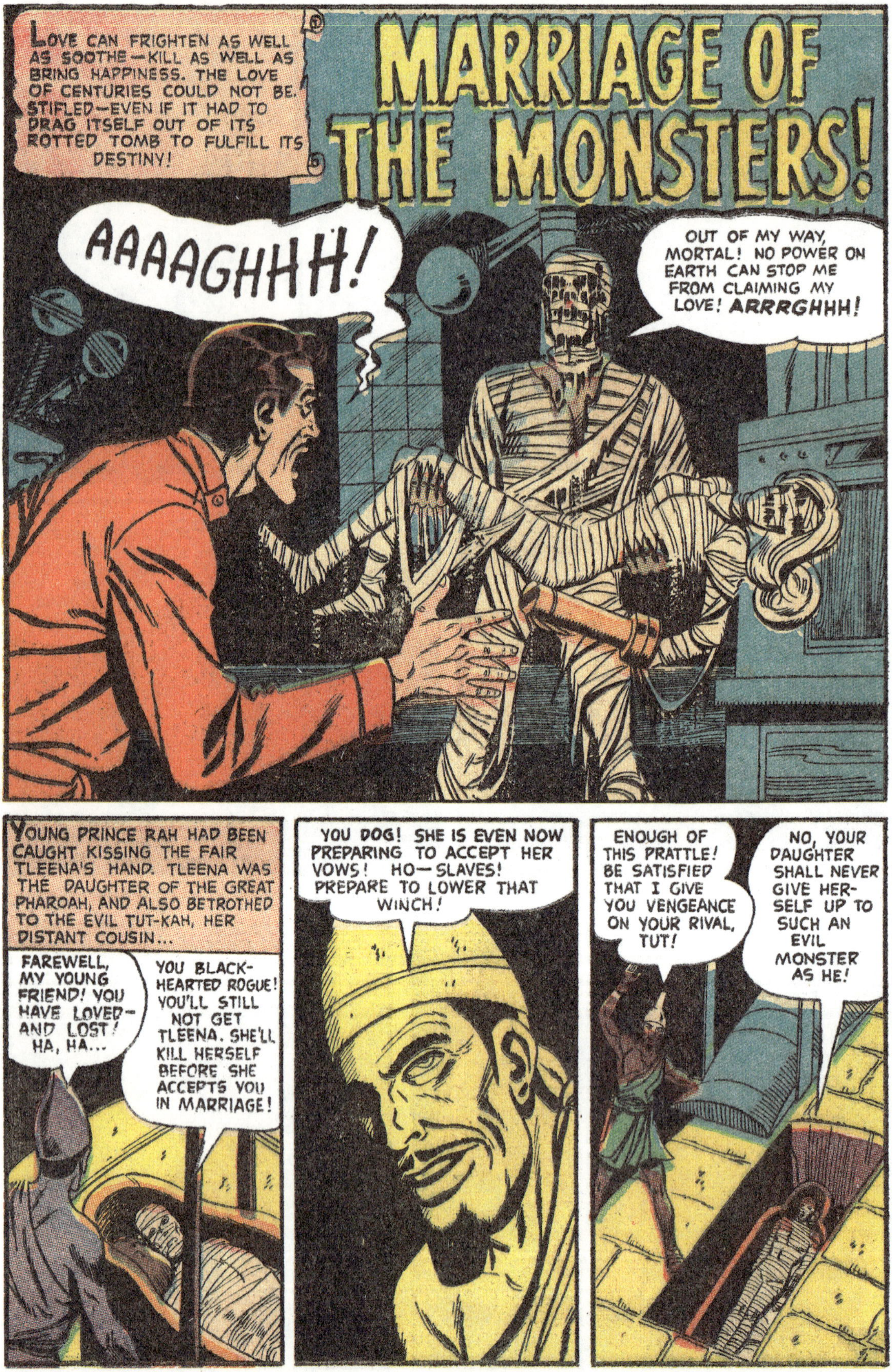

LOVE CAN FRIGHTEN AS WELL AS SOOTHE—KILL AS WELL AS BRING HAPPINESS. THE LOVE OF CENTURIES COULD NOT BE STIFLED—EVEN IF IT HAD TO DRAG ITSELF OUT OF ITS ROTTED TOMB TO FULFILL ITS DESTINY!

MARRIAGE OF THE MONSTERS!

AAAAGHHHH!

OUT OF MY WAY, MORTAL! NO POWER ON EARTH CAN STOP ME FROM CLAIMING MY LOVE! **ARRRGHHH!**

YOUNG PRINCE RAH HAD BEEN CAUGHT KISSING THE FAIR TLEENA'S HAND. TLEENA WAS THE DAUGHTER OF THE GREAT PHAROAH, AND ALSO BETROTHED TO THE EVIL TUT-KAH, HER DISTANT COUSIN...

I SHALL NOT WAIT FOR YOUR SCREAMS, PIG! I SHALL KILL YOU MYSELF!
OUR PRINCESS TLEENA WISHES TO SPEAK, OH, MASTERS! BOW TO HER!
GONGGGG!

HAIL! OH, MY FATHER—IN YOUR JUSTICE YOU HAVE COMMITTED A GREAT WRONG! YOU ARE CONDEMNING A MAN WHO SOUGHT ONLY TO WIN MY LOVE! KNOW, ALL OF YOU, THAT I LOVE RAH—NOT THE EVIL TUT!

KNOW—GREAT PHARDAH—THAT YOUR DAUGHTER BELONGS TO ME—OR I SHALL BRING DOWN MY MIGHTY LEGIONS AGAINST ALL OF EGYPT! WHAT SAY YE NOW, TLEENA?

THEN THERE IS NO CHOICE FOR ME BUT TO KILL MYSELF! RAH—MY SWEET! I SHALL JOIN YOU IN DEATH!
OHHH! SHE HAS KILLED HERSELF! TLEENA IS DEAD! OHHH...

AY, SHE HAS KILLED HERSELF, TUT! NOW YOU MAY CRUSH THE LIFE FROM MY BODY, BUT I STILL CLAIM HER FOR MY SWEETHEART!
LOWER THE COFFIN UPON HIM! BURY HIM WITH BURNING SAND! QUICKLY—SO I MAY HEAR HIS AGONIZED SCREAMS!

SHOVEL THAT DIRT OVER HIS FEATURES! LET HIM SUFFOCATE! HA, HA...
BARROOOOOMM!

KNOW YE, TUT! WE SHALL HAVE OUR REVENGE! YOU HAVE KILLED US—BUT YOU SHALL NEVER KILL OUR LOVE! SOMEWHERE—SOMETIME, WE SHALL RETURN! YOU WILL NEVER SEPARATE TLEENA AND I...

SO CENTURIES WENT BY— AND THE TOMB OF THE TWO LOVERS SANK LOWER AND LOWER INTO THE BOWELS OF THE EARTH. DEATH HAD CLAIMED THEM —ONE INSEPARABLE — EVER CONSTANT AS TIME ITSELF...

THEN 3000 YEARS LATER— DR. JACOB MESSNER DISCOVERED A SCIENTIFIC PRINCIPLE THAT WAS TO BRING HIM SUCH DISREPUTE—AND DEATH !!
PREPOSTEROUS! NO ONE CAN BRING DEAD CORPSES TO LIFE! HE 'S INSANE! THROW HIM OUT!
YOU'LL SEE! YOU FOOLS— YOU ARE TOO BLIND TO RECOGNIZE GENIUS SUCH AS MINE!

HA, HA— YOU'RE NOTHING BUT A CHARLATAN, MESSNER! GO BACK TO YOUR WEIRD EXPERIMENTS AND YOUR SMELLY VIALS! HA, HA!
BAH! LAUGH NOW— BUT YOU SHALL COME TO ME ONE DAY, BEGGING TO TAKE ME BACK! I'LL SHOW YOU ALL!

JACOB MESSNER HAD FOR YEARS WORKED ON THE PRINCIPLE THAT LIFE COMES FROM ELECTRICAL ENERGY. NOW HE WAS ABOUT TO PROVE IT...
THIS MUMMY IS PERFECT FOR MY EXPERIMENT! THE MUSEUM WILL NEVER FIND OUT WHO STOLE IT —ONE OF THEIR OWN MEMBERS! HA, HA... EVERYTHING IS READY!

HA, HA— SOON IT SHALL BE ALIVE! SOON I SHALL WIN EVERLASTING FAME FOR MYSELF!
CRAACKLE...
SNAP...
SNAP...

BUT THREE LONG, TRYING HOURS LATER...

BAH! IT HAS NOT MOVED AN INCH! IT IS BUT A DUMB CLOD OF PROTOPLASM! I'LL FLING IT BACK TO THE MOULDY COFFIN WHENCE IT CAME! I HAVE ANOTHER SPECIMEN TO WORK WITH!

NOW WITH THIS ONE I SHALL TRY A DIFFERENT APPROACH! I'LL CONNECT THE ELECTRODES IN A CONTINUOUS SERIES. THAT SHOULD GIVE ME MORE ELECTRICITY! HA, HA— I SHALL SUCCEED!
3

WHO DARES DISTURB OUR REPOSE? I SHALL THROTTLE THE MORTAL THAT HAS CALLED US BACK FROM THE BEYOND! AIIIE! IT IS TUT! HE LIVES AGAIN THROUGH HIS DESCENDANT!

ONCE AGAIN, THE HUM OF GIANT GENERATORS BEGAN THEIR WHINE OF EERIE PROTEST! BUT NOW, BLENDED IN WITH THEM WAS A CACOPHONOUS DISCORD OF INHUMAN PAIN...
OHHHH... WHY DO YE TORTURE US? LET US BE! DO NOT TORTURE US SO!
HA, HA! IT MOVES! I'VE BROUGHT BACK LIFE FROM THE DEAD!

SUDDENLY...
W-WHAT WAS THAT?
THUD!

MESSNER GRABBED A FLASHLIGHT AND WENT DOWNSTAIRS TO INVESTIGATE, LITTLE REALIZING THAT HIS NEMESIS WAS NEAR. HE HAD JUST ARRIVED BACK AT HIS LAB, WHEN—
YOU HAVE CREATED YOUR EVIL ONCE AGAIN, TUT! TLEENA AND I HAVE BEEN BROUGHT TO LIFE! BUT YOU'LL TORTURE US NO MORE! WE SHALL HAVE OUR REVENGE!
YAAAA!

YE SHALL GIVE US YOUR OWN ELECTRICAL ENERGY! WE SHALL TOUCH LIPS, TLEENA AND I—WE SHALL MARRY AND THEN JOIN EACH OTHER BACK IN THE BEYOND! THIS SHALL BE YOUR DOOM!
DON'T WALK UNDER THAT ELECTRODE! WE'LL ALL BE ELECTROCUTED! AIIIEEEEE!

YAAAA!
ZZZZZZZ ZZZ

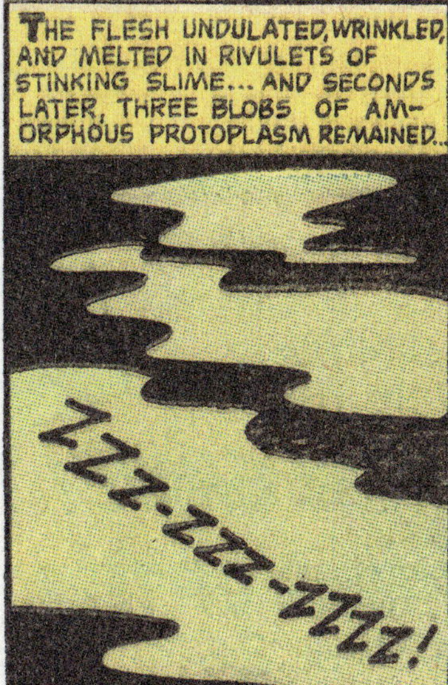
THE FLESH UNDULATED, WRINKLED, AND MELTED IN RIVULETS OF STINKING SLIME... AND SECONDS LATER, THREE BLOBS OF AMORPHOUS PROTOPLASM REMAINED...
ZZZ-ZZZ-ZZZZ!

...AND TWO CHARRED BONEY HANDS JOINED TOGETHER, FOR RAH AND TLEENA WERE JOINED AT LAST!
THE END

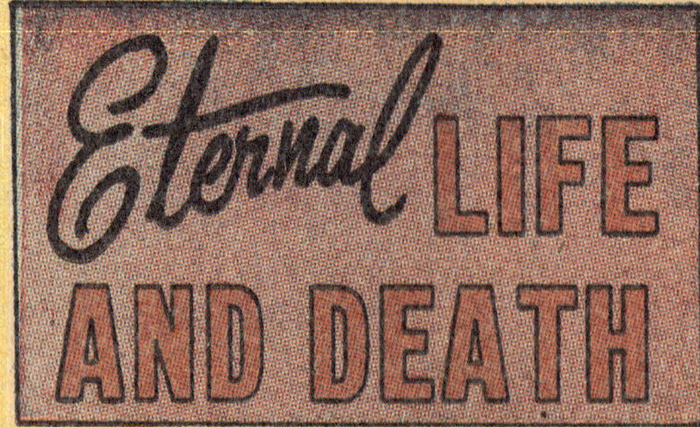

Dr. Clayborne's voice was hushed, almost reverent. "This is it, Stewart!" he whispered, holding aloft the test-tube filled with amber-colored liquid. "The secret of eternal life—right here in my hand! All these years of research, of experiments . . . all these years of being laughed at, ridiculed . . . all of it is worthwhile now . . ."

Jeb Stewart stifled a yawn. He was bored stiff with the doctor's harangue. He'd heard it so many times before. Clayborne and his eternal life nonsense!

"It's almost like a movie or a book!" Stewart thought jeeringly. "The mad scientist and his devilish experiments! Even *I'm* here—the ever-faithful assistant . . . !"

"Stewart!" Dr. Clayborne's voice cracked like a whip. "You're not paying any attention to me! I'm telling you of the greatest scientific discovery of all time, and *you're not even listening!*"

Stewart's patience cracked. "Look here, Dr. Clayborne!" he snapped. "You pay me to assist you with your so-called experiments! You pay me well, so I give you all the assistance you want! But what I *think* of your wacky experiments is my own business! You're *not* paying me to be a cheering section for all your half-baked 'discoveries!' Eternal life . . . *baloney!!*"

Every last bit of color drained from the doctor's face. He tried to speak and couldn't. "You . . . you . . ." he choked, "you . . . Judas . . ." A shrill, spiraling, maniacal scream tore from his throat With one leap he was on top of his assistant, a gleaming blade in his hand. Again and again and again the blade descended, plunging like summer lightning into Jeb Stewart's back.

"NO! AIEEEE!" the dying man screamed. Bright red blood spurted from his lips . . . he gurgled . . . choking on his own blood . . . and then he screamed no more. Long after his body lay still, the blade plunged again . . . and again . . . and again.

Till at last, his insane fury spent, Dr. Clayborne fell back, gasping from his exertions. A faint smile twisted his lips. "Perhaps I've been too harsh with you, Stewart!" he told the corpse at his feet. "After all, you're *still* the perfect assistant—even now! How clever of you to realize that once *I* had the secret of eternal life, I would require a *subject for demonstration purposes!* Yes, indeed, Stewart—I'm grateful to you!"

Still smiling, the mad scientist carefully filled a hypodermic needle with the precious amber fluid. He completed the injection into Stewart's still-warm arm quickly and easily . . . and sat back to wait for the results.

They were not long in coming. Jeb Stewart stirred—groaned—and staggered to his feet! His eyes were black, empty caverns with no light behind them as he looked dazedly about . . . his body was taut and rigid, and he moved like a kind of mechanical monster . . . but he was most assuredly *not dead!*

"I've done it! I've done it!" sobbed Dr. Clayborne in ecstasy. "I killed you, and now I've brought you back to life! I am your master! I am master of the world . . . !"

The living-dead man turned at the sound of the voice. In the empty sockets of his eyes blazed a sudden terrible flame. He moved . . .

"NO! NO! STAY BACK! YOU FOOL! ONLY I CAN GIVE YOU BACK TO DEATH! OTHERWISE YOU ARE DOOMED—DOOMED TO ETERNAL LIFE—DOOMED TO WALK THE EARTH FOR ALL ETERNITY . . . NO! AAAARRGHHH!"

Dr. Clayborne's broken body crashed into the experimental table as it fell, knocking the tube of amber liquid to the floor. Then the only sound to be heard in the laboratory was the opening of the window, as a blood-soaked, robot-like creature slipped out into the night . . . and into eternity . . .

SOLDIERS
SAILORS
WACS
MORTARS
MARINES
PT BOATS
HOWITZERS
TRUCKS
CANNONS
BOMBERS
TANKS
CRUISERS
BATTLESHIPS
PT BOATS
MARINES
WAVES
WACS
SAILORS
SOLDIERS
SOLDIERS
SAILORS
WACS
WAVES
MARINES
PT BOATS
BATTLESHIPS
CRUISERS
JETS
50 COMBAT ACTION PLASTIC TOYS
$1 POSTPAID
Your Own TASK FORCE
Now you can be Commander in Chief of this complete task force. Have pitched battles, gunnery drills, deploy your troops for attack and defense. Here's a complete army 50 pieces in all including soldiers, sailors, marines, PT boat, Howitzers, tanks, planes, and ships. You'll be thrilled and delighted with this complete task force Nothing else like it!
LOOK WHAT YOU GET. SOLDIERS · SAILORS · MARINES · WACS · TANKS · JEEPS · PT BOATS · BATTLESHIPS · JET PLANES · BOMBERS · MACHINE GUNNERS · HOWITZERS · TRUCKS · BAZOOKA MEN · RIFLEMEN
Here's a great collection of military toys yours for just a single dollar bill. You'll have hours of fun and pleasure with this wonderful set Every piece made of plastic in realistic scale. Precision formed of Styrene...nothing like it has ever been offered at this price Rush your order now. 6" long die cut cannon that shoots harmless bombs included in your order NOW!
FREE 6" LONG DIE CUT SHOOTING CANNON!
Supplies Limited! Don't delay Rush name and address and $1 for each set. Your complete 50-piece task force will be shipped by return mail. Sorry no COD's. Rush your dollar today.
FIGHTING FORCE Dept. 11
1860 Broadway
New York 23, N.Y.
I enclose ________ at $1 per set.
Rush your 50-piece Fighting Force set prepaid.
Name ________ Age ___
Address ________
City ________ State ________
MACHINE GUNS
BAZOOKAS
RIFLEMEN

WE DARE YOU TO READ THESE TALES OF TERROR and SUSPENSE
NOW PUBLISHED MONTHLY
THE BEST IN SHOCK MYSTERY
GET THEM EVERY MONTH
TALES OF TERROR AND SUSPENSE!
CHAMBER OF CHILLS
WE DARE YOU
TO READ THESE EERIE TALES OF SUPERNATURAL HORROR!
WITCHES TALES
STRANGEST TALES OF FEAR AND SUPERSTITION!
BLACK CAT MYSTERY
TALES BEYOND BELIEF AND IMAGINATION
TOMB OF TERROR
THE MARRIAGE OF THE MONSTERS!

Bill Halloran was lost . . . lost in the vast, icy wilderness of the Antarctic.

He had left Janssen's reconnoitering party to check on the robot weather stations which they had set up along the coast of Adelaide Land. But now he was caught in a labyrinth of snow.

The day had been beautiful and clear. But as frequently happens in the Antarctic, sudden storm winds gusted across the glacier plains, whipping up fine snow spray that blanketed the 24-hour South Pole sun. The wind blew like thunder—at 200 miles per hour. And in a moment, Bill's tractor had been completely disabled.

He had gotten out to seek refuge on the leeward side of the tractor, and that was his mistake,—the shrieking wind had blasted him off his feet! Heavy, choking snow dust rushed at him, and he stumbled away—aimlessly—blindly!

Then as suddenly as the storm wind had exploded, it evaporated, and again the seemingly eternal sun bore through settling snow dust. Bill shook his head to clear the daze.

And he was stunned again . . .

The tractor was nowhere in sight! All landmarks that were along the weather station route on Adelaide Land, were apparently gone. He could not find the angular pressure ridge nor the undulating knolls.

He was lost. With the sun almost overhead, he had no sense of direction, and anyhow at the South Pole, there was no direction! His solar compass, which would have helped him find his way to the coast, was in the now gone tractor.

It was useless to stay where he was, so he trudged on and on in the hardening snow. The cold was biting and incredible, and all the woolens he wore were no protection.

Time passed with agonizing slowness. Exhaustion began to tell, yet Bill simply had to keep moving . . . or death would take its toll.

Suddenly he saw something rise from the snowfields. His mind swirled in a pool of emotion as he made out its half-human, half-beast form! He was afraid to trust his senses. He might be seeing a man, he thought, and his exhausted mind had been the monster's creator.

He called out aloud.

The thing stopped and looked at him. Bill turned and ran, stumbled, picked himself up, and ran toward the thing.

It waited until Bill was only a hundred yards away, and then turned slowly . . . and ambled toward the icy wilderness.

Bill doubled his steps, and the thing fled still faster. Bill stopped with despair. The thing stopped and looked at him. Bill's senses were blurred and he could hardly make it out. but he was sure it stood on its two feet . . . and wore some white fur!

Bill called once more. The thing did not answer. Bill stumbled toward it. The thing retreated again, and Bill sat down with despair. He sobbed like a baby.

The thing drew closer to him. Driven by blind, urgent despair, Bill lunged toward the thing. He felt soft white fur and gripped it with the desperateness of a lost soul. The thing shook itself free and retreated a few paces.

And then Bill's thinking came to a halt!

A strange transformation was going on under the Antarctic sun. White fur began to grow on Bill's face and then his arms and body! And white fur disappeared from the thing very slowly, and an ancient sad man took its place!

The man took Bill's clothes and then turned resolutely toward the Adelaide Land coast. He walked firmly, leaving Bill behind to rise slowly and begin his sentence of fate.

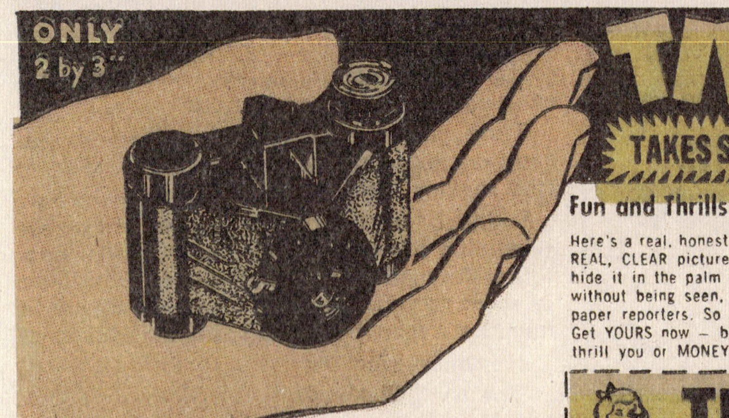

TINY MIDGET CAMERA

TAKES SECRET PICTURES

1.39

Fun and Thrills Galore for You!

Here's a real, honest-to-goodness camera that takes REAL, CLEAR pictures – yet it's so SMALL you can hide it in the palm of your hand! Take SECRET pictures without being seen, of friends or enemies – like F.B.I. men or newspaper reporters. So EASY – anybody can use it! Just AIM and CLICK! Get YOURS now – bargain price only 1.39. GUARANTEED to satisfy and thrill you or MONEY BACK. Send COUPON below.

Fits in palm of hand!

- EVEN A CHILD CAN USE IT!
- TAKES DANDY, CLEAR PICTURES!
- POCKET SIZE — ONLY 2 BY 3 INCHES!
- TAKES REAL ACTION PHOTOS!
- QUALITY GROUND LENS!

Here's one of the world's SMALLEST cameras. Just the same you get beautiful, jumbo 2 x 3 enlarged photos from standard, low cost 828 film. Also – Kodak COLOR pictures – real, NATURAL looking pictures of friends and family that live on in your memory for years and years. Takes ACTION shots of sports events, school affairs, races, accidents, boats, nature scenes, etc. EASY – just AIM AND CLICK! Nothing complicated! GUARANTEED to satisfy you or full price back. SEND NO MONEY – pay postman only 1.39, plus postage on arrival. SAVE MORE – Send only 1.39 with order and get a NICE GIFT in your package besides! RUSH COUPON NOW – Don't miss this GUARANTEED BARGAIN!

CONSUMERS MART, Dept. 35-G-32
131 West 33rd Street New York 1, N. Y.

TRIAL COUPON

CONSUMERS MART, Dept. 35-G-32
131 West 33rd Street New York 1, N. Y.

GENTLEMEN: Send me the GUARANTEED MIDGET CAMERA that takes SECRET pictures. I will pay bargain price of only 1.39, plus postage, on delivery. If I am not thrilled and satisfied during a full week's trial you will send back my 1.39 without fail.

NAME ______________________

ADDRESS ______________________

TOWN ______________ STATE ______________

☐ SAVE MORE MONEY and receive a delightful GIFT free of extra charge! Just send 1.39 – not ONE PENNY extra – with this coupon. We will pay all postage charges. Same MONEY-BACK GUARANTEE, of course.

BOTH NOW ON SALE! BE SURE TO GET YOUR COPIES!

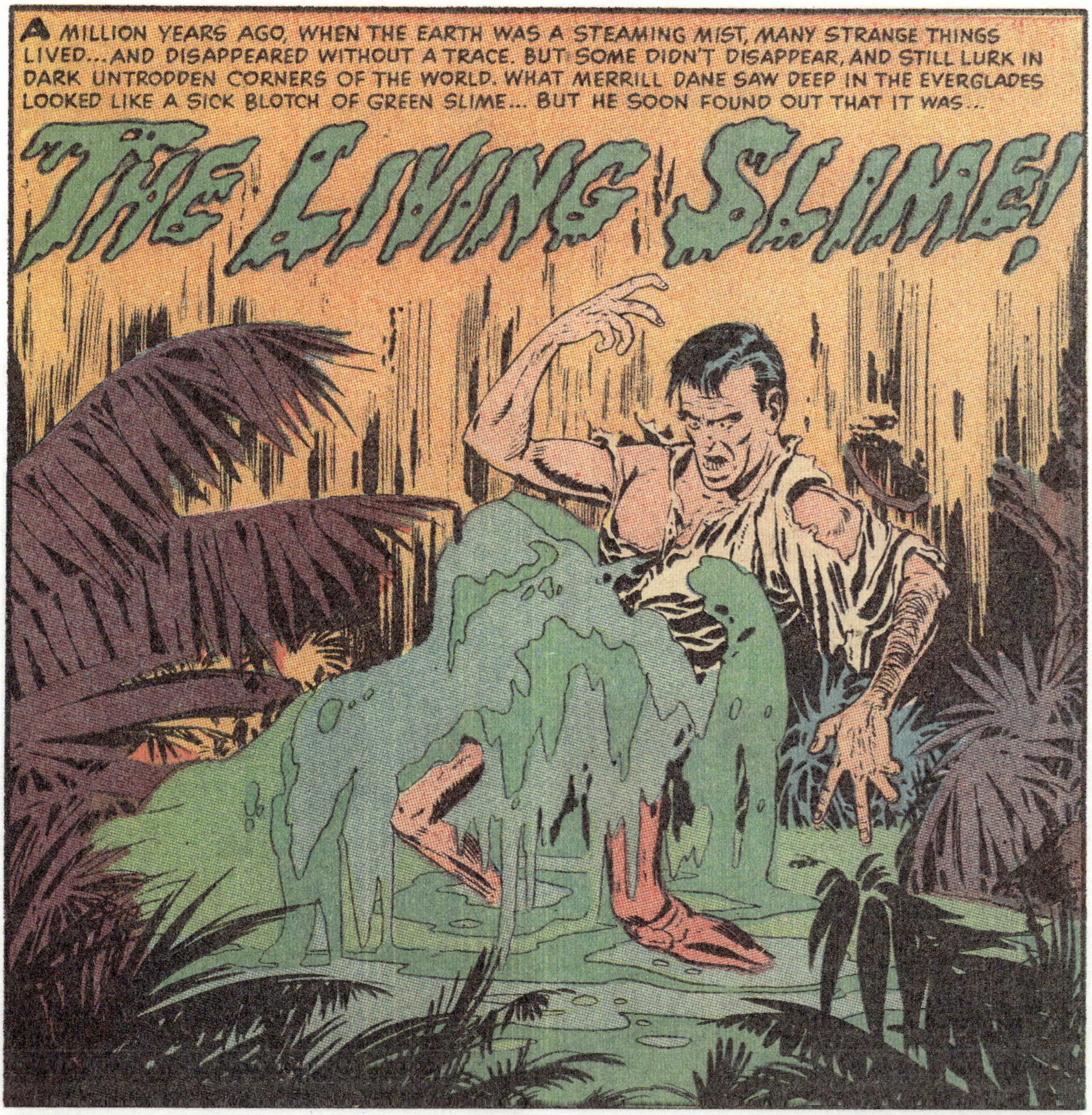

A MILLION YEARS AGO, WHEN THE EARTH WAS A STEAMING MIST, MANY STRANGE THINGS LIVED... AND DISAPPEARED WITHOUT A TRACE. BUT SOME DIDN'T DISAPPEAR, AND STILL LURK IN DARK UNTRODDEN CORNERS OF THE WORLD. WHAT MERRILL DANE SAW DEEP IN THE EVERGLADES LOOKED LIKE A SICK BLOTCH OF GREEN SLIME... BUT HE SOON FOUND OUT THAT IT WAS...

THE LIVING SLIME!

AS DANE GULPED QUICK PAINFUL BREATHS INTO HIS ACHING LUNGS...
THAT STRANGE GREEN MIRE! I...I'VE NEVER SEEN ANYTHING LIKE IT BEFORE!

IT...IT'S REACHING FOR THAT RABBIT...CLUTCHING WITH INCREDIBLE SPEED!

IT'S EATING HIM... TURNING HIM INTO UGLY GREEN SWAMP STUFF LIKE ITSELF!

SUDDENLY...
THE BLOODHOUNDS! THEY... THEY'LL TEAR ME TO RIBBONS!

DANE FLED IN WILD PANIC, UNAWARE THAT HIS FOOT BRUSHED THE EDGE OF THE LOATHSOME GREEN OOZE!
I'LL NEVER MAKE IT! MY LEGS.. LIKE LEAD!

AND THEN...ONLY A FEW MOMENTS LATER...
WH-WHAT'S HAPPENED? I--I'M RUNNING FASTER THAN THE WIND...BOUNDING THROUGH THE AIR LIKE...LIKE A RABBIT!
2

DANE EASILY OUTDISTANCED THE BLOODHOUNDS, AND SOUGHT REFUGE IN THE HUT OF A SWAMP SQUATTER WHERE...
THAT GREEN SLIME... THE EVIL SWAMP STUFF! GET IT OFF!

WH-WHY? WHAT'S WRONG?
LOOK BEHIND YOU, MAN! LOOK BEHIND YOU!

HURRY! BEFORE IT GETS HERE! IT ALWAYS GETS BACK ITS OWN... EVEN THE TINIEST SPOT... AND IF IT'S ON YOU, IT'LL SWALLOW YOU, TOO!

DANE HURRIEDLY WIPED OFF THE UGLY SMUDGE, AND FLUNG THE RAG AT THE LOATHSOME, CRAWLING OOZE!
WH--WHAT IS THAT DEVILISH STUFF?
IT GOT WHAT IT CAME FOR. NOW IT'S GOING BACK!

NO ONE KNOWS...'CEPTIN' THAT IT'S EVIL... AND ALIVE! THEY SAY IF YOU TOUCH IT SOON AFTER IT'S EATEN A LIVING THING, YOU KIND OF ABSORB SOMETHING THAT WAS PART OF THAT LIVING THING!

IT MUST BE TRUE... I GOT IT ON ME AFTER IT FED ON THE RABBIT, AND I WAS ABLE TO RUN LIKE A RABBIT!

DANE RESTED AT THE SHACK FOR A FEW DAYS, AND THEN...
DON'T FORGET... YOU BETTER NOT MENTION THAT GREEN STUFF TO NOBODY OUTSIDE THE SWAMP. THEY'D THINK YOU WAS CRAZY!
I WON'T ... AND THANKS A LOT, OLD TIMER!
3

DANE FLED TO A DISTANT CITY WHERE HE CHANGED HIS NAME AND SECURED EMPLOYMENT...
I COULD REALLY GET PLACES HERE...IF I HAD A HEAD FOR FIGURES LIKE JONES! IF THERE WAS ONLY SOME WAY I COULD ACQUIRE HIS TALENT...
R. JONES GEN. MANAGER

...BUT MAYBE I CAN! THE SWAMP STUFF... BACK IN THE EVERGLADES! IF I COULD GET HIM THERE, AND...HMMM... JONES AND I ARE GOING TO GET REAL FRIENDLY AFTER TODAY!

SOME DAYS LATER...
FUNNY THAT WE'RE BOTH INTERESTED IN HUNTING...I KNOW A SWELL PLACE...ALIVE WITH GAME. LIKE TO COME OUT WITH ME THIS WEEK-END?
RIGHT! IT'S A DATE!

THAT WEEK-END, WHERE THERE WERE NO WITNESSES BUT THE GRIM SHADOWS THAT WRITHED SULLENLY ON THE STREAM.
AMBROSE! WH-WHAT ARE YOU... AAAHH!

AAAGHHH!
HA-HA! IT'LL SUCK YOUR LIFE FORCE OUT--SO THAT I CAN ABSORB IT!

MOMENTS LATER...
MUST REMEMBER...HAVE TO WIPE IT OFF IN AN INSTANT!

IT...IT'S AMAZING! I...I CAN THINK WITH SUCH CLARITY NOW! THAT PROBLEM I COULDN'T SOLVE AT THE OFFICE YESTERDAY--THE SOLUTION JUST LEAPS INTO MY MIND!
4

WILLIAM AMBROSE ALIAS MERRILL DANE, CONVICT AT LARGE, WON HIS PROMOTION ...BUT HE STILL WASN'T SATISFIED...
THIS JOB IS PEANUTS. THE GREEN POOL CAN MAKE ME THE GREATEST MAN OF ALL TIMES!
GENERAL MANAGER

HE BIDED HIS TIME UNTIL HE BECAME A LEADING MEMBER OF THE COMMUNITY, AND THEN INVITED THREE MEN TO HIS HOME...
GENTLEMEN, I'VE INVITED YOU HERE SO THAT I CAN SHOW YOU THE MOST AMAZING SIGHT EVER! IT WILL MEAN A LITTLE TRIP!
HMMM...YOU'VE GOT A SOUND REPUTATION, AMBROSE. I'M GAME.
COUNT ME IN.

SOME TIME LATER, AT THE GREEN POOL...
EVANS...THE WORLD'S GREATEST SCIENTIST... CALKINS...A LEADING POLITICIAN, AND GENERAL WRIGHT, THE MILITARY GENIUS! WHEN I PLANT THEM THERE AND REAP THE HARVEST OF THEIR SKILLS, I'LL COMBINE ALL THEIR GENIUS IN ONE MIND...MINE!
WELL, AMBROSE... WHAT DID YOU WANT TO SHOW US?

YOU'LL SEE! STEP FORWARD ALL OF YOU...INTO THE GREEN POOL!
THE MAN'S MAD!

LET'S HUMOR HIM. THE WORST THAT CAN HAPPEN IS THAT WE'LL SOIL OUR CLOTHES IN THIS HARMLESS MUCK!
ALL RIGHT IF YOU SAY SO... BUT I DON'T LIKE THE LOOKS OF THAT STUFF! SOMETHING TREACHEROUS... AND EVIL ABOUT IT!

AAAAAGHHHWH

MOMENTS LATER...
NOW TO ABSORB THEIR GENIUS...BECOME THE GREATEST MAN ON EARTH!

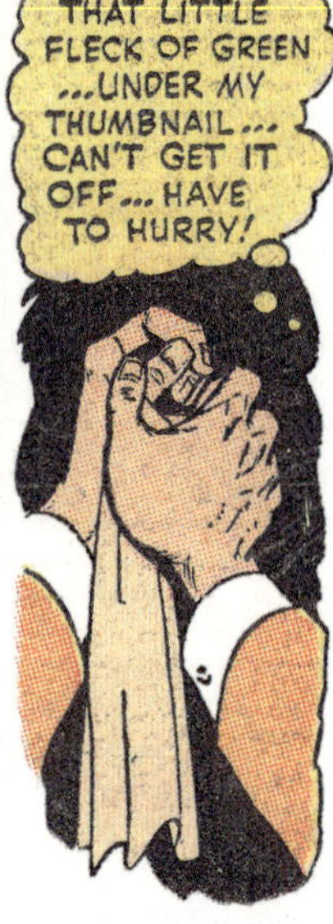
THAT LITTLE FLECK OF GREEN ...UNDER MY THUMBNAIL... CAN'T GET IT OFF... HAVE TO HURRY!

IT... IT WON'T WASH OFF! NO! NO! WAIT!

GO BACK! GO BACK!

LET ME GO! LET ME GO!

RELENTLESSLY, THE PUTRID TORRENT WASHED OVER HIM, AND THEN, ITS TERRIBLE HUNGER SATED, RECEDED SLOWLY...
THE END
6

FOUR SAW THE LEGENDARY FACE OF UNUTTERABLE DOOM-- AND EACH ONE MET A FATE TOO HORRIBLE TO DESCRIBE! BUT ONE AMONG THEM WAS THE TRUE GHOUL FROM THE BEYOND! WHO WAS IT? WHO ALONE OBEYED...
HEAD OF THE MEDUSA
I--I'M CHANGING! HAIR IS SPROUTING ON MY FACE! AAAGGHH!
ALL OF US WERE SCIENTISTS. HUGO HOFF, RICHARD DARE, AND I, JACK CROWL. VIVIEN MADE A CHARMING AND VERY EFFICIENT FOURTH. WE HAD TRAVELED FOR MONTHS INTO IMPENETRABLE JUNGLE-- AND NOW WE SAW IT!
LOOK! GOOD LORD--IT'S TRUE THEN--THE LOST CITY OF ILLIUM!
THE "LAND OF THE GODS"! WE'VE DONE IT! OUR EXPEDITION TO UNCOVER ANCIENT RUINS IS A SUCCESS!
OHHH-- THAT HORRIBLE FACE! I CAN'T MOVE! EEEEEE!

I THREW A GRENADE INTO THE CLOSED CORRIDOR, ALLOWING THEM TO ENTER THE TEMPLE...
BARRRRROOOOM!
LOOK! YOU'VE OPENED UP SOME SORT OF SECRET PASSAGEWAY INSIDE!
CAREFUL, EVERY-ONE! STAY CLOSE TO EACH OTHER AND BE EXTREMELY ON GUARD! I-- I SEEM TO HAVE A STRANGE FOREBODING OF DANGER!
MOMENTS LATER, WE HAD ALL ARRIVED AT ONE OF THE MOST GIGANTIC CAVERNS I HAD EVER SEEN IN MY LIFE! HUGE DISTORTED OBJECTS WERE RANGED ABOUT IN A SEMI-CIRCLE TOWARDS A LARGER MORE GROTESQUE IMAGE...
CAN YOU MAKE OUT WHAT IT IS?
I DON'T SEE IT TOO CLEARLY IN THIS GLOOM!
AIIIIEEEEE! LOOK! LOOK!
THE SIGHT OF THAT HORRIBLE, MONSTROUS FACE FILLED ME WITH A DREAD THAT FROZE THE BLOOD IN MY VEINS! SUDDENLY--A NUMBING SENSATION SHOT THROUGH MY SPINE. I WAS SLOWLY BECOMING PARALYZED--AND THERE WAS NOTHING I COULD DO ABOUT IT!
EEEEEE! WE'RE TURNING INTO STONE!
I'VE GOT TO DESTROY THAT HEAD!
2

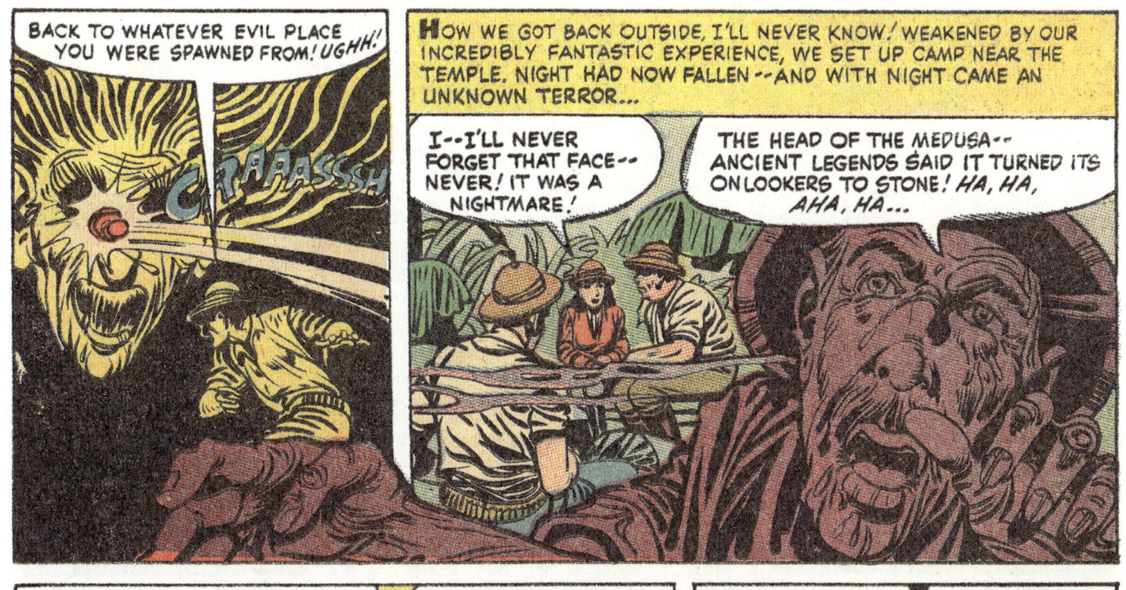
BACK TO WHATEVER EVIL PLACE YOU WERE SPAWNED FROM! UGHH!
CRAAASSSH
HOW WE GOT BACK OUTSIDE, I'LL NEVER KNOW! WEAKENED BY OUR INCREDIBLY FANTASTIC EXPERIENCE, WE SET UP CAMP NEAR THE TEMPLE. NIGHT HAD NOW FALLEN--AND WITH NIGHT CAME AN UNKNOWN TERROR...
I--I'LL NEVER FORGET THAT FACE--NEVER! IT WAS A NIGHTMARE!
THE HEAD OF THE MEDUSA--ANCIENT LEGENDS SAID IT TURNED ITS ONLOOKERS TO STONE! HA, HA, AHA, HA...

AIIIIIEEEE! RICHARD IS CHANGING! OH, MY GOD! HE'S TURNING INTO THAT HORRIBLE CREATURE!
DON'T BE AFRAID, MORTAL! LET ME TOUCH THAT LOVELY, PULSATING NECK OF YOURS! ONE TINY BITE... AND ALL WILL BE OVER! HA, HA, HA...
IT'S GOT VIV! SHE'S BEING CARRIED INTO THE JUNGLE! DO SOMETHING! SHE'LL BE KILLED!
HEAD FOR THE TEMPLE--QUICK! THAT'S THE ONLY LOGICAL PLACE IT WOULD TAKE HER!

WE FOLLOWED IT INTO THE INNER-CHAMBER OF THE RUINED TEMPLE. SUDDENLY, UNABLE TO ESCAPE ANY FURTHER, THE FRIGHTENING CREATURE THAT HAD ONCE BEEN A MAN, TURNED ON US, CLAWS OUT, FANGS BARED--READY TO KILL!!
ARRGGHH!
KILL IT--HURRY!
YES--! WE HAVE WITNESSED A TERRIBLE TRAGEDY! RICHARD DARE IS NO MORE!
OH, DICK--
LET'S GET OUT OF THIS GOD-FORSAKEN PLACE! AND FAST!

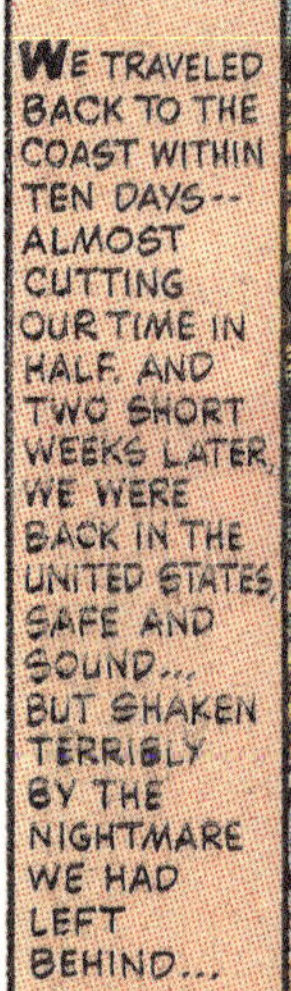
WE TRAVELED BACK TO THE COAST WITHIN TEN DAYS-- ALMOST CUTTING OUR TIME IN HALF. AND TWO SHORT WEEKS LATER, WE WERE BACK IN THE UNITED STATES, SAFE AND SOUND... BUT SHAKEN TERRIBLY BY THE NIGHTMARE WE HAD LEFT BEHIND...

ALL OF US HAD DECIDED NEVER TO MENTION RICHARD DARE'S TRUE FATE. SO DEEPLY HAD OUR EXPERIENCE UNNERVED US, THAT EACH OF US PARTED TO DIFFERENT TYPES OF WORK WITHIN THE CITY. THEN, ONE DAY, I RECEIVED A CALL FROM VIV...
JACK--SOMETHING HORRIBLE HAS HAPPENED! IT'S HUGO! COME OVER RIGHT AWAY!
ALL RIGHT! AT ONCE!

VIV GAVE ME AN ADDRESS AT WHICH I WOULD MEET HER. I GOT THERE IN ONE HOUR FLAT, BUT MY SURPRISE WAS EVEN GREATER WHEN I SAW WHERE I WAS...
VIVIENE! MY LORD-- WHAT ARE YOU DOING HERE IN AN INSANE ASYLUM? WHERE'S HUGO?
IN THERE, JACK! OHH--THIS MUST BE A HIDEOUS DREAM, IT HAS TO BE!
GOOD HEAVENS! WHAT? HOW?
HUGO NEVER GAVE UP TRYING TO FIND OUT WHY RICHARD DARE HAD TURNED INTO A MEDUSA-GHOUL! HE MUST HAVE FELT HIMSELF CHANGING, TOO--HE HAD HIMSELF COMMITTED--AND THEN WHEN HE SAW IT WAS HOPELESS, HE HANGED HIMSELF!
BUT WHY HUGO AND NOT US? VIV--I'VE HAD MYSELF EXAMINED BY SPECIALISTS ALL OVER THE COUNTRY. NOT ONE CAN FIND ANYTHING WRONG!
HUGO LEFT BEHIND A DIARY. HE THINKS THE GAZE OF THE MEDUSA IS LIKE SOME POISON THAT CHANGES THE CHEMICAL COMPOSITION OF THE ONLOOKER'S BODY AFTER A CERTAIN LENGTH OF TIME! OH-- WHAT ARE WE GOING TO DO?

THERE WAS NOTHING TO DO--BUT HOPE AND PRAY--AND WAIT! THEN ONE MORNING, ON MY WAY TO WORK, I PICKED UP THE EXTRA EDITION OF A SCREAMING NEWS-HEADLINE...
"FIENDISH CREATURE ROAMS CITY STREETS! NONE SAFE FROM MURDERING GHOUL!" NO! IT CAN'T BE! IT JUST CAN'T BE! I--I'VE GOT TO ACT FAST!
NEWS
IDEA AFTER IDEA--PLAN AFTER PLAN WENT THROUGH MY MIND. I KNEW WHO THE GHOUL WAS! I COULD SEE THE ACTUAL EVENTS OF HOW THE CREATURE LAY IN WAIT FOR ITS VICTIMS AT NIGHT! MY MIND SHUDDERED AT THE THOUGHT!
DO NOT RUN, PUNY ONE! YOU CANNOT ESCAPE THE MEDUSA! HA, HA, HA!
HELP! HELP! DON'T TOUCH ME! AIEEEE!

STOP!
YOU'LL NEVER GET AWAY!
ANOTHER NECK HAS BEEN BITTEN --ANOTHER'S BLOOD COURSES IN MY VEINS! THE MEDUSA ALWAYS CONQUERS-- EVER-- EVER--AND FOREVER! HA-HA-HA...
I RESOLVED TO FIND VIV THAT NIGHT... FOR THE GHOUL COULD BE HER, NO ONE ELSE! BUT JUST AS I REACHED HOME, THE PHONE RANG AND HER FRIGHTENED VOICE BEGGED ME TO MEET HER NEAR THE OUTSKIRTS OF THE CITY. AND A HALF-HOUR LATER...
OHH--THANK GOD IT'S NOT YOU! I--I THOUGHT YOU WERE THE...
YES, I KNOW, AND I THOUGHT YOU WERE THE GHOUL! BUT THEN WHO COULD IT BE, VIV? DO YOU SUPPOSE HUGO HAS--COME BACK?
NEITHER OF US KNEW! BUT WE MEANT TO FIND OUT! I HAD DONE RESEARCH ON THE MEDUSA IN THE LIBRARY. LEGENDS SPOKE OF AN EFFECT IT PRODUCED IN CERTAIN PEOPLE WHO COULD THEN, AS GHOULS, NEVER BE DESTROYED! PERHAPS HUGO WAS THE ONE! SO, LATER THAT NIGHT...
HAVE YOU OPENED THE CRYPT YET, JACK?
I--I THINK IT'S STARTING TO GIVE WAY!
CAN I HELP? PERHAPS IF YOU USE THAT CROW-BAR, IT MIGHT WEDGE IT OPEN!
NO! IT'S MOVING! ONE MORE HEAVE AND I'LL...
HA HA HA HA HA
YOU! BUT WHY DID YOU WAIT SO LONG TO REVEAL YOURSELF TO ME?
BECAUSE IT WOULD BE ABSOLUTELY PRIVATE HERE... SO NICE AND QUIET--SO COMPLETELY PERFECT FOR--DEATH!! HA, HA, HA, HA...

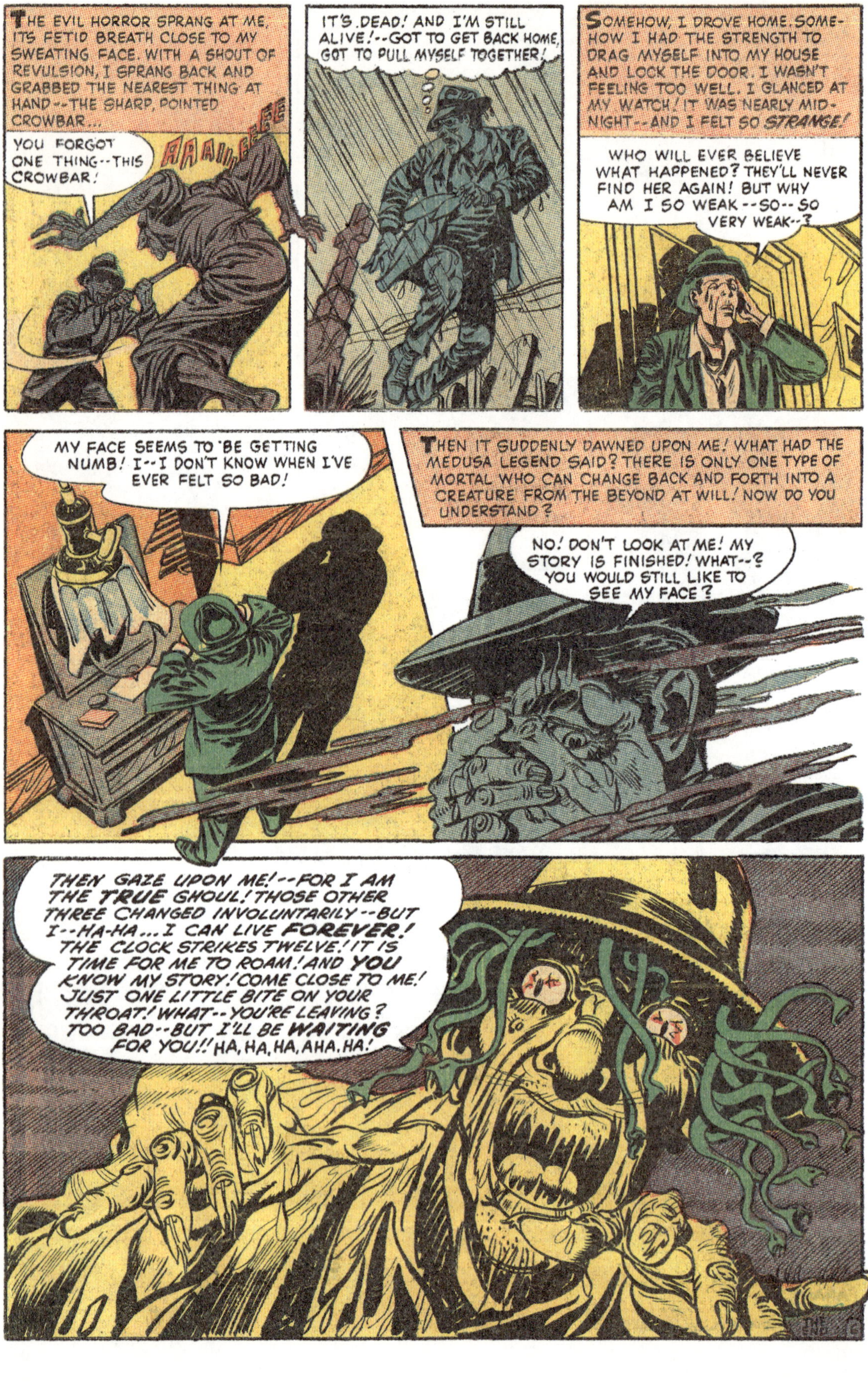

SOMEHOW, I DROVE HOME. SOMEHOW I HAD THE STRENGTH TO DRAG MYSELF INTO MY HOUSE AND LOCK THE DOOR. I WASN'T FEELING TOO WELL. I GLANCED AT MY WATCH! IT WAS NEARLY MIDNIGHT--AND I FELT SO *STRANGE!*

MY FACE SEEMS TO BE GETTING NUMB! I--I DON'T KNOW WHEN I'VE EVER FELT SO BAD!

THEN IT SUDDENLY DAWNED UPON ME! WHAT HAD THE MEDUSA LEGEND SAID? THERE IS ONLY ONE TYPE OF MORTAL WHO CAN CHANGE BACK AND FORTH INTO A CREATURE FROM THE BEYOND AT WILL! NOW DO YOU UNDERSTAND?

NO! DON'T LOOK AT ME! MY STORY IS FINISHED! WHAT--? YOU WOULD STILL LIKE TO SEE MY FACE?

THEN GAZE UPON ME!--FOR I AM THE ***TRUE*** *GHOUL! THOSE OTHER THREE CHANGED INVOLUNTARILY--BUT I--HA-HA... I CAN LIVE* ***FOREVER!*** *THE CLOCK STRIKES TWELVE! IT IS TIME FOR ME TO ROAM! AND* ***YOU*** *KNOW MY STORY! COME CLOSE TO ME! JUST ONE LITTLE BITE ON YOUR THROAT! WHAT--YOU'RE LEAVING? TOO BAD--BUT I'LL BE* ***WAITING*** *FOR YOU!!* HA, HA, HA, AHA, HA!

THEY LAUGHED WHEN I STARTED TO TALK!

HA HA

HA NA - LOOK WHO'S TRYING TO TELL A JOKE

PEOPLE TELL ME THAT A FOOL AND HIS MONEY ARE SOON PARTED, BUT I WONDER HOW THEY EVER GOT TOGETHER IN THE FIRST PLACE.

OH, JACKIE! YOU'RE **WONDERFUL!** WHERE DID YOU EVER LEARN TO TELL JOKES LIKE THAT?

HA HA HE HE

YOURS **FREE** WITH EACH ORDER OF "FUN PARADE ANNUAL" AND "HELLO BUDDIES ANNUAL"

HOW YOU TOO CAN TELL FUNNY JOKES

How often have you wished you could tell a funny joke and tell it the way the experts do? There are hundreds of times you can win a point by telling the right story at the right time in the right way. It's easy when you know HOW! The editors of FUN PARADE, one of the nation's funniest humor magazines, have written a simple guide titled "HOW TO TELL FUNNY JOKES." It is written in simple language and tells you completely HOW TO TELL FUNNY JOKES, where to find material, how to improvise, how to change a joke so that it fits your story and many other revealing secrets. Now for the first time offered anywhere.

FOR PUBLIC SPEAKERS
FOR TEACHERS
FOR WRITERS
FOR SCHOOL PLAYS, CLUB SKITS, ETC.

EACH VOLUME 192 PAGES

BOTH VOLUMES ONLY **$1.00** PLUS FREE "HOW TO TELL FUNNY JOKES"

CARTOONS BY AMERICA'S FAMOUS CARTOONISTS!

Here are only a few of America's leading cartoonists who illustrate some of the jokes appearing in "FUN PARADE ANNUAL," and "HELLO BUDDIES ANNUAL"—You'll recognize their signatures on cartoons in the leading humor magazines and in newspapers from coast to coast. DAN FLOWERS, AL ROSS, REAMER KELLER, ANGELO, DAVE BREGOR, DAN G. BROWN, E. SIMMS CAMPBELL, SWAN, LARIAR, KIRK STILES, HENRY BOLTINOFF, WENZEL, VIC HERMAN, SALO, MILOKINN, ALI, ATKINS, R. GUSTAFSON, JEFF KEATE, CHARLES STRAUS, CRAMER, SCOTT, LINDA & JERRY WALTERS, ERIC ERICSON *and many others.*

SEND FOR THIS WONDERFUL COMBINATION OFFER TODAY

MONEY BACK GUARANTEE

After you have examined these fun packed books and you are not entirely satisfied, you may return them to us, within 5 days in good condition and your dollar will be refunded. You may keep the booklet, "HOW TO TELL A FUNNY JOKE." Don't wait. You can't lose. Send your order today.

FUN PARADE INC. DEPT. WT
1860 BROADWAY NEW YORK 23, N.Y.

MAIL THIS ORDER TODAY!

FUN PARADE INC., DEPT. WT
1860 BROADWAY
NEW YORK 23, NEW YORK

Yes, please send me postpaid your free booklet "HOW TO TELL FUNNY JOKES." Here is my dollar for the TWO ANNUALS, FUN PARADE and HELLO BUDDIES, each 192 pages.

PRINT NAME ______________________

ADDRESS ______________________

CITY ______________ ZONE IF ANY ______ STATE ______

SORRY, NO C.O.D.'S OR ORDER OUTSIDE U.S.A.

SEND NO MONEY—Try at our risk!

Here's a LIFETIME BARGAIN for you! Compare with domestic binoculars selling up to 10.00 for clarity, light weight and rugged construction! Just look thru them once and you'll be convinced of their quality You will be thrilled with the GERMAN KLARO-VIS lens that give you TERRIFIC MAGNIFICATION POWER, a wide field of view and sharp, brilliant detail! Smooth SYNCHRONIZED centre focusing mechanism gives you quick, easy adjustments Light weight – easy to carry with you – yet they are so STRONGLY made that it is virtually IMPOSSIBLE TO BREAK THEM in normal use! Yes, this is what you have always wanted - now yours at an unbelievably LOW PRICE – while they last!

BIG SIZE — BIG POWER — BIG VALUE

Please do not confuse the KLARO-VIS with crudely made Binoculars claiming 18 MILE RANGES! These are NEW and so DIFFERENT, made by GERMAN ARTISANS You receive BIG POWER, BIG SIZE and a BIG LIFETIME BARGAIN!

A LIFETIME OF THRILLS AWAITS YOU!

When you own this power-packed instrument, distances seem to melt away you always have a "ringside" seat at boxing matches, races, baseball or football You get an intimate view of nature, the sky at night, distant sunsets, birds and wild animals, distant boats, seashore scenes, etc. You see what your neighbors are doing (without being seen). Carry them with you on hunting trips too!

FREE TRIAL OFFER — ENJOY AT OUR RISK!

We want to send you a pair of these super-power glasses for you to examine and enjoy for ONE WHOLE WEEK – without obligation. You take no chances. Test them . . use them as you like. Compare them for value and power with binoculars selling up to 10.00. Then YOU be the JUDGE! If you're not thrilled, then return and get your MONEY BACK! Don't send ONE PENNY – pay postman only 3.00 plus postage on arrival. Do it today – WHILE SUPPLY LASTS. Don't miss the fun and thrills another day RUSH THE TRIAL COUPON RIGHT NOW.

MAIL COUPON FOR HOME TRIAL!

CONSUMERS MART, Dept. 35-G-134
131 West 33rd Street NEW YORK I.N.Y.

GENTLEMEN: RUSH your guaranteed KLAROVIS Super Power Field Glasses for a whole week's home trial – FREE of obligation and your SURPRISE FRIENDSHIP GIFT. I will pay postman 3.00 plus postage on arrival. I shall enjoy them, and use them for a whole week and if not satisfied with this thrilling bargain, you are to send my 3.00 back. The surprise Friendship Gift is mine to KEEP even if I return the KLAROVIS!

NAME____________________

ADDRESS____________________

TOWN__________ STATE__________

☐ EXTRA SAVINGS FOR YOU! Send 3.00 cash, check or money order with this coupon and we pay ALL POSTAGE costs. SAME MONEY-BACK GUARANTEE!

YOU can WIN this big 15" Silver Trophy as Roger just did
When I enrolled I was a skinny, sick weakling. I was shy with girls because I had nothing to show off. A few weeks after starting the Jowett Course my body was the best in the neighborhood. Now I get respect and admiration from every fellow and girl I meet.
Roger D. Hirsch
Aren't YOU as SICK and Tired as I was of being SKINNY
CHICKEN-CHESTED
SPINDLE-ARMED
NARROW-SHOULDERED
SHORT-WINDED
WEAK, HALF-ALIVE
JEERFD, BULLIED
?
There's that skinny scarecrow ROGER. Let's pass him by!
Then do as I did...
MAIL THE COUPON BELOW
I gained 53 lbs. of mighty muscle
I added 6½ inches to my CHEST
3 inches to each ARM
And the rest in proportion — ALL IN A FEW SHORT WEEKS by using the JOWETT SYSTEM
for building Real HE-MEN
ROGER HIRSCH was an 112 lb. 6 ft. weakling LOOK AT HIM NOW!
Come on, PAL, Now YOU give me 10 pleasant Minutes a Day in your own home . . . and I'll give YOU a NEW HE-MAN BODY for your OLD SKELETON FRAME.
says GEORGE F. JOWETT
World's Greatest Builder of HE-MEN
NO! I don't care how skinny or flabby you are; if you're a teen-ager, in your 20's or 30's or over; if you're short or tall, or what work you do. All I want is JUST 10 EXCITING MINUTES in your home to MAKE YOU OVER by the SAME METHOD I turned myself from a wreck to a Champion of Champions.
YES! You'll see INCH upon INCH of MIGHTY MUSCLE added to YOUR ARMS. Your CHEST deepened. Your BACK AND SHOULDERS broadened. From head to heels, you'll gain SOLIDITY, SIZE, POWER, SPEED! You'll become an ALL-Around, ALL-American HE-MAN, a WINNER in everything you tackle—or my Training won't cost you one solitary cent!
George F. Jowett Whom experts call "Champion of Champions"
• World's wrestling and wt. lifting champ
• World's Strongest Arms.
• 4 times "World's Perfect Body" Winner.
FREE! If you mail coupon NOW
1 MUSCLE METER
2 JOWETT'S Photo Book of Famous Strong Men!
His amazing book, "Nerves of Steel, Muscles of Iron," has guided thousands of weaklings to muscular power. Packed with photos of miracle men of might and muscle who started perhaps weaker than you are. Read the thrilling adventures of Jowett in strength that inspired his pupils to follow him. They'll show you the best way to might and muscle. Send for FREE gift book of PHOTOS OF FAMOUS STRONG MEN
NOW LET ME MAKE YOU LIKE ROGER A WINNER IN EVERY WALK OF LIFE
WHAM
DARLING, THAT BULLY WON'T PICK ON YOU AGAIN.
JOE WALLOPPED ANOTHER HOMER! HE'S SURE TO BE CAPTAIN NOW
JOE YOUR NEW ENERGY AND APPEARANCE SURE DO A GOOD JOB. YOU EARNED YOUR PROMOTION.
JOES JOWETT HE-MAN STRENGTH AND BUILD WON HIM THOSE STRIPES
Develop YOUR 520 MUSCLES Gain Pounds, INCHES, FAST!
Friend, I've traveled the world. Made a LIFETIME STUDY of every way known to develop your body. Then I devised the BEST by TEST, my "5-WAY PROGRESSIVE POWER" the only method that builds you 5-ways fast. You save YEARS, DOLLARS like movie star Tom Tyler did. Like Champ Roger Hirsch did. Like MANY THOUSANDS like you did. SO . . .
MAIL COUPON NOW and GET
This may be Your LAST chance to GET AMAZING
NATIONAL EMERGENCY OFFER
All these 5 Picture Packed COURSES on He-Man Building for only while supply lasts!
10¢
MILLIONS have been sold for $1 and more
FREE Photo Book How you can Become an All-Around All-American HE-MAN
How to Build MIGHTY ARMS
How to Build A MIGHTY CHEST
How to Build A MIGHTY GRIP
How to Build A MIGHTY BACK
How to Build MIGHTY LEGS
How to BECOME A MUSCULAR HE-MAN
BOTH FREE!
1. Photo Book of STRONG MEN
2. MUSCLE METER
DEPT. HS-29
"Jowett Courses greatest in World for Building All-Around HE-MEN". —R.F. Kelley Physical Director
JOWETT INSTITUTE OF PHYSICAL TRAINING 230 FIFTH AVENUE, NEW YORK 1, N.Y.
Dear George: Please mail to me FREE Jowett's Photo Book of Strong Men and a Muscle Meter, plus all 5 HE-MAN Building Courses: 1. How to Build a Mighty Chest. 2. How to Build a Mighty Arm. 3. How to Build a Mighty Grip. 4. How to Build a Mighty Back. 5. How to Build Mighty Legs—Now all in One Volume "How to become a Muscular He-Man." ENCLOSED FIND 10c FOR POSTAGE AND HANDLING (No C.O.D's).
NAME ______ AGE ____
ADDRESS ______
CITY ______ ZONE ____ STATE ______

It's thrilling fun to be a magician! But it's twice as wonderful to be a money-making magician, to baffle all your friends and family. With this amazing money machine you can perform real, mystifying magic. Think of the excitement when plain sheets of paper are placed in the machine, and as the rollers revolve, **OUT COMES HONEST-TO-GOODNESS MONEY TO SPEND.** There's a magic trick, of course, that only you will know. You'll be one magician in tremendous demand to perform your money magic! The whole family will find this remarkable money-maker thrilling entertainment. Rush your order NOW. **SEND NO MONEY.** Remit with order and we pay postage or C.O.D. plus postage.

FREE! WITH EVERY BANK ½ lb. TIN PEANUTS — PLANTERS Cocktail PEANUTS

PEANUT BANK

•NEW! •EXCITING! •SAVES MONEY —SERVES PEANUTS •BANK HOLDS UP TO $20. •INSERT COIN HERE

MR. PEANUT VENDER-BANK

- 7½" HIGH!
- HOLDS PENNIES, NICKELS, DIMES!
- DOUBLE LOCK AND KEY!

Exciting saving bank serves peanuts while you save pennies, nickels, dimes! Comes with top hat, dashing monocle, a ½ pound vacuum can of delicious roasted peanuts, double lock and key. Drop in a coin and flip back the ear — out pops a generous amount of peanuts. Made of sturdy, durable plastic, MR. PEANUT VENDER-BANK is ideal to start the kiddies saving (holds upwards of $20 in coins.) Wonderful for parties, entertaining, family fun. Easy to refill.

IMAGINE ONLY $2.98 COMPLETE

Imagine Only $3.49 complete

Turn the key and the car is off! You can make it go wherever you wish because it's a genuine 3 gear motor car that shifts into first, second, third or reverse . . . And if you want to stop, keep your hand on the steering wheel and pull on your brakes! It's the miniature version of a grown-up convertible with all of the same features . . . long, slim lines, real rubber walled tires, a plexiglas windshield, straight running board, and two front headlights! Comes already assembled in bright modern colors.

A wonderful new doll in washable rubber Wonderskin whose hair is so lifelike it can be waved in any style and rewaved just like your own. A perfect playmate for the "Junior Mother" of the house. Complete with real Hair-wave kit which consists of . . . plastic curlers . . . rubber waving bands . . . waving end papers . . . plastic comb . . . and bottle of hair wave lotion. Ginger is 11 inches tall. Her soft cuddly body which can be bathed will give the "Junior Miss" an almost real baby sister to play with.

- HE'S OVER 19" TALL!
- MOVES HIS MOUTH,
- ARMS AND LEGS! REAL COWBOY OUTFIT!

Hey kids — here's your chance to become a master ventriloquist — in a jiffy! Imagine — you can make *HAPPY the* COWBOY actually talk! (In your own voice, of course.) Pull the string in the back of his head — watch his lips move — hear your own words coming right out of *HAPPY'S* mouth! See how real he looks—rigged up in a cowboy *hat*, washable *plaid shirt and western pants*. . . Show off your skill at parties — at school! *SEND NO MONEY*. (C.O.D. you pay postage. Remit with order, we pay postage.)

SEND NO MONEY C.O.D You pay postage. Remit with order. We pay postage.

SEND COUPON!

NOVELTY MART, Dept. HA-3
59 East 8th Street, New York 3, N. Y.

Gentlemen: Please send me the following:
Enclosed find: ☐ Check or M.O. ☐ C.O.D. plus postage.

☐ Money Machine $1.98 ☐ Peanut Bank $2.98
☐ Motor Car $3.49 ☐ Ginger $3.98
☐ HAPPY THE COWBOY $2.98

Name______________ ______________

Address______________ City______________ State______________

NOVELTY MART 59 East 8th Street, Dept. HA-3 New York 3,